# bone
# and
# blood

# Margo Gorman

# bone and blood

## A Berlin Novel

Matador
9 Priory Business Park
Kibworth Beauchamp
Leicestershire LE8 0RX, UK
Tel: (+44) 116 279 2299
Fax: (+44) 116 279 2277
Email: books@troubador.co.uk
Web: www.troubador.co.uk/matador

ISBN 978-1784620-370

British Library Cataloguing in Publication Data.
A catalogue record for this book is available from the British Library.

Patrice lyrics from Nile Album ©Patrice

Typeset in Perpetua by Troubador Publishing Ltd
Printed and bound in the UK by TJ International, Padstow, Cornwall

**Matador** is an imprint of Troubador Publishing Ltd

| Fowles in the Frith | Birds in the forest |
|---|---|
| The fisshes in the flood | Fish in the river |
| And I mon waxe wood | And I must go mad |
| Much Sorwe I walke with | Much sorrow I walk with |
| For best of boon and blood | For best of bone and blood |

(Medieval English lyric)

Chapter One

# That Place

*Hard to tell. Hard not to tell. Now it's too late. I didn't want to burden you with such a story, Katharina. I didn't want understanding, pity or disgust from anyone then. I don't want it now. But I wanted you one day to have the letters I never posted to Mary, I wanted you to have Anna's enamel can. Am I just a selfish old woman? Wanting to speak to you from my grave? Brigitte looked around. Did I speak aloud or in my head? These days I can't always tell.* The voile curtain waltzed closer and swept away again. Ghosting memories of the dead Katharina waiting to be buried. Ghosting memories of the stiff corpse of Anna in the camp so long ago.

The sound of the tram promised to take Brigitte for Kaffee und Kuchen— the steamy music of Coffee and Cake in her head. She should have asked Yola to close the window – up, down, over – the handle with so many variations and Brigitte could manage none of them. Nothing. Nix. Katharina was as proud of it as if she had made it herself. She loved to pull back the curtains and open both windows fully.

'It's like having a balcony without having to move from the room,' she would say every time, 'You need more fresh air, Mama.' And what good was fresh air now? What good did all the wandering in the Wald do her now?

Brigitte groped on the table beside her. Her hand was

surprised to touch softness. She turned too quickly and the pain shot up her leg to her spine. She shifted slightly to escape some of it. Ach so, it was the leather pouch of her mother's rosary beads – resurrected from a dusty drawer the day Katharina told her. They gave her an excuse at least to sit and mutter to herself. But not now. She checked her bar of chocolate was there – milk, not her usual bar of black chocolate melting memories of bitter cold. Not many Irish people liked it. Surprised when she brought them dark chocolate, reminding her of the ways she had grown away from who she had been. Milk chocolate to-day because she wanted to have some to offer Peggy's son – if he came. The packet of Taschentücher was in its place. What do you call them now in English: you don't call the paper ones handkerchiefs do you? So many words escaped her grasp these days. But she wasn't afraid of losing her memory. She wished for it. She craved and feared the blank depths.

She wanted familiar fears like the fear of Katharina crinkling her forehead in frustration. The fly spray was also in reach on the table.

'Mama, must you spray that poison? Think what you're doing to the air you breathe, not to mention the ozone layer.'

She loved the way her daughter spoke English, an accent like none other: not German, not foreign, but not Irish either. Brigitte ignored her words. She hated flies more than death itself. She hated them because they could always find food. The more death there was, the more they swarmed. Katharina knew nothing about flies. She saw only a single fly or a few small summer flies rise up from the rubbish. Brigitte knew the fly spray was a weapon against the death and decay you couldn't see but the flies could always find. Sweeping heaps of them

2

from under the cupboards and beds on her free day. The child crawled around with her – using her bottom shuffle to propel her forward. Quicker than a crawl. Chuckling at mama. She made it a game for the child and prayed she would grow up remembering the chuckle but fearful she wouldn't. Anna was forgotten then so why did her ghost come back now?

The sweet relief when your worst fear took over. Release. The other night when she woke too late to regain control of the warm wet flow. Relief. It was almost worth it even though she had to strip the bed herself, wash and dry the mattress before Yola came. She laughed then and now again with the memory – the hairdryer had never been used for her hair but had come in useful after all. They said it was your short-term memory went first and early memories could come back. Early memories would be all right but those memories of numb horror must stay in their place. She wanted those letters buried now, or burnt. Better if it could be both. Who to ask? Not Monika. Cremation she said. What about Anna's enamel can for the ashes? She couldn't ask. Not Monika.

She touched the small frame of the photo of her daughter's face; the only photo Katharina would allow to be on display, because it was so small. She wasn't even smiling; but she was there and Brigitte smiled at her. The remote control for the TV was in its place too although she didn't watch the news these days. And her glass of water – the blue sunshine water of Greece shining through from the Untertasse. Under-cup not saucer. But there is an English word; Katharina told her. The blue Greek sea held the word for her.

'They call them coasters in English but maybe it's an American word. Do you like them? I'll buy them for you.'

'No I don't want them.'

'Don't want them or don't like them?'

'I like them but I don't need them.'

Katharina was frustrated with her. 'I'll buy them for you as a memento. You never buy anything for yourself.' Brigitte let her buy them to bring back the smiles and the walk down the hillside smelling of wild oregano, thyme and rosemary. She didn't say, 'I prefer the others.' Let Katharina choose.

Her tablet box was there too – filled carefully every Sunday. She preferred to do it herself. She touched the hard leather of her wallet beside it. Well it was a cross between a handbag and a wallet – big enough for her important papers and the money she needed to give to Yola and with a wrist strap so it was easy to carry if she needed to use the stick. The bag was another gift. Not a gift – a cast-off.

'I don't use it anymore, Mama. It would be better for you than your handbag.'

True enough, it was handy for her when she took the shopping trolley. On the days when she went shopping alone. Not now.

'Why do you have to have a hand bag with you all day when you're inside? And with so much stuff in it. I gave you a small one so it would be light. Now you fill it full. Most of what's in it you could put in the bureau. No one's going to steal anything from you here. Yola will think you don't trust her.'

Her movements brought Yola from the kitchen. Brigitte was distracted by the face of her old friend, Mary, glimpsed through Yola's curious compassion. How good to see you, Mary. Leitrim half-lilt. Half-tilt with the hills of Donegal and Ben Bulben brooding over them. Sharing the years of knowing nothing. Eighty-one was too young for Mary. She would have liked to go to send her off but she couldn't face Ireland again.

A wake with the constant flow of neighbours, tea, sandwiches and sympathy. No wake here for an only daughter. Monika knew nothing of wakes

Waiting. She hated it because it brought her back to hell. Silence is better than making a story of it. Better than Anna's voice in her head coming back after all these years. 'Guck mal!' The children said it. Look! They laughed when Brigitte mixed up the words Kuchen and kochen. Looking and cooking. 'Guck nicht hoch!' Anna said and pushed her head down. Others strained above her head at the window of the block. She could not move. Could not see .

'Eine Frau?' Anna had said then. Horror snapped the door shut. She muttered, 'Nicht unser Fleisch und Blut': Not our flesh and blood. Did 'Fleisch und Blut' mean the same for them as for us? Blood was for relatives so not me for sure. Not even German and certainly no witness to Jehovah. My guardian Anna must have forgotten my foreignness in the moment of the story. The whisper passed through her in the hours following. Surely misunderstood. Not possible. Even a group in anger could not do such a thing. In her block when one was caught for breaking some rule and everyone was punished, they suffered together: there was no attempt to put blame on the one.

Anna talked with her taut body – willing me to see the sight as a warning. Desperate eyes reflected in the raw damp mirror image. Some patches of skin on my own hands amidst the raw flesh. Wishing for more callouses. But no blood on our hands. So little flesh on the bones. No flesh and blood. Not mine. She shut her eyes then. Fear of the people who created the Lager; fear of the dead woman; fear of the guards who stood by and let them do the work and condemned them all as animals. They could whip them as animals and go to Mass on Sunday. Anna told her the story of "Die Arme" later in breathless whispers. Anna spoke simple clear German. The problem was not the words. There are no words for telling such a story. Shut your eyes and shut your mouth.

In the Lager, she had vowed she never wanted to see her own flesh and blood again. No leakage of horror to her family. The dream of Berlin would hold her always. Not enough courage to take her life or the unborn life. Another unkept promise to herself. She touched the bag with the store of tablets. Now she would be sure. At least she would die in one piece. More bone than flesh. More bone than blood. She would bury those memories with Katharina.

Her daughter put bone back into a bloody handful of life. She loved the child so much it hurt.

'Why don't you visit Ireland?' Katharina would ask, her broad brow holding her logical mind.

Why don't you? Brigitte would not ask later. Why this? Why that? Rather why than how. 'How was Ireland? How was the camp? How was the war?'

'Mama, why do you punish yourself? What for?'

Brigitte would breathe again the despair in the air. Ducking and diving in the words to keep the conversation alive. 'I wonder why the word for "Lager" in English is "concentration camp". I thought concentration was paying attention.'

Long ago in the dictionary days, games of kniffel, board games and laughter. Long before she met Monika – the Jules who captivated her. Days of long hair and songs against war, against America. Her hair hanging down as she leant over the book.

'Oh now I see the link. It can mean bringing power, troops

or prisoners together in one point, not just the power of attention.' Katharina studied and the more she studied the angrier she became. 'Tell me, what did happen in those days? Tell me, Mama. It'll help you. It'll help us.'

How could telling help? Comfort now in the confirmation of despair.

'Are you awake, Brigitte?' Mary would have said Biddy. No-one called her the old name here. Sometimes she felt like Bridget but Bridget was young and Irish. Brigitte is someone different, a German mother, an old woman. She had to put up with Yola because Yola needed money and Katharina paid her. Sometimes she had the voice of a Blockova. Once she said the word aloud and Katharina flicked it back to her sharply, 'What's a Blockova? That's a Polish word isn't it? Where did you learn Polish?' 'I don't know the English word for it. Why do I need a word for somebody who does not exist in English? In German they were called Blockälteste,' she answered with an answer that was no answer at all.

Katharina cut a fine slice of cheese carefully, controlling her exasperation at the point of the knife. 'Oh I remember that word all right. You and your riddles and misinformation. You told me once 'Blockälteste' meant matron. I made a fool of myself in school with that English teacher. I'll always see her look of pity. It wasn't your lack of German. You and your half-telling.'

'There are things they don't teach you in school.'

Matron – someone who cared for people, looked after them. She could not explain how the distortion of everything, even the words in your mouth and the thoughts in your head, were their greatest victories. Postponement had saved her but for what had it saved her? To sit here now with a blockova all to herself? She had succeeded for so many years to keep the Blockälteste's face buried. Was it Yola who resurrected those times? Was it the white face of Katharina when she carried the news of her illness? The desire to sink her head again into the smell of stale human flesh. 'Why am I here? I'd be better dead.'

These days dawn sneaked in wearing Anna's face and whispered Anna's explanations. The rat-scratches of sound were a counterpoint to the blaring of Appell. The blockova would offer her bread and sausage again but this time she would refuse. She would say no. No to the pure light of day offering hope; no to the dusky grappling behind the block; no to the slab of musty bread from inside the breast of a jacket; no to the queue for the watery turnip soup; no to the wake-up call: No Appell.

She must wait until the time was right. She would save some of the tranquillisers and sleeping tablets they gave her now. She would have to find out how many she would need. There must be no mistake. She wished now for the comfort of her own mother. There were so many mothers then. When she presented the tiny stiff bodies with the old man's face to the mothers, did it bring back for them the time of conception? She had wished for marriage and children for Katharina. With grandchildren she could bury it forever. The burden would be easier for them to cast off. Young people look to the future. Grandchildren would turn the world over again. Some-one to defend her against the memories. To hold in her arms a child who was born in a world without war. Not this world then because there is always war.

If only Katharina had not met that Jules. Unnatural life. Monika looked so German. And Monika's father, what did he do in those times? Too late to ask or even wonder.

She'd rung Irma, who had offered to come for the funeral. Brigitte insisted no. It would be too much for her – all the way from Vienna to Berlin after her operation. But to hear her voice was something. Irma was lucky – she had grandchildren. In the days of memorials after the wall came down, she came back to Berlin and visited Brigitte on the way. They talked not of those times but about her grandchildren and now Irma sent their photographs every year on the 8th May if she did not come herself. No grandchildren for Brigitte. Would grandchildren be a comfort at this time?

## Chapter Two

# Snow in August

Aisling reached out to shuffle forward the music searching for something to put her feet on the floor. Sharon Shannon pulled her back and forward with memories of Dad buying her complicit beer. Bitter enough to the tongue but delight in her throat at the sharing. Her brother, Michael, and Mum hated the diddle-de-do of the accordion and screamed with mock pain at the "Man of Constant Sorrow", but it brought her comfort and raised her to her feet to look in the mirror.

Did she look a bit paler than usual? She felt like she had a bit of a hangover. She didn't remember having a lot to drink. Was it usual to feel a bit hung over after it? Maybe she had more than she thought. Sometimes she wasn't sure how much she'd pretended last night and how much was the real effect. She dived into bed again and reached for the new notebook she had bought herself. Maybe she shouldn't have been so cheap. She'd got it in an "everything for 2 euro" shop. It wasn't bad quality paper and she liked the hardcover black with red binding. She planned to put photos of her and Matt on the cover – faces amidst the telescope and planets and covering the Science Work Book words. Blank page opposite lined page so when she didn't feel like writing she could draw. This time for herself only. No sharing, no matter how much she laughed to herself.

No-one to share with anyway. Blown it with Maeve and Matt away.

She missed Matt and his ramblings about electrons and neurons and fields of potentiality. He claimed there was a basis in physics for all the sub-atomic particles of humanity past and present being linked to all the particles of existence past or present and in theory we could tap into it through our consciousness of it. Sometimes she wasn't sure how much Matt was pulling her leg but she enjoyed the science fiction feel to it. No-one, not even Matt, would get access to this journal. No pretence.

20th August 2005. *No words came so draw the dance of death. Mum dancing around Michael memories. Dad dancing around one ear cocked as if he's listening but his eyes and hands texting away.*

Aisling threw down the notebook with the cartoon strip half finished. Words were too banal like some gossip dialogue overheard in the pizzeria. She needed a joke with a jag and none came. No notebook. Try earphones and closed eyes but that led to an unwelcome re-screening of last night.

Cathy had called for her at the pizzeria – she'd arranged to get off at 10.30. It was Matt's last big night with them before he went off to Venezuela. When Cathy saw that she was about to sneeze, she shouted at her. 'Don't! You'll waste it. You crazy cow! That's half of my line.' Cathy had wangled an invitation to Matt's farewell party at the club through Aisling. Matt would never have invited Cathy. Arms linked, Cathy kept needling about whether Matt was gay or not. How else could anyone explain his failure to look into her cleavage when she presented it under his nose? She wanted him, gay or not. Did Aisling? No! So Aisling was ally no 1 on the project of hooking him.

The only motivation for Cathy to share her line. Eyes

closed now she could feel the lights in the club sparkling on her skin. They met at Cathy's house in Blackrock. Her parents were away for the weekend. The novelty of the black marble in the bathroom and getting into a new set plus her first trip to the club in Stillorgan added more edge. When it hit her, it was a fantastic feeling as if she was inside the rainbow and looking at herself in it at the same time. High as a kite, they all laughed at that, the laughter echoing inside her head.

Sparklers all the way to the club but Matt wasn't smiling. Are you on something? Dragging him into the light and music, dancing and laughing with him. Did she really tongue him or was that someone else? She hoped not because he would be sure then to think that she was on something. They didn't do tonguing. His face echoed near hers now. He was too good a friend to get into any sex thing. In a way she hoped Cathy was right and he was gay because she didn't want to lose him as a friend and a steady girlfriend would mean problems.

'Don't look down,' Cathy had said later.

Why did she say that? Once Aisling did but it made her feel dizzy and sick. Looking up was better. Glamorous glass bouncing light back into her head. Dancing on air and beating out the blue, green, purple, red light from her head out of her feet. At one time she felt like she was skiing down a slope. Snow sharp on her face. Smug in saloppettes and taking a corner like a pro. Off-piste, out of bounds and the thrill of it whooshing through with blood bringing patches of colour to her face. The best feeling yet. It still beat snow on a line. 'Snow in August,' she laughed into Matt's ear when she danced closer to hear what Cathy said to him.

'Can I come and see you in Venezuela – I've heard that there is a great night life there.'

Matt looked Cathy straight in the eye, 'Depends who you talk to. Cokeheads can have sparkling lights and puke in the gutter anywhere – no need to go to Venezuela. Getting their kicks while someone else is getting kicked for them. They're the link in the chain that keeps all the racketeers going – dinner-party druggies, who fund child prostitution, people trafficking and the rest.'

'And global warming maybe too?' Aisling intervened. Cathy laughed as if she didn't hear, or didn't care, and danced off.

'You didn't tell me he was such a Holy Joe,' she muttered in her ear later. So Cathy didn't get her fling with Matt. Another friendship lost. Though if Maeve had an inkling of her name in the same breath as Cathy's there would be even less of a chance of rekindling those ashes.

Shit! It wouldn't have mattered if Matt were still around because he was best of all for hanging out with. Would Maeve ever forgive her? Not that there was anything to forgive for Gawd's sake. Both of them were drunk when it started. It didn't mean anything. She wasn't thinking of him as Maeve's father – he was just a man with a hard-on. If he'd left it at that and hadn't bloody stalked her – taking her for cocktails so as they could screw in the back of his BMW.

And of course she couldn't tell Maeve about getting rid of the evidence. Her mother didn't even want to know who the father was. The fact that he was married and old enough to be Aisling's father was the killer factor. Her mother said no-one was to know. NO-ONE NOT EVEN MAEVE. Did she guess? Not even Dad knew the reason for the girlie weekend in London. The whole weekend was hell – even the shopping they had to get to bring home as evidence of innocence. Aisling pretended to have more pain than she had. She did have cramps and bleeding but it was more like a bad period. She hated shopping when she had her monthlies. Mum insisting that she wore those ridiculous pads instead of a tampon post sprout removal.

Vacuum extraction. Thankfully in the early stages. Thanks be to Mum and her extra eagle eye. The clinic was efficient. Mum prattling about her days in London. Women's rights including the right to abortion. No clinic in Ireland. The waiting room full of dreary mistakes didn't take her on. Aisling tried to nudge her to shut it.

Another side to the perfect mother managing family and career back in Dublin. They never talked about it after. Confidential is confidential, Mum said. Nobody should be put in the position of keeping such a secret not even Dad. Nobody to talk to about her regrets. Sometimes she wandered around Mothercare imagining herself shopping with the baby. 'Loser,' she said and drew a series of abortion stories for mothers of monsters. Strips on how the world would be different if Hitler, Mussolini and Stalin had been aborted.

Her nose felt sensitive. She took a small mirror from the top drawer of her bedside locker and looked up it. Nothing unusual there. An image of photos of the inside of peoples' noses completely worn away came back from some health lecture. 'Don't be such a baby,' she mouthed at the mirror. No more. Been there, done that. Matt had made her promise before he said goodbye. He knew she didn't make promises so why did he ask? It'd do her head in whether she kept it or not. She'd told him she didn't take much – it wasn't a full line or anything and she'd sneezed too.

'Just as well,' he said, 'If you get into it, the only thing you can be sure about with coke is that you'll want more. Having a good time depends on the coke, not on you or on anybody or anything else.'

'Speaking from experience then are we?' Aisling regretted the sarcastic tone. The last thing she wanted was to fall out with Matt now – especially just before he headed off to work on some street project in a dangerous part of the world.

'It wouldn't make sense for me to try it, if I know it would make me want more and it would mean I'd become just another cokehead.' Matt shrugged, 'I've seen enough of what it has done to my friends and I don't want it for me. It's up to you to decide for yourself. Just don't come crying to me saying it's the only thing that makes you feel alive.'

'It does though – make you feel alive, I mean – though not as good as skiing.'

'Well, if you need coke to make you feel alive it's your choice. Why not stick to skiing?'

'You're talking like we have choice in everything. Most things we don't.'

'Too right, most things we don't, so where we do have a bit of choice, it's worth something. All I'm saying is you have a choice to become a cokehead or not, now. If you get addicted to it, the choice is gone.'

Matt didn't need to be right but he often was. She couldn't remember what he said next. Was that the coke? If only he was still here. She looked at her bedside clock. He'd be on the flight to Shannon already. She'd be bawling in a minute if she didn't do something. Time for breakfast but maybe a shower first.

Chapter Three

# Dublin Discussion

'You should go.' Mary pulled the cord of her bathrobe tighter before opening the oven to take out the warm ciabatta. Recreating the normality of Saturday morning breakfast with the Review section of the Irish Times. Hoping the smell of coffee would tempt Aisling down.

'Won't you come too? I'm not much good at that sort of thing,' Diarmuid tossed his mobile phone from one hand to another.

Mary carried the smell of coffee to the table in the stainless steel percolator, the genuine article bought in the Italian shop. 'Diarmuid, would you put that damn phone away until after breakfast at least. And you know there's no way I can go to a funeral, when I don't have to. It would bring it all back.'

'And it won't for me I suppose.'

'Well, it's different and it's your cousin who has died, not mine.'

'Why should I go to be with an aunt that I've met about three times in my life at funerals? Aunt Bridget, or Brigitte she calls herself now, went to Germany before I was even born. It would be quite enough to send a Mass card. I don't even know if she's still a Catholic, for God's sake. I know nothing about her. I don't speak German. What use would I be?'

'Well, your mother thinks someone should go to represent the family and for once I think she's right. She's lost her only child.' The lines around Mary's mouth and eyes tightened making her look older than her 50 years.

'Some child; her daughter was nearly sixty.'

'Still her child.'

'I think I'll ask Willie: they must have loads of direct flights to Berlin. I've got his mobile number here. He might even get there and back in a day. If not, the most he would have to stay would be one night,' Diarmuid scrolled down his contact numbers.

'Willie? Are you serious? Your brother Willie should be banned from funerals, weddings and all social occasions until he has dried out completely. He's worse than your Uncle Michael or maybe you thought of asking him to go? Maybe your mother asked you because she wants to make sure that Willie *doesn't* go. She knows that you're the only one she can trust who's close enough. Your sister Val is hardly going to fly over from New York to the funeral of a cousin she hasn't met and your brother Conor would hardly take the time to go to his own mother's funeral never mind someone he probably has never even heard of.'

Aisling switched off the music she used to drown out calls for breakfast and crossed the landing. The kitchen door was open. She could hear them arguing, ignoring Lisa Hannigan playing in the background. Good music and her favourite track. Lisa the exception for overlap with Mum's taste in music. Not enough to drown him out. She wished she had the house to herself. The face looked at her from the mirror again. She wanted space to shake off his white face, looking at her, just looking. She covered it with a towel to stop it dissolving into water.

17

She had pushed him under often enough. It was her favourite sport in the swimming pool when they were on holidays in the apartment in Spain. He didn't dare call out or tell. He would thrash in silence. Then he learnt to hold his breath. She would count silently to the point that she knew he would be bursting and the squirming would start. He would come up then, his eyes reproachful but only air in his mouth. He never came in the pool when she was there before him. He would leave after she caught him if he didn't manage to escape before she got in. She loved it when he was there, floating on the airbed, and didn't see her at all until she tipped him off.

They were arguing last night when she came in from work. Some story about a strange aunt of her father's in Berlin. The aunt was even older than Granny. Her daughter had died. Chug-chug, a new thought made his face dissolve and vanish down the plughole. Why not? She would offer to go to the funeral with her father. Better than being stuck in Dublin with her Mum. The job was beginning to bore her. She would be glad to get away from it for a few days.

Aisling abandoned the shower and pulled on a bathrobe, her bare feet drying on the stair carpet before she reached the kitchen. Maybe she should ring Aunt Lizzie first. Her mother's sister, Elizabeth, who was the main organiser of family events, hated being called Lizzie. Everyone loved that she hated it. She was too efficient and bossy but indispensable on an occasion like this. At Michael's funeral, she had organised everything and everyone – even Gran.

'I'll go if you like,' she sat down at the other end of the table with her back to the glass wall and the jungle on the other side. It was the only part of the house that she liked. This corner where the tropical plants in the new conservatory were reflected in the mirror on the wall created an extravagance of green and provided speckled sunlight for the whole kitchen. Hothouse feel from outside in. It caught enough sun to bring summer warmth to the damp August morning.

She reached down to stroke Mitten, who had roused himself from the basket in the sunspot. He'd started out as Mitten Too from the day she said, "I'm going to call him Mitten too," but he'd rubbed and licked his way to the number one spot. She didn't forget number one Mitten. Mitten Too was a reminder every time of the sensation of soft, limp flesh, warm in her bare hands. Feeling a mess of raw meat, guts, furry blood, something squashed. Concentrate on the dry furry coat that kept it together. Hearing again his voice – it's dead. "Mitten's not an it," she retorted and held the flesh up to him, threatening to throw it at him so that he would run away frightened. He did. Run away to Mammy. He always said Mammy. She used Mum like everyone normal did. She hated it because it was his way of claiming her for himself. If he hadn't chased Mitten onto the road, she would be still alive. Their mother could only thank God that it was Mitten and not Michael who had run out in front of the car. She had nightmares even now. Giving birth to Mitten who came out as squashy limp flesh.

'You what?' Her mother looked at her, distracted by something missing in the backcloth of greenery – a part of the house where there were no memories of Michael – an extension outwards and upwards instead of moving house. Aisling knew it was her father's way of forcing her mother to sort out Michael's things and to move on from his death.

'I'll go to the funeral of this cousin.'

Now that she had the idea, Aisling wanted it agreed. She was mentally making a list of things she would need. Surely with a funeral there wouldn't be time for her mother's usual dithering. No time for those deflected memories to be centre spread again. Her mother looked at her uncomprehendingly.

'I thought I could go with Dad and then stay around for a few days – have a look at Berlin.' Aisling kept her voice level – a new discipline – a sugar coating on her impatience. A way to get out of this ridiculous Mum-sitting. She had to move out of the flat because of the to-do with Maeve but she'd have found something else if it wasn't for bloody Michael.

'You! Go to Berlin?' Motherly incomprehension.

Aisling looked to her father. She was sure she could rely on him for this one. She had her information. If he wanted she would go alone. Would prefer it in fact.

He leapt at it, 'She's right, she could go – if it's only a family representative we want – why not? She'd be great and even knows German, which is more than you could say for me. Didn't she get honours in her Leaving Cert! Great idea! Why didn't I think of it? I must ring and find out when the funeral is. We can get some tickets arranged and a hotel. You could stay until the weekend – or until it's over. We don't even know when the funeral is yet.'

'You mean that both of you could go? Maybe you're right. It would be company for you.'

'Well, it's up to Dad. I'd like to go that's all,' Aisling kept her focus on getting out of here somehow soon.

'Well you know my view on it. I'm not convinced that anyone needs to go,' Aisling gave her father a warning look and he added hastily, 'but it would be great if Aisling agreed to represent the family. It would be a good opportunity for her to see a bit of Berlin too while she was there. There's no rush on her coming back. There's certainly no need for me to go as well.'

'But Aisling's never been to Berlin,' she turned to Aisling, 'You've never even met Aunt Bridget. Where would you stay in Berlin? And what about your job?'

Her mother's anxiety hit the highest note on the wind chime above Aisling's head. Treating her like a child. Ridiculous! Mental fragility or not.

Aisling darted under the defences, 'Job! You must be joking; there's a queue of other students waiting to pick it up.'

'Well it was good of Jim to take you. You can't just throw it back in his face like that.'

'Look, Mum, I know he made it seem like a special favour to you and Dad because you are regular customers but waiting on tables is not highly sophisticated work and he's not paying me any more than anyone else. There are plenty more where I came from.'

'I thought you liked it.'

'It's fine; the tips are good and I can walk to work. I've nothing to complain about but I wouldn't pine if I never had to go back in the place again. It's a holiday job and Jim's used to people like me coming and going. I was thinking of taking a couple of weeks off anyway. I have a bit saved. Living at home, working in the evenings .. and all… means that I've hardly gone out.'

'Well, I still think the two of you should go.'

'Now Mary, there's no way we're going to go and leave you here on your own. Aisling's talking a lot of sense – it would be a good experience for her. Why not a couple of weeks in Berlin – the amount we'd save on my flights and hotel would keep her going for a bit longer?' Her father turned to her, 'It might even give you some ideas about what you want to do when you finish your degree.'

'Yeah, it might.' Aisling kept her voice bright but was careful to make no concessions to her father's attempt to score a goal for himself. She had only just finished her first year in DCU and already they were planning her future. She hadn't told them yet how wrong the course was for her. She wasn't nerdy enough for it. When she applied, Marketing and Business seemed the way to go, to combine her drawing with techno tools. Bound to be a money spinner too. Get a well-paid job in a global operation or set up as a freelance. Wrong choice. There was not a single person interested in hand-drawn cartoon graphics and their potential for use in marketing products. She knew if she went back next term, she wouldn't last. Wrong time to tell the parents. Maybe after Berlin.

'It's only a funeral! Why would she hang about Berlin after that? You'd be on your own, Aisling – it's not like you'd be with one of your friends.'

'Well there's Aunt Bridget too,' her father was struggling but keeping his eye on the ball.

'Now it's Aunt Bridget – before it was a complete stranger whom you met a few times at funerals. You said it yourself; she's a woman in her eighties. It's hard enough to persuade Aisling to go and visit your mother in Drumcondra.'

'That's different.'

'I don't like the idea of her all alone in Berlin.'

Aisling came in fresh, 'Mum, I can look after myself. I'll find a student hostel or something on the Internet. And I don't even need Dad to find me a flight; I'll get that on the Internet too. I'll just go and have a look now.'

'She's right, Mary. It would be a good experience for her. As you said, she's never been to Berlin. Aunt Bridget would appreciate a younger person around.'

'Everybody has good ideas – the breeding ground for disaster,' Mary wiped condensation from the new window and put on the fan to expel the droplets of 'smother mother' in the air. She knew they thought it. No point in letting Diarmuid see how worried she was about Aisling too. She had good reason to be. Michael's death came so quickly after the other business.

Aisling's father gave her the raised eyebrow behind her mother's back. It was the signal to back off. Be the other grown up. Bloody Michael. Even dead she had to dance around him. She hated him. The fishing trip was their father's idea. He had to live with his decision to turn over in bed that morning. Michael was probably glad of the chance to top himself. Nobody even breathed suicide but Aisling knew even if they didn't. No tragic accident. He'd left everything too tidy – even tidier than you would expect from Michael. The torn out pages from his journal clinched it. She was sure the pages had bits about her he didn't want anyone else to read. And all that sugary stuff about Mum and Dad – even about her – in the last few pages, she didn't believe it for one minute. It was all too neat – almost like a suicide note without admitting to the suicide. Now her mother had him practically canonised. She hated all this pussyfooting around. She hated him for not being there.

'Whatever… I'll go and have a look for flights.'

'Good idea, I'll come up in a minute.'

And so it was. Special offer on a direct Aer Lingus flight to Berlin. Too good to miss. Aisling waited just long enough to hustle her mother into confirmation before reserving it. Booked for two weeks. It was really cheap so even if she had to change it later, it would be no problem. Nobody knew when exactly the funeral would be.

'The funeral could be any day. We have to go for it.'

When he got enough agreement, his relief bounded upstairs and whipped out his credit card. Done. He rang his aunt then to offer his sympathy and tell her Aisling was coming. The aunt was insistent Aisling should come and stay with her. The spare room was hers as long as she wanted. Aisling was annoyed about that. She didn't really want to stay there, but she'd sort that out when she got there. And it would be handy to have somewhere to stay when she arrived. Her parents had never been to Berlin either. It was going to be her place, her show.

Her mother was annoyed at the speed of it all of course. To distract her Aisling asked her what to wear to the funeral. Borrow something dull enough. Leave her father texting. She knew the script. There was a big match in Croke Park at the weekend that he wanted to go to but daren't mention it as a reason for not going to the funeral. He would be texting Desie telling him that he could make the match after all. Desie's wife Maureen would ring Mum to suggest they meet up and go for a walk while the boys went to the match.

They were all so predictable and BORING! 'If I thought that was all there was to look forward to when I'm as old as them, I'd top myself now too.' Berlin might be something different with a bit of luck. A chance to rebury the fucking ghostly face that looked at her from the mirror. Time to ring around to find someone to cover her weekend shifts at the restaurant. Then to let Jim know about the funeral and maybe she wouldn't be coming back to work. A quick dash on the DART to get a Guide to Berlin.

Lots of stuff about the Berlin wall. If they wanted it as a tourist attraction they should have hung onto more of it.

Anyone who really wanted to visit the remains of the Berlin wall, should start in the States. Their final holiday as a family had been in California and they'd seen a huge chunk of the wall in the County Museum of Art in LA. Not a replica apparently; the real thing shipped out. There were chunks of wall all over the place. A cartoon strip materialised in her head around the nursery rhyme about the war of the Roses, or was it the Napoleonic wars? The one where the duke marched his men up and down hills pointlessly – a satire on his lack of skill in battle. The comic strip would be a global search to locate the Berlin wall. Where is the wall now? Who cares? When it was up it was up and when it was down it was down. When it was only half way up, it was neither up nor down.

Chapter Four

# Shades of Ireland

Nod. Nod into open eyes and the feel of the rosary beads murmuring decades of joy. I can see my mother's face. I can feel her in the beads that she gave me. I can hear her thoughts in my half sleep. Joyful mysteries carry her to her rest. Yola shouts me back, "Möchten Sie etwas?" Do I want anything? Shaking the inside feeling awake.

Yes. I want Katharina. I will lift the phone and ring her Handy to hear her voice again. Monika will know. When will I cancel it? She asked me. I said nothing. I don't understand this daughter death. This morning I smelled her in her jacket. How can material hold her still when her skin and bone cannot? Now is the time for Yola to ask me if I want coffee and cake on a tray or will I come to the dining table. Sit alone or with her? I have no family now.

The family in Ireland evaporate with daily excuses of circumstance. Peggy rings me again to say how sorry not to be fit to travel. Someone will come. Diarmuid who drove me to my mother? I need flesh and blood. Yola dusts my record of Johnny Cash "Flesh and Blood needs Flesh and Blood and you're the one I need." Only Katharina. My secret love song for her. Did she know? She asked if I missed my family in Ireland. Only my mother, I told her. Why not visit? Impatient when I postponed time and time again. When my mother was ill in bed, Katharina bought the non-refundable ticket for me, knowing I could not waste it. Why not go, Mama? Why not? You worked so hard all your life. Now you have time.

My only Flesh and Blood is gone. Do I want a stranger in my house? I would prefer to have Katharina's body here and then the strangers could come and shake my hand. Waiting to bury my daughter and wishing I could be buried with her. Efficient Monika could arrange a double funeral. Yola would help. She comes every day now except Sunday. Katharina arranged that. Did she know then she was going to die?

Brigitte saw Katharina's face white and anxious arguing with her. Her hair colour the colour of drying turf, dark as the earth but reflecting the light on the bracken trapped inside it. But Katharina didn't look Irish – her hair fell from her face just below her jaw, smoothed into shape, German straight and determined. Her blue eyes were set apart above high cheekbones – no soft boggy Irishness around the eyes. At first the single stray grey strands rebelled but they were pulled out. When the grey strands became too many, first she cut it, and then she dyed it. Once she dyed it a deep aubergine colour. Defiance. When she lost weight and her hair was cut short; when she was ill; Brigitte could not look at her: she saw too many deaths in her face.

They went together shopping for wigs. They laughed together that day and went to Café Buchwald for Kaffee und Kuchen. They both loved Café Buchwald. Katharina could hardly finish her cake although they had no lunch. She played with the strawberry cheesecake and talked of her memories of the first time her mother took her there and the other times too. Brigitte wanted to ask Katharina did she ever take Monika there, but she could not. She wanted to keep the wig buying day as a happy day, to store it with other happy days. A day of crisp, speckled leaves skittering ahead of them down the street. A little girl holding her mother's hand skipped the joy of loving back into life. A pause to admire the small pumpkins displayed among the yellow and red-brown chrysanthemums of autumn. 'I'll get some of them for you.' The wonder of chestnuts, kurbis and pinecones arranged on the windowsill. German homework on the table between them. Katharina correcting the bad habits of Brigitte's German grammar. English for laughter and fun. German for work.

The wig was for Katharina's 60th birthday . Monika didn't know about it. Katharina wanted to surprise her. No celebration now. She will wear it in her coffin instead.

'It's better than going to the hairdresser,' she laughed when she got a wig that reproduced the colour of her own hair. The wig might have fooled Monika but it would never fool Brigitte. It was too neat. There were no stray signs of rebellion. Katharina shook its cloak-like cover over her face to conceal the death in her dark eyes. Once, on the rare occasion that she stayed during her cancer death sentence, Brigitte found her in the bathroom, wisps of hair floating off her skull as she knelt by the toilet bowl. Brigitte said nothing and left her there. That was how they were together. How they had always been for so long now. So little to say because there was too much left unsaid for too long.

Brigitte hated Katharina's way of thinking and not saying. Her white face a silent accusation. How could Brigitte have told her the worst about that place? It would sully the life she'd rescued from dirt and death.

'There's nothing you need to do. Monika will do it all,' she said once.

'I couldn't do it anyway,' Brigitte told herself. 'I always knew someone else would do it for Katharina because I would go first, of course.'

Glad of Monika for that at least. Not those memories of the worst times when Katharina did not visit for weeks.

'I might as well be dead.' Did I mean it then? I mean it now for sure. Then, I said it to hurt my Katharina. I was angry when she went with Monika to Greece. Did they walk the same sunsets as Katya walked with me? 'Not so much as a postcard,' I said to her. I lied. One did come but I hid it. She put it in an envelope so that it would come faster. I know that too.

'I might as well. I don't understand, Mama? What do these words mean?' Her eyes and nose wrinkled into the question like when she was a child. I was angrier then because there was no German life in that. I could not tell her it was my mother's voice speaking those words not mine.

'I might as well be dead for all they care.'

I knew it was a lie but still I went to my mother when she was weak and waiting to die. Now I have no-one to see me off. Self-pity, you selfish old woman.

Yola says she will stay until someone comes from Ireland. Yola talks of the farm in Poland. 'Heimweh,' she said, patting her chest. And you? Homesick? No I lied. Do I miss my Heimat? She did not know any word in English for 'Heimat'. To her it meant something more than home, a place where you belonged. I tell her I don't belong in Ireland for sure. But I am a foreigner in Germany. I need no heimat.

I do not say. Better to be heimatless than pitted one against another. Rounded buttocks of one nationality. Skinny Hintern of another. An outcast torn limb from limb eats the soul if you have one. Better not to be typecast guilty or innocent. Trapped in hate, I am the same. Let whomsoever who is not guilty throw the first stone. The greatest victory of any Reich – to take the fear of the other and twist it in our gut to make a holocaust of hope. I am the same but different too I hope. Katharina is my difference. Katharina was my difference.

'I love you, Mama.'

She liked to say those words in English. Always. Even at the worst times.

I tell Yola I miss half-knowing people. Neighbours who might turn the knife in your back but might help you in a crisis. Here you know people or they are strangers. There, there were people that you knew to see, knew to hear about, knew to say hello to but not much more. People whom you hardly knew but you would go to their wake if they died.

There was nothing like a good wake to help you face life in death. A lie. Or maybe a mix of truth and lie. In truth Brigitte didn't miss the trudging around the countryside to the homes of half-known neighbours or distant relatives to pray, gossip, laugh and cry over a corpse that she barely recognised. She was glad to leave that Ireland behind when she came to Berlin as a slip of a girl.

Since the death of her mother, Peggy kept up regular contact. Funny that it should be Peggy who would ring more and more often.

'The phone is my little luxury,' she would say and share details of her children, grandchildren – neighbours even. It was Peggy she rang first to tell about Katharina. Liam's voice, when she did ring, was full of accusation that she kept in touch with Peggy and had told her first. Liam was always her favourite – he was her baby when he was born. She was ten years old – old enough to help nurse him. It was Brigitte who could get him to sleep in the big bed before his older brothers joined him later. It was Brigitte who would change the bed in the middle of the night as the others fumed at him piddling again. When their mother died, he had turned mulish and bitter and refused contact with all the family except Brigitte because she had come when called.

She went because Peggy told her Liam was at the end of his tether and would hardly speak to any of them. Their mother needed someone to stay there at nights and Liam could not spend every night, disturbed by her distress. None of the others would share the burden. The oldest, Michael, was away in England and just as well because he would not be much use anyway as he needed looking after himself. Apparently he had a fondness for the bottle. Peggy was in Dublin and claimed she was needed to look after her son Conor who was still living at home and her two grandchildren, Aisling and Michael, after school. John-Joe and Marion lived a mile up the road, but neither could bear to leave their comfortable modern house to be there in the old house with a range hungry for heat, and a wind under the door that could cut corn. Her brother James was in Boston making his fortune. Brigitte remembered the night before he left, the determination on his face that he would be the equal of anybody and come back with dollars in his pocket or not at all. Ireland was too full of quisling arse lickers for him to continue to live there. He made his money all right and married an Irish woman over there who came from a family with roots in Galway. He rarely came to Ireland but offered great hospitality to anyone who would go to him. He had found work for all of John-Joe and Marion's children and they rarely came back now either.

Liam must have been desperate when he rang Peggy. Not

a one of them expected Brigitte to come back after so long away. None of them knew it was just after Katharina had moved out. Brigitte had no need to work. Her pension was more than enough.

'Why not go?' Katharina said, and she was happy to arrange it all. Peggy's son, Diarmuid, picked her up at the airport and drove her to Leitrim. She sat in the front seat of his BMW, grateful for the periods of polite silence. At every corner, no matter how remote, there were new houses being built or shopping centres or retail outlets. It was all too fast, too comfortable and unfamiliar.

The old house at home was smaller than she remembered. To make conversation, Diarmuid puzzled over how they had all fitted into the three bedrooms upstairs. At the time theirs was one of the biggest houses. There were plenty of bigger families in smaller houses. Liam had done his best to transport their parents' bedroom from upstairs to what was once the good room downstairs so that it would be familiar. When her grandmother lived and died there, it was still called the parlour. Now it was mother's room. Diarmuid paced around the kitchen drinking the mug of tea and eating sandwiches they'd bought in the garage where they stopped. He stayed barely an hour before heading back to Dublin. The whole country seemed to have shrunk to a small island with incongruous houses on every corner.

Shake their hands now for Katharina's wake. Daughter death mixing with mother death. Alone with her mother in the old home, her mother became the child. She was in a half-sleep a lot of the time that first week after Brigitte arrived. It was hard to know if she was conscious – even when Brigitte was spooning water and food into her mouth. In the moments of fullest consciousness, she would call for Liam to bring her porridge but did not look surprised when it came in the hands of Brigitte. Brigitte fitted in with the rituals Liam had set up for himself. Yet there was time enough for her to find her own routine around Liam and the carer who came to wash and change their mother. Brigitte prepared meals for herself and Liam. She baked, cleaned the house, washed and dried the sheets and nightclothes. Back to the days of survival with her baby.

She spent time by the bedside just talking quietly about her own life unsure whether her mother heard any of it. Putting things in place. Say it aloud even if she is sleeping. Let her go with 'I love you, Mammy'. Harsh words. Hard thoughts go with the words. The last time she said those words was as a child. Then the eyes flickered and lips said 'I love you too, Biddy'. When did I last say to Katharina, 'Ich liebe dich.'? Too long ago. I will never tell how I learnt to love the German father in my Katharina. 'I love you' were empty words before she came. The child and the angry adult in her gave me back the words love and hate

Murmuring familiarity, Hail Mary, Holy Mary. Mother of God. My two loves. My mother and my daughter. I haven't a heart big enough for more. Yet there is room for shame there and guilt. A clear out needed. Time to declutter, Mama, Katharina would say, using an English word I have never heard before.

During those days they thought would be the last, Liam would often come and sit with her in the kitchen and they kept the range on all night. Brigitte sometimes fell asleep there on the sofa unless Liam decided the few hundred yards to his house weren't worth the bother, and then she left the sofa to him and

33

climbed the stair. During the day, she was glad to see him come and sit with their mother. She liked time alone outside walking the lanes, watching the lake change in the light.

Their mother surprised the doctor by regaining a level of awareness and attention in the second week Brigitte was there. Liam had a brief moment of joy when he arrived in one day to find his mother back in her armchair by the range watching the door. She recognised Brigitte and called now for Biddy as well as Liam. The old mix of rebellion, frustration and love that had been buried for half a century came back. Merging Mother, Daughter, Mother. Scrubbing baby nappies in cold water in post-war Berlin. Changing her mother's nappy at night, wiping her bottom. Never able to forget the dysentery days with skitter hardened on her legs as she worked in the cold. Waiting with the others in a queue for the blast of ice to dislodge it. Protected here by the supply of large nappies Liam picked up from the health centre in his van. Grateful if a neighbour sat with Mammy and Brigitte could come with him to save his blushes. Changed, clean nightie. Comfortable. Mammy took her hand and kissed it. This was not the Mammy she knew. It was Hannelore kissing the hand of farmers in gratitude for fried potatoes. The Lager was there and far away at the same time. The two worlds crashed together.

'I'm sorry for sending you away.'

Quatsch. Nonsense. Brigitte bit her tongue. I was the one who went and left you here at the mercy of the parish pump. Irish eyes are smiling. German whips are cracking. Both guilty. Both innocent

'No, Mammy. No, Mammy, no. You didn't send me. I wanted to go.' No more to be said. 'All in the past now. You did your best for all of us. Shall we say a decade of the rosary?'

No word of the scandal in walking out with a protestant boy from Manorhamilton. Brigitte had long forgotten him. Poor Mammy. He wasn't the reason for going and not coming back. She had told Mammy that Katharina's father was a Catholic. Would it be a comfort or hurt her more? A married man. None of it matters now.

She tried to tell Katharina later but the words would not come. The grief shocked her. Missing Mammy after all these years. Memories of the early days in Berlin. A happy missing in the days when she swung herself onto the tram and thought if Mammy could see me now. Mammy alive and busy. Back to the days of no Katharina. The time between and the day Katharina came with news of cancer. Time of being Mammy. She wanted to look after her baby again but Monika took over. Did Katharina want her to or did she do it to please her? No pleasing Mama.

Katharina and Monika. We want to live together, Mama. Forty she was then. Too old to have children. Too late to marry. Forty years and then nothing. At least Brigitte had her work for a couple of years more. Then nothing. Nix. There was no reason not to go to Ireland to look after her own mother. Those weeks in Leitrim it was good to be needed. A second stroke drew the inevitable closer. The hospital was rampant with infection. Better off at home. A steady decline with a very low level of consciousness blurred the days into forever. There was no jealous fighting for the right to sit up at night any more. Liam was always in and out of course. Even Marion – give her due – took her turn to sit with their mother in those last days. One early morning while Brigitte prepared the mixture the doctor had prescribed to substitute for food, she heard her mother call 'Mammy, Mammy, Mammy'. It was not the first time but now it was followed by a murmured litany of names of people already dead. Yet there was no sign of full consciousness. It was more like talking in her sleep. Brigitte felt her bones say 'Ring Liam'.

Within minutes, she heard the key turn in the front door. 'Is she gone?' Liam asked it like an accusation but she shook her head. They sat one on each side of the bed and waited for the doctor who took one look and said, "It won't be long now" before leaving again. The next two hours they waited with the rattling breath, wondering which would be the last. When it came, it was more of a final shudder than a breath.

Waiting there by the bedside for something to happen next, for someone to come who knew what to do. 'Death is always sudden no matter how long you wait for it.' It was Mary's voice and Mary's hand in hers. Then Mary's son turned up and Mary said, 'I'll go and make a nice cup of tea. You'll take one too Jim, won't you?' She last saw Jim when they were at school together; he looked now like his own father. Puzzling through the blur of sleeplessness. Why is he here in his dark clothes talking to Liam before they had put the word out of her mother's death? Then she saw his father in him – his father with the taxi and the hearse. His father dead, he was the undertaker now. In his wake, neighbours she hadn't seen for sixty years came, carrying food and murmuring: sorry for your loss; died at home; in her own bed; of all of them you look the most like her; long life; hard work; good death; lucky you could come from Germany mingling with the hail Mary, holy Mary, mother of God. Girls, she had been to school with, turned into their own mothers.

Where shall I put this? Where shall I put that? What about your mother's bedroom upstairs? Brigitte could nod and leave them to it. Later after a rest in her mother's bed, she brought them two clean white sheets, the last from the pile she had ironed under her mother's eye of approval on those days she sat up. Two linen sheets, saved from a pile inherited from Biddy's grandmother, who was given them when she left service when the old woman she looked after died. Biddy replacing the arms her mother had used to wash and iron those sheets before her father died. She put her face between the stiff sheets, breathing the smell of a clean death. She was glad her mother had that.

Peggy-now-Margaret arrived late and then went to bed, tired after the long drive. It was John-Joe, now Joe, who was so like her father, who did most to bring her mother's presence back into the house as it emptied of neighbours. Joe made her life and death merge with his talk of the Celtic tiger and the days when her father turned from cattle to sheep and Liam going back again now to cattle. Cycles and rotation. She stepped back from the arrangements. It was down to Liam and so it should be – he was always her mother's favourite and hers too. Peggy, please-remember-to-call-me-Margaret-not-Peggy, was last as she had to come from Dublin. Her son would pick up James from Boston on the way. Liam was business-like and good-humoured but she knew he was the one who would grieve most. The one who came every morning for all those years of her mother living alone. Peggy was quick to point out that he had to come anyway to feed the cattle he had on the farm. Self-interest is quick to spot self-interest. No shame in that.

Brigitte kept that image of the last rosary, with all her siblings together for the first time in half a century, as a comfort when images of the past brought their ghosts into the present. Peggy led the rosary. James stood at the head of the coffin. He died in the States three years later, as lavishly as he had lived, by Peggy's account. Michael's large red nose was beacon to how he had spent the small fortune he had earned in the building trade in England. John-Joe, now the local big time business man, stood beside Michael, looking lost without his wife, Marion, beside him. He had taken over a petrol pump in the village street and turned it into one of those garage-supermarkets. His children sold the business and the big house when Marion died at the height of the property boom in Ireland. Apparently he was now in a nursing home. Beside him, Liam with his jaw set. Liam who thought more of the animals on his farm than he did of his brothers and sisters who had let him down so badly in their mother's final months.

There was a comfortable finality in leaving for the last time. It wasn't the narrowness of the place. She was surprised to find how much things had changed. Young women who had children outside marriage were accepted now. There was none of the dramatic, 'Don't come and darken my door again with your bastard.' The ritual of Sunday Mass was still observed but very few young people were there. Everybody had cars. They shopped and shopped in shops that had not existed before. They visited less. It seemed as if the Irish family she had left behind didn't exist any longer for anyone.

When she got back to Berlin, she felt once more the joy of public transport, of anonymous city lights and department stores. She looked up friends and organised outings for Kaffee und Kuchen. Back to the days when she first swung her way on trams in search of the best coffee and cake. The grief hit her later. She swung between the past and present, between despair and moments of relief, knowing she would never go back to Ireland. When Katharina worried about her in the down days, she said, 'Maybe I will' – just to please her.

## Chapter Five

# Gran

They were all going over to Gran's – to offer their sympathy.

'So what relation is Brigitte to me, Dad?' Aisling asked when they were in the car.

'I don't know whether there's a name for it. Maybe great-aunt? She's your Gran's sister and you're going to represent your Gran – don't forget that.'

'So her daughter, Katharina, is your cousin.'

'That's right. I think it means she'd be your second cousin or maybe it is first cousin, once removed. Ask your Gran.'

'What age was this Katharina?'

'Well she was born in 1945, so that would make her nearly 60. Poor woman – worked hard all her life by all accounts and didn't live until she could pick up a pension. I can't think of anything more galling.'

Diarmuid opened the front door with his key and called out, 'Mother, it's us.' Gran was sitting in her usual position in her armchair by the fire watching TV. Her father had taken that into account.

'She'll throw us out when the 'Late Late Show' comes on. The TV will be off because she'll not want us to know that she's going to watch it at all. Anyway Aisling has to get to bed early if she's going to make that early flight.'

Her dad knew that Gran wouldn't be best pleased with him letting Aisling go alone – that was probably the reason for the odd look that came in her direction – but Aisling wasn't prepared for the disapproval to overflow onto her.

On a Friday, her Gran always looked like she was dressed for Sunday Mass. She took a taxi every Friday to get her hair done and after that she would meet her friend, Anna, for coffee. She would stay dressed up for the Late, Late Show and would allow herself a little glass of sherry or port or Bailey's. She must have kept to her usual Friday routine. The lamb-white cap of curls and the fact that she was still wearing a silk scarf around her neck were sure signs. The scarf was one that Aisling liked because it was the colour of a vivid sky shot through with bits of scattered cloud. She had probably spent most of yesterday evening choosing the combination of clothes – blue blouse, grey cardigan and skirt with its two front pleats combining with the cameo brooch at her throat.

Gran went straight into her Dad, 'So you're too busy now to go to a funeral. I'll have to make sure that I die at a convenient time myself if I want any of my relations to be there.'

'Oh come on, Mother, if it was Aunt Bridget herself, I would make more of an effort but I don't even know this cousin and it's not as if she's bothered much about us over the years.'

Her Dad's tone always carried the defensive guilt of a little boy. Why did he have to justify going or not going to his mother?

'Oh, it's very easy to speak ill of the dead.' Aisling loved to see her Gran making her dad squirm and she made the mistake of letting a smile show.

'And I don't know what you're laughing at – if the funeral was in Belleek rather than Berlin, you'd hardly volunteer to go.'

Aisling had long ago learnt to say nothing and just wait a while. It was too soon to tell Gran her hair looked well. 'Will I make a cup of tea?' Distraction was the only way to deal with Gran when she was in one of her moods. That question didn't need an answer. It just meant she could head off to the kitchen.

'Nobody even asked if I wanted to go myself,' she heard her Gran say as she left the room.

So that was it. Her father and mother exchanged glances. Aisling left the door open so that she could hear them from the kitchen.

'Well, it's not too late. But you said last time we went to Spain that you hated travel and you would never get on a plane again.'

'That was different: that was holidays. This is a funeral.'

Aisling was glad they couldn't hear her giggle, which reached the surface as the kettle boiled. She hunted around the drawers for one of Gran's stores of Marks and Spencer's chocolate biscuits. She usually sampled a few. Her dad had brought a few scones from the fresh bread stand in the garage. He and Mum would cop it for that too, the mood that Gran was in. She would be sure to give out about everybody buying scones instead of baking them 'and the price those places charge.' She hoped she wasn't serious about going to the funeral – that would be a rather different trip. She buttered the scones and brought in the tray.

'Oh fresh scones – hardly homemade, I suppose.'

'No, Mum, they have so much fresh stuff for sale, it's easier to buy than to bake when you only want a few.'

'What did you pay for these?' Gran looked from her dad to her mum.

'I don't remember, Mother.' Diarmuid answered quickly.

'Yes, it's all very well for some – more money than you know what to do with. But when you're on a tight budget like I was when you were growing up or now on my pension, you wouldn't dream of buying what you could bake yourself. Kathleen told me she paid 48 cents for one the other day. I said, 'More fool you, Kathleen; you can bake them and freeze them you know. If it weren't for these pains of mine, I'd still be doing that. God knows maybe I should. If I could sell them at that price, I could supplement my pension.'

At least the topic had shifted. And it would soon be time for the 'Late, Late Show'. But Gran wasn't ready to let go that easy. 'I suppose you haven't even said a prayer for her. That's gone out of fashion too – like going to Mass. Poor Bridget. It's hard to be so far from your own at a time like this.'

'I thought we'd say a few prayers with you, Mother – maybe a decade of the rosary.'

'A decade indeed. So now the Rosary is rationed.'

'We can say the whole thing if you want.'

Aisling hoped her father caught the wordless Dad-you-are-such-a-hypocrite glance she shot at him.

'You lead then.'

The entertainment of her father forgetting the first half of the Hail Mary was nearly worth kneeling there with one eye on the clock. Luckily her Gran didn't expect any of them to remember what the sorrowful mysteries were. By the time it got to the 4th mystery and Aisling's turn, she could rattle off the Our Father and the ten Hail Marys and the Glory be to the Father in record time.

The last time she had said the rosary was when Michael died. Her Gran was there at the house waiting for them when the undertakers brought him back to the house. Most people didn't have a wake in the house these days. Most people in Dublin anyway, though they probably did in the country still. When they brought Michael back from Leitrim, Gran and Mum both wanted a wake so there was no question of not having one. Her Mum wanted Michael to come home with them one last time even if it was in a coffin.

Aisling wished now she had slowed down her decade of the rosary as she saw that her Gran was the one now with her eye on the clock – the Late-Late Show would start any minute. It would be fun to see her squirm a bit for a change. What about this second cousin in Berlin; would there be a wake? Hardly likely. It was an Irish thing, or a country thing anyway. Aisling knew nothing about her and had never heard the name of any uncle. He was probably dead.

'What about her husband, is he dead too?' Aisling's question hung in the air for a few seconds and her Dad gave her one of those – not in front of Gran looks. Well she should have been warned if there was something she shouldn't ask about.

But her Gran wasn't a bit put out; the ads were still on the telly, which she'd switched on the minute they had finished the rosary. 'Poor Bridget never got married. As far as I know, she adopted Katharina, one of those poor war orphans. Bridget gave her the very bread out of her own mouth by all accounts – not that she got a lot of thanks for it. But sure if it was thanks we were waiting for, we'd wait a long time.'

'Are you sure you don't want me to make arrangements for you to go, Mother? It's not too late if you really want to. It can be done; we could get you a wheelchair to take you through the airport.' Her father knew rightly the offer was just a gesture.

'Me in a wheelchair! How could you, Diarmuid?' Her Gran knew too.

Diarmuid's voice was warm with satisfaction now, 'I think it would do Aunt Bridget good to come home for a while when it's all over and she'll not do that if we all go over there now. I'd be happy to pay for that if you want to invite her.'

'Yes, I'll ring her again to-morrow.' That was it – another sly glance at the clock on the mantelpiece. Count down to the "Late, Late Show" and they could excuse themselves.

'I'll have an early night to-night, I think.' Gran could be a real hypocrite too sometimes.

Aisling waited until they were in the car before she asked, 'So what's all this about Katharina being an orphan? So she's not a real cousin?'

Her mother spoke for her father, 'I think it's what your Gran wants to believe. No-one really knows the full story but Katharina is Bridget's daughter; that much is sure. There were so many different stories, we never knew which one Bridget told to make it easier for her parents; which one was the truth; and which one was pure fabrication. Your uncle Liam always said that the father was in the German army.' Her mother imitated his Leitrim lilt but made it slower, 'And what could be wrong with that – weren't we all fighting the British then?'

She switched back to her own voice, 'There were other stories about an American soldier but Katharina was born too soon after the end of the war for that. Anyway whoever it was, it's fairly sure they were never married. That's probably why Bridget never came back to Ireland. Well they couldn't to begin with. Berlin wasn't the easiest place to travel to. Even when it came to our time to travel in the late 60's, your Gran was never keen. She used the excuse of the wall going up and people being killed. She made it sound as if Aunt Bridget was right in the middle of it. The real reason was that as long as Bridget was in Berlin and didn't have much contact with the family, there was less scope for scandal. Anyway, from accounts we heard, Berlin seemed to be stuck in a time warp.'

'I'm surprised you didn't make an effort. I thought that would be just up your street, Dad – a bit of living history. The Berlin Wall came down some time in the late 1980's, didn't it?'

'November 1989. I'm surprised you don't remember that date. The end of the German Democratic Republic and the unification of Germany followed on really quickly. It was the death knell of the Soviet Bloc.'

'I was only born in 1983 remember. I wasn't watching the news at 6 years old. And the Soviet Bloc is history now.'

'I suppose so,' her dad frowned and she could hear him slipping into history lecture tone which she mocked internally in half listening mode, 'Your aunt was in the bit of Berlin controlled by the Allies at the end of the war but she was close to the Wall by all accounts.'

'So I'll be visiting an interesting specimen of social history. I'm surprised you're not coming with me.'

'Well I would love to but… '

'Just think, Diarmuid,' Her mother sighed, ' Michael was just born.'

Danger zone of life BMD and life AMD – life-before-Michael-died and life after-Michael-died. Dad kicked the ball back into history.

'No need to be sarcastic, young lady. Remember, it *is* part of living history not something only in schoolbooks. And apparently Berlin has a real buzz these days. Now it's the capital city again. Seat of government. Media hub and so on.'

'Be careful of what you say about the war to Brigitte. She was in some camp for a while during the war – somewhere near Berlin,' her mother added.

'A prisoner-of-war camp? What did she do to get in there?'

'Well, it wasn't a prisoner of war camp – more some sort of labour camp. They rounded foreigners up apparently.'

Her father butted in, 'Where did you hear that, Mary, surely I would have known about it?'

'I don't know the full story but apparently your uncle Liam talked to her a lot when she came over to look after your grandmother that time.'

'Oh, Liam! Well it could be hard to sort the fact from the fiction. You'll have to be a bit more tactful than usual, Aisling.'

'Look who's talking!'

'Don't worry. Just don't ask too many questions. Let Aunt Bridget tell you what she wants.'

Aisling said nothing – a funeral, a relative older than God and historical research; maybe Berlin could be more boring than being stuck at home. Still it wouldn't be for long and it would make the break from being the good daughter. There must be clubs and cool places to hang out in Berlin. Maybe the buzz her father talked about had some connection to the Love Parade. Berlin was bracketed in her memory with the Love Parade. She reminded herself again to Google it. She'd have time to look at the guide at the airport if not before. It sounded as if there would be a few skeletons in the aunt's cupboard worth a rattle too. Gran always censored out the more colourful bits of family history except maybe when she had a few sherries at Christmas.

## Chapter Six

# God Demands A Holocaust

The best of both would be good. In Ireland they took you from deathbed to the grave in three days. Here in Berlin there was so much to arrange and it took so long. Monika wanted Katharina in her family's grave and now it was Monika who arranged everything.

'And who will do it for me?' she asked herself again and again and told herself not to be such a stupid, selfish, old woman. Someone would. How many pills would she need to be sure? The worst would be to survive and need them even more than she did now. So many days of getting up, eating and sleeping while Katharina's cold body lay somewhere alone. Brigitte would have liked Katharina here with her in the flat but it wasn't done. Instead she was kept in a fridge. Brigitte knew she would have to see her in the coffin but how? Who would take her? Not Monika, that was sure. She pinned her hopes on Peggy sending someone. She would get the pills ready. When to take them? Before Peggy sent someone or after? Before would be better. She didn't need them all those years. All they needed to do was arrange her funeral. Monika would help. She and Katharina would get cremated together. The groping and grovelling for bread in conception would be merged with the years of joy with the child who brought back the will to live. Anna would read again from the book of Wisdom 3.1-6.9. The word sounding holy, a sacrifice. She heard it first in Anna's German. The Old Testament was not read in the Ireland of her childhood. Later Katharina found it for her.

> "God has put them to the test
> and proved them worthy to be with him;
> he has tested them like gold in a furnace,
> and accepted them as a holocaust."
> Words of blood.

Flesh of my flesh. A love child or a bastard. Her father would not have allowed her to bring up her bastard in Leitrim. They chose to believe the whirlwind romance with an American soldier. No questions asked about why she didn't follow him to America. When Katharina was old enough to go there alone, she visited once. She said she hated Ireland because Ireland didn't fight the Nazis.

Waiting for death – a series of small steps to be remembered. You could make it seem dramatic but the last breath was only another breath, no more, no less – the last breath of many breaths. Monika was with Katharina when she died. She didn't send for me. Just a phone call. It was what Katharina wanted, she said. It wasn't right. Not even a priest. A new death brings back memory of old deaths; brings a moment to join being and non-being. Father O' Dwyer who wanted to talk to her about her mother over a cup of tea when she wanted silence. It was only afterwards she realised he needed to know what to say in the sermon and it would save him asking another time. Who should do the readings? Should the coffin be light or dark? A foreign New Ireland question – would her mother want some make-up on? She made up what she didn't know like the silent simulation of a well-known hymn.

'It was that night that I stopped believing in life after death,' she told her friend Mary who waltzed in the window for Katharina's wake. 'Why then and not in that place?' she asked aloud. 'Why did the two worlds come together that time when they had been happy to survive in separation for so long? Was it the pointlessness of it all? Good, gut, guttural-good both better than nice. There is no nice death but a wake would still be good. It would be good to listen to stories of ghosts and spirits, stories of the past. Memories. Good memories. There are not many of those memories left now in Ireland. Where have they gone if not to an afterlife? Good and God. Was it then that I stopped believing in God too?'

All those years she had hung on to her belief that God and Good were somewhere still. Nobody would have blamed her if she had lost her faith a long time ago in the Lager. Nobody who knew or who could imagine it. Then she used to wonder what sort of God could do this but she found him still among the Bibelki, the Jehovah's Witnesses. She could even see him in Günter when his face was close to hers – even when she saw him once with his belt in his hand, bending over that woman eating from the ground like a dog. She could see him demanding more than any human was capable of and taking away more than any human could imagine. The strange logic of the camp.

She could see God in the woman he whipped too. Thanks to her mother. 'Remember, you are no better or worse than anyone can be. If you keep yourself from the worst in them, you keep yourself from the worst in you. There, but for the grace of God, goes me or you.' Her mother's voice in her ear. Surviving. Anna's heavy breathing in the other. A little bundle of bones and yet such a strange noise as she left them behind.

She lifted the photo album to bring back the memories of Katharina making her First Communion. When her eyes closed again, it was Günter she saw striding up the aisle. She knew Günter was a Catholic and went to Mass every Sunday and prayed but she had never seen him in a church. It was only a picture she created in her mind. She never stopped asking herself how he could go to Mass on Sunday and do as he did the rest of the week. Maybe Günter prayed for these people whom he saw as no more than animals. She was lucky to be with the 'Bifos' or she would have died too. Günter respected the Bibelki. They managed to stay clean and mostly they refused to die of dysentery like so many of the others. He respected them more than the Communists, who were better organised. But it was the communist, Irma, who brought back the will to live, when Anna died. In Irma's company, wanting to live became a habit again. A bad habit now that she wanted to die, even though there was nothing to leave and nothing to go to.

Good strong wake laughter was what she needed then and now – not this civilised tidy planning done by Katharina from her coffin. A wake. A nice cup of tea to sip or slurp. A nice cup of tea – those were the words from her mother's last days. Biddy tried to make everything nice for her. She would sleep again after a few spoonfuls of warm sweet tea. She wanted her sister Peggy to come. Her sister Peggy had always been able to be nice, to find niceness, to make niceness. She has a fine Dublin house and fine Dublin family and fine Dublin ways. She has coffee with Irish women in Dublin, who have never been to Leitrim or maybe passed through it once without knowing but some of them have been to Berlin. Not Peggy.

Yola hovered, 'Frau Duignan, would you like some coffee and cake?'

Brigitte said yes to please her. Kaffee und Kuchen. Yola spoke English. One of the reasons Katharina wanted Yola to help her was she liked to speak English. She was delighted when Brigitte corrected her. The big bonus for her was that she was paid to have the opportunity to learn English in Berlin. 'Your daughter was good and kind. Why does God take the good and kind people?'

Brigitte could hear Mary's laugh like crackling in an old wireless. He won't come for us too quick then will he? She wanted to laugh with Mary not cry with Yola but the tears came more easily. Tears and more tears. She wished Yola were gone. If she were alone the tears would dry up. I will die alone. She reached for a tablet – something that would help her survive now but not leave her short of a supply for her need to die later.

Play it again, Katharina, who laughed although she didn't like Johnny Cash.

Diarmuid will not come after all. Peggy's granddaughter is on her way. A strange young woman. Down to earth, Peggy says. She will find her own way. No need to involve Monika. Good. What is she looking for? Not the funeral of my Katharina, I am sure. At her age I would not choose to be with a bad-tempered old biddy. Berlin? Like me? Running too. I made a mistake; I said she could stay in Katharina's room. I am not ready for that. I will pay for her to stay in a hotel. I will have no need of my savings soon. I wanted Diarmuid. I could leave him to make arrangements for me to follow Katharina. My bones shriek but no-one hears.

'Someone comes from Eerland?' Yola hovered within earshot when Peggy rang. Brigitte didn't correct the pronunciation of Ireland; she liked it so.

'Yes. My sister said someone will come to-morrow.'

'Your sister will come?'

'No she is not strong enough to travel. Her granddaughter will come.'

'I make prepare in the morning.'

'Thank you, Yola. I am tired now. I will go to sleep soon'

'I left you some evening bread on the tray.'

'Thank you. I don't need any more.' Brigitte was too weary to tell Yola once again that "Abendbrot" did not sound right when translated into "evening bread". She wanted supper with Katharina – any Katharina who would come from behind the curtain. She would not come out until Yola left. Finally Yola did leave and Brigitte was alone waiting for Katharina. She sat by the candle and flowers that Monika had brought to her. She cancelled the image of Monika, stiff in her own sorrow, hugging it to herself. She had tried to embrace Brigitte when she came with the flowers but it felt wrong. Katharina had said once – she could be a second daughter for you. Such nonsense, she was no flesh and blood. When Katharina went to live with her, it killed forever the chance to have a grandchild and a future in this place. Brigitte turned over the photo of Katharina and went into the kitchen.

There it was – her supper on a tray. The tablets in a box each according to the time and the day. 'So you don't have to go looking for them, Mama.' Did Katharina say that in German or English? Brigitte found the two languages mixed themselves in her brain, as she got older. Sometimes she didn't know which one she had spoken. She blinked at the white modern lines of the kitchen. Each line from Katharina's careful pencil on squared paper. They took it to the big store where a neat young man put it on a computer. She thought Katharina might stay that time. It was her kitchen even now.

She filled a glass of water to take her tablets and took it with her to put on the bedside table. Katharina liked to speak English to her. It was the one thing that she seemed proud of – her English-speaking mother. When Brigitte spoke her own strange mix of the two languages, Katharina would laugh. Brigitte heard that laugh now as she got into bed – it came from Katharina's room. She told herself not to go looking. It was better to know that Katharina was there than to go in and find her absent.

It was not memories of Katharina that woke her from her short sleep. It was not Katharina's face that came to her in sleep. That came when she woke. In her sleep it was those images again – gone for such a long time that she thought that she had burnt them forever. Images without the words she had hoped to share but never did – those were there still, stuffed in the drawers of her memory. Images of bone and blood that she couldn't bring herself to share with her own flesh and blood. Katharina was so angry when she didn't want to bring life to those images again. She had failed in that too.

Katharina screaming as she went through the dark curtain to the crematorium. The smell of burning flesh which I will not smell. Left with only ashes to bury. Monika will arrange it all, Katharina had said. It's not as if we want a big family grave. It would be ridiculous and anyway if you decide to go back to Ireland. She stopped then leaving those images hanging there that she would not put into words because it meant acknowledging them as reality.

It was easier not to talk. Easier not to face the hurt of belief or disbelief. Better to keep counsel. Easier to leave a hole there in your story than to risk what telling the story will do. So she was right to keep her own story. Surely everyone knows how the potential for cruelty in all of us is mighty. Some people like to think they would die first before they would kill another human being. How wrong they are! They told us in school of the Saint who chose death instead of rape. On the holy picture it is so clear. It doesn't show the doubt, the hunger that eats you inside, the mixed-up-ness of feelings. The image of those nightmare days has stayed so long in my bones I know it to be true. It is possible and it did happen. How could I tell my little Kathy such a story? Katharina didn't like to be called Kathy but now I can call her what I want.

Those years when she wanted so much to be younger than her years – when people saw her and Katharina and asked if they were sisters. Such pleasure in that. Years when she could disbelieve such death. Greece, twenty-five years ago – feeling young among those married women who became solid matrons overnight. She and Kathy wore shorts and linked arms in the street – the holiday was a present for Brigitte's 60th birthday and her retirement. Time anyway for retirement – the Americans were leaving in droves even then. Happy for once – a lifetime from now. The past scattered onto the sea. And then one day I was old. It happened so suddenly. And with it the great excuse of being old – everyone doubts the memory of old people. And who was interested anyway in such a story? Now it is too late. Kathy is gone. I will vanish.

The heavy motor bike in the street dragged the loud siren of the Lager back into the present. So why does this image fight its way into my thoughts in these days. Bull's-eyes white with some black somewhere. Not so strong as brandy balls. Are you one of those that suck them until they are gone? Or do you forget and crunch on it with your teeth. Bulls' Eyes that popped out. My memory of Anna's story mixes with the images without words.

It wasn't what they said. Dog, pig, Hund, Schwein. Unless they are right and we are all animals. Better to believe what happened is not possible, she told herself often. Once she referred to the story to a stranger who came with Irma, who said she too had heard such a story from the women in her block. The woman nodded. 'There are testimonies to such a story in the research with survivors.'

Shaking inside again – she had forgotten the strange, shaking feeling bringing cold from inside, not just from ice of the shower jet alternating between a trickle and full blast. Shaking but making herself stand there still while skitter ran down the inside of her legs. She learnt German early from Anna. Durchfall easier to spell than Diarrhoea. Falling liquid brown. Nowadays, she put one of those big nappies on before going for her afternoon nap. No brown stain of fear on the sheet when she woke. Anna's warning. Vorsicht! Careful to pick off the lice carrying disease. Anna– her Bibelki, who was best at finding and cracking every last louse. The cold shower night and morning was the best defence against the louse. Anna loved Brigitte's hair. She delighted in spreading her fingers through the soft, woody-brown curls with chestnut lights. Kastanien – Licht. Every night she told her how lucky she was they had not shaved it off and insisted on checking every hair for lice.

Often Brigitte would fall asleep before Anna was finished. It was hard to know if letting her keep her hair was an arbitrary choice because of the chaos of the camp or recognition of her red star status. Chaos of the times, because many of the politicals had shaved heads. Not a real red star, Anna was quick to realise. A country girl come to the city. Irish not English. Her hair was one small protection against the cold and the push towards a grovelling place on the ground waiting for everyone. One small protection against being one more of those human skeletons, who looked like apparitions not people.

How so many vermin could thrive there amidst so much cold and death was a puzzle. She made him cut off half of it and plaited it into a scarf as a birthday present for Anna. Even when Anna's body was stiff and naked on the death trolley, they left Brigitte's hair around her neck mixing with long wisps of Anna's. Shaking now. Not from cold. She would be more comfortable in bed.

'Was I too young then?' Not too young for death when so many died. This grand-daughter of Peggy's who comes. What age is she? Years do not bring age as fast as war. There is no mercy in war – or death. Aisling – a sister of the boy from Peggy's fine Dublin family. Tragic. Accidents can happen of course. Peggy described the wake. How tired she was on her feet all day, making coffee and finding vases for flowers in the house of her son where people called after the death. Did they have a wake at the house? Bringing the boy back to the old house and the undertaker coming there for him to bring him to Dublin. When Mammy was dying, Peggy had to look after this girl, Aisling. One more excuse for not being there to nurse Mammy.

Brigitte was the only one who could go to look after their mother. Katharina living with Monika. No job. A pension. She was the one who could save their mother from the nursing home. They didn't expect her to go of course. The arguments were marshalled ready for the nursing home – even Liam had agreed. They were grateful to her – grateful for the face-saving and postponing any dispute about the home place or about money to fund a nursing home.

Her brothers and sisters avoided her eyes at her mother's funeral. Did their gratitude put a new barrier between Brigitte and them? Maybe they saw the renewal of her fear of sliding down into the cesspit where your body loses control over its functions. Maybe it was their expectation of her speedy return to Berlin. They would rather fight about the old place and everyone would take sides on that – one pitched against the other – guarding their bitterness against death and decay.

She wished Peggy would come now but she knew she wouldn't. My own flesh and blood. Fleisch und Blut. Had she learnt nothing? In death there is no flesh and not a lot of blood. The blood comes before death. It is the bones that are stronger and our bones are all much the same. Bone torn from bone by other women. Or kicked to death? All suffering. All anti-socials. But someone to protect her from Monika's sorrow – her face looking like death itself – and to protect her from Yola who cared more than any flesh and blood. Or cared only about Katharina's money. Both and neither true.

Chapter Seven

# Berlin

'Take a taxi from the airport,' her mother said, pushing a 50-euro note into her hand when they said goodbye.

No way, Aisling thought. She hated the way her mother treated her like a child sometimes. Since she was back living at home, it was as if she'd never left. She'd checked on the Internet and there was a train from the airport to Berlin. She got out in Alexanderplatz – she could see from the map that it was a central point for lots of different trains – S-Bahn, U-Bahn. Taxi from here maybe? First browse for a map of Berlin. The smell of food was everywhere, tempting her. She stopped at a stall selling slices of pizza and ate her way around the station. Maybe she could linger a bit more before finding the aunt. She sent a text to her Dad – landed safely – on the way to Aunt Bridget. Time for a quick café latte at an Italian café, while she looked at the map she had bought.

Hopefully the text would keep her parents off her tail. This funeral business kept them too close for comfort. Her mother was bound to ring the aunt at some point. Aisling was weary of constant anxiety and glad to escape it for a while. The conversation she had with her aunt, when her father passed the phone to her the day before, was short but Aisling managed to get a bit of information. Her aunt had said she was near the U-Bahn station, Bern..something Strasse on line number U8. She'd seen U8 somewhere. It looked easier than finding the exit for a taxi and maybe faster too. It was only when she was on the train that Aisling realised she hadn't seen a ticket office or bought a ticket. She still had the one from the airport so she could produce something. Fingers crossed that the first thing wasn't being caught at the other end.

She was happy she'd saved the taxi fare – more money to add to her own savings and the stash her father had promised to put in her account so that she could afford to stay. If she'd planned the trip for herself, she'd have had to pay it from her allowance. Profit so far good. It was more fun to find her own way and to take the U-Bahn to Bernauer Strasse.

When she emerged she found herself among high houses with layers of apartments – she looked for the street sign in case she was off in the wrong direction – Strelitzer Strasse. It was a bit of a shock to see some buildings so old and dilapidated after the city slick of Alexanderplatz. The renovated ones reminded her a bit of the new places down on Dublin quays. She found Hussitenstraße and the apartment block. The names were all on the entry phone system – Duignan – an Irish name among all the German names.

When Aisling said her name she could hear Dad's aunt say 'Come in – up the stairs on the left.' Inside the entrance door, she saw no stairs. She paused in the big high hall – there were lots of windows and entrances around a sort of internal courtyard. She had expected to be inside, not out again. Strange. She went through the first door on the left where there was a staircase. She heard a voice above her, 'I'm here, Aisling.' The tone had familiar echoes but her name was pronounced with a foreign intonation. Her father had warned her that his aunt was more German than Irish now and not to expect her to be like Gran.

True and not true, Dad. The aunt was a bit of a Gran replicate in features and stature – it was the hair and the clothes that were really different. She wore black, loose trousers with a synthetic crease and a long, black sweater with slits up the side. That and the dark grey hair flat to her head made her look square and manly. Maybe that's why Gran would never wear trousers even in the house and why she nearly always wore fine clinging jumpers – short sleeved ones when it was warm, long sleeved in the winter and a fine cardigan as an extra layer. If she was going out, she put on 'an outfit' even if it was only to the local shops. She wondered if Gran's hair would look the same as this replica without the perm.

'You are Aisling?' The voice was warmer than Gran's but further away too – like it came from toes toasted by stories around a turf fire. Not a city voice. She held out her hand. At least she's not one of these slobbery old dears, Aisling thought to herself as she offered hers in return – like her mother's aunt Maggie, who smelled of a mixture of fancy soap and perfume on the first whiff which was drowned on the second breath by a smell that reminded Aisling of flea markets. Aisling couldn't work out what to call her. Aunt Bridget? That didn't feel right so she said nothing. Her eyes were red and her skin a light grey, about the same colour as her hair. She could do with a lesson from Gran on a bit of carefully applied make-up.

'You don't look a bit like Diarmuid,' the woman sounded very Irish and puzzled on this note. Aisling wanted to laugh out loud. She couldn't imagine how she could ever look like her dad with his round face, thin hair going grey and the bit of beer belly. Even Michael hadn't looked a bit like him.

'Come, come, I am keeping you standing there,' she ushered her in waving her stick. There was another woman hovering in the background, who came forward into the hallway and offered to take Aisling's white cotton jacket. Aisling shuffled off the jacket, dropped her rucksack in the hall and followed her aunt.

'You will have a cup of tea after your journey?' Was it a question or a command?

The aunt's tone was odd – young and not young, Irish and not Irish, country and not country. Something about her reminded Aisling of old black and white films. She led her through the door on the left, which was obviously the living room, and her aunt carried on through an archway into a dining area. Through the open door to the right, Aisling could see what looked like the kitchen. The table was set – a white cloth with 3 places set in fine china. There were rolls, different breads, cheese, cold meats and smoked salmon. Aisling was sorry she had grabbed a slice of pizza. The place really reeked of coffee – a good omen, as it was Aisling's favourite smell.

'I don't know what food you like,' the aunt was hesitant and unsure.

'This looks great. I love grazing on cheese, ham, salami and all that stuff.' Better to be casual at the start – ward off any expectations.

'Perhaps you would like to use the bathroom before you ring your parents.'

'Yes thanks.'

The bathroom was white tiles and chrome, very clean and tidy but not that modern. The whole apartment had an old fashioned feel in spite of the modern white and plain flavour. In the dining area of the big living room, a layer of white voile full length to the floor screened the windows facing onto the street – no sign of a T.V. – but old pictures on the walls and a tall rubber plant in a corner. On a small table beside it, there was a vase of flowers, a crucifix and two lit candles. Perhaps an altar for Katharina? The aunt's work or someone else's? She kicked herself for missing the chance to say she was sorry about her daughter. What were the words? 'Sorry for your loss.' Sounded stupid. Losing someone like you mislaid them somewhere. She'd say something later. It was obvious anyway: wasn't that why she was here?

The woman, who the aunt introduced as Yola, brought in a pot of tea in a Chinese teapot with a straw handle but did not join them at the table. Maybe she was a sort of maid. No coffee in spite of the smell. Aisling was left with the aunt sitting in silence looking at her.

'Dad is sorry he couldn't come. He didn't want to leave Mum alone and she's not able for a funeral. Gran would have liked to come but she's not very good at flying.' Such a lie. Gran had made the long haul to the States only last year.

'I didn't expect it. I was so sorry to hear about your brother. Katharina too but she was too ill to travel. I didn't expect anyone but I am glad of someone. It helps to have someone from my family here.'

Heavy number. Aisling thought. Was there a concealed guilt-trip there somewhere? She wondered whether and how to ask about the funeral.

'Katharina was living with her friend. She is organising everything. She will tell us when the funeral is – perhaps Friday.'

Was it the accent or was the 'friend' a bit loaded –maybe a hint of Gran in that emphasis? Who was the friend?

Aisling did some calculation as she cut her bread into small even squares – a slice of cheese and a slice of salami. She wished for some background noise to camouflage the sound of the knife and the munching of her teeth through the bread. She'd expected it to be a bit sooner. What would she do between now and Friday? Surely she couldn't just sit here and wait to Friday – that was nearly a week. Her aunt drank the tea and nibbled at a bit of smoked salmon. She had the phone on the table beside her – another un-gran sign. Gran refused to even answer the phone at meal times. The phone hardly had time to ring before the aunt answered it.

'Diarmuid. Yes she's here. Sorry, I should have thought to get her to ring you right away. I'll pass the phone over.'

'Fine, Dad. No problems. Did you get my text? I'm sitting here in front of a mini-buffet. No, I don't know yet. I'll ring you later if you want. Tell Mum everything's O.K. Apparently the funeral might be next Friday.'

Aisling could hear her mother in the background 'Next Friday – how will she manage 'til then?' She said good-bye and hung up. She'd talk to her mother later when she'd worked out her survival plan.

Yola came back to hover around. 'You want more tay?' Aisling nearly laughed out loud at the 'tay' – it sounded like Mrs Doyle from Father Ted but at least she spoke English. She ate and drank more than she wanted. When the aunt suggested that she might like a rest after her journey, she was delighted to escape. Yola fussed around and then said she was leaving and would come back early the next morning.

The 'spare' room was big enough to hold a single bed, a table desk under a high window and a wardrobe full of clothes. Someone – Katharina? – had stuck a notice board on the side of the wardrobe covered in old photos but you couldn't see it from anywhere else in the room.

Aisling lay on the bed and plugged herself into her I-pod. She must try the adapter for the charger too. She'd brought the docking station but she'd have to suss out how the aunt would react first. She must've dozed off a bit because she didn't hear anyone come in but she heard another voice in the living room when she roused herself. Maybe this new arrival would give her enough cover to be able to escape for a few hours.

When she went in, a woman with pure white cropped hair was sitting at the table. She looked a good bit younger than Aisling's mother, who dyed her hair, but she was probably of a similar age. It was a funky style but didn't look like she was trying to look younger. I must tell Mum she should try a different hairstyle, Aisling noted. This woman looked annoyed. So were they arguing?

She stood up, 'I'm Monika, Katharina's friend.' She put out her hand.

'Hello Monika, I'm Aisling – second cousin.' Aisling felt a bit foolish when she said that. It probably meant nothing to Germans.

'You had a good journey?'

'Yes fine thanks.'

'It is good you could come. We were making arrangements just now about the funeral.'

'You mean you are here to tell me that there is no room in your grave for my daughter after all.'

Monika turned her pale face with the skin stretched taut over her high cheekbones to Aisling, 'We have a problem. There are too many roots from a tree in the grave. We cannot bury a coffin in the earth. So we must arrange a cremation first.'

'Too many roots!' Brigitte made a sucking sound through her teeth to show the contempt for this. Too many roots indeed! Some strong German tree which had seen more life than herself was dictating how Katharina would be buried. It was bad enough before. Katharina had told her Monika would make the arrangements in that distant way she used for such communication about her own death. 'Monika will make the arrangements for me when I am no longer here.' She wanted to correct her, 'When you are gone' we say, but the words choked her.

There was no way to answer Katharina when she spoke in that matter-of-fact way as if she was arranging an invitation to coffee and cake. Monika would do that too, she supposed. The funeral guests would be taken somewhere for coffee and cake. Without her, she promised. She'd take a taxi to their favourite place – alone if this girl from Dublin wouldn't come with her. Katharina and her notes in German for Monika. Her own mother left in the dark.

Cut out of her death as she was cut out of her life. Katharina burnt to ashes. The thought of it brought the smell back and the sight of the stiff body of Anna on a trolley waiting to go there. She wanted dignity for Katharina. Not Monika here alive reinforcing Katharina's absence. A mother should not bury her own child. Was Katharina's pain so much greater than all she had suffered to bring her into this life?

'We can have another grave surely.' She hated herself for the pleading tone in her voice.

'There is so much paperwork to get a new grave, Brigitte,' Monika sighed and put her head in her hands for a few seconds, then raised it again. 'When we talked about it, Katharina said if my family did not wish her to be in our grave, she would prefer to be cremated and her urn placed in the wall.'

Was it true what she said? Did Katharina not know how much her own mother hated cremation? And if so, why did Katharina not say it to her too when she spoke of the arrangements? All she would say was, 'Monika will arrange it all. It would be too much for you.'

Paperwork. Why Katharina turned the place upside down for her Birth Certificate. Her expression. Father unknown. Like so many years ago. Now Monika's family could say yes or no to her daughter in their grave. Too many roots was just an excuse. Not enough roots was more likely. Katharina lived always on the surface of the earth – immediate. Her strong passion for one cause or another. Her impatience with the world. She worked always for others with no thought of herself. How dare they refuse her a place in their earth!

'Well, if Katharina wanted to be cremated, it should be OK, then, shouldn't it?' Aisling filled the silence. She liked this way of talking about arrangements. It made it more real somehow.

'Burnt to ashes and stuffed in some hole in a wall!' Brigitte sucked through her teeth again.

There was a fair bit of Gran there in that response. Aisling smothered a smile.

'We can arrange that Katharina's ashes are buried in our family grave. She is in the earth then at least.'

'And what if your family say no?'

'There's no question of that: my mother and my brother both love Katharina. They have already agreed to do whatever you want. It's what you want.'

'Humph! What I want. As if it matters what I want,' Brigitte fought the tremble in her voice and the wetness of her eyes. So they had got round her after all. Katharina would be cremated and put in Monika's family grave. The worst of all options. 'You do what you think. Katharina appointed you. I have no say.'

'I know it's hard for you,' Monika's voice was gentle now. 'I know Katharina found it hard to talk about these things. We all do.'

She turned to Aisling, 'It seems as if the best is cremation and burial in our family grave. We will put a special stone there on the grave with Katharina's name.' Aisling saw her hesitate then dive in, 'We will have to wait for the cremation.'

'Wait?' Brigitte's eyes narrowed.

'Yes. I will find out how long.'

'And Katharina? She must wait in some fridge with a tag on her toe?'

'It's not like something out of a 'Tatort'; it is quite usual that it takes time to make arrangements,' Monika showed a bit of mettle in her tone but quickly turned conciliatory again, 'You will have the opportunity to visit her. I can arrange it.'

Would the carrot work? The aunt had one of Gran's mulish expressions on her face. It made Aisling want to smile. She wanted to warn this woman there was no chance of winning against that expression. She'd better be careful or she'd get caught between the two of them. If it came to taking sides, she'd take the aunt's but ideally she'd find a way to escape while this Monika was there.

'You mean that if I want to see my daughter one last time, I have to agree for her to be cremated and buried in your grave.'

Monika could barely conceal her exasperation, 'I did not say this. I am presenting you with the choices we have to make. Often, in this country, people do not go to the... ' she looked for a word and couldn't find one, 'to see the person in the coffin but I thought you may like it because this is what they do in Ireland.'

'Well, it is the custom in Ireland for everyone to visit the house and pay your respects to the dead.' The aunt's stone-grey face was set even harder than Monika's, 'It is not allowed in this country. '

'So a wake is not allowed here. Just as well,' Aisling thought, 'They'd be fighting about where to hold the wake.' Her desire to escape was increasing. She certainly did not want to be involved in organising some German version of a wake even if it was in a morgue. She assumed a bright tone, 'I thought I might go out for a little while to get some fresh air. I know you have lots to sort out.'

'Aisling, you could come with me to see my daughter one last time?' The aunt's expression was a mixture of bossy and persuasive. A sure winner.

Monika looked from one to the other. 'Could you go to the place with your aunt, if I arranged it? Sorry I don't know the English word? Bestattungsunternehmer.'

Aisling guessed, 'Do you mean a funeral parlour? Well I don't really know my way around yet. I've just arrived and I don't know much German.'

'English is not a problem. They speak English. It's even better when you know some German. In any case, Brigitte knows German and you would take a taxi there and back. I will write the address for you now and ring you when I have arranged it.' Monika kept her remarks directed at Aisling. 'It is good that you are here. Brigitte needs her own family at this time.'

Aisling shrugged, 'O.K.' She could hardly say no in the

circumstances. She wasn't that keen on this Monika either, in spite of the funky hairstyle. She could see that getting caught between these two was worse than being the meat in a Gran-Mum sandwich.

## Chapter Eight

# Funeral Parlour

Brigitte was even more brusque than usual on the phone. When she finished, she kept repeating an address as she looked for a pen to write it down. Aisling guessed it was Monika with the address of the funeral parlour. Her first bit of sightseeing in Berlin. Alternative or what? A few words of explanation to Aisling, a phone call for a taxi and Brigitte was ready and waiting. She was moving quicker than Aisling had seen her move so far. She should do it more often – it took years off her.

The view from the taxi was pretty boring – broad streets, boring buildings and advertising but nothing that looked like a centre. No doubt the taxi driver avoided the centre. The aunt sat beside her, stiff with stubbornness, or maybe fear. When they got there, the aunt looked at her watch and told the taxi-driver to come back in half-an-hour. They went in through the entrance and found themselves in a little reception area that looked more like an estate agents than a funeral parlour.

The aunt spoke in German and the round, comfortable woman on reception made reassuring noises. In complete contrast to her, there was a tall, thin, male assistant with square glasses and a decently gelled haircut, who came to take them into a little room at the end of a corridor where the coffin lay open. Thankfully the door was open because the place had no windows and was stifling in spite of the air-conditioning – set for cool of course. They had Katharina to themselves. Aisling was impressed at her Gothic style. Blackish-brown straight hair – too sleek to be her own surely but she didn't sound the type to wear a wig either. The face whiter than white but the lips with a bit of lipstick. Born 8th September 1945 she read on the lid standing by the coffin. So Katharina was nearly 60 when she died – already an old woman. The aunt just stood there for long silent minutes– no tears or prayers. Brigitte was not the old biddy Aisling had expected from her father's description of Aunt Biddy. Her composure in spite of the pain was worthy of respect.

Finally she spoke, 'It helps to see her. I wasn't with her when she died you see. It helps to take it in. Lipstick. She is no longer here.' The aunt's tone was matter-of-fact. She produced a shuffle of yellow, discoloured paper; 'I want you to put this in the coffin for me.'

'Me? Don't you think it would be better if one of the staff did it? I might wreck the… ' Aisling stopped – what word to use? 'Display' came to the tip of her tongue but 'corpse' sounded worse.

'I want you to do it.' The aunt passed over the sheaf of paper. Aisling tried to lift the corner of the satin cover on the body to stick the paper in but it seemed to be stuck down. The aunt had turned away to sit on a chair against the wall. The tall skinny young man, who hovered outside the door, was speaking to her. Aisling was tempted to stuff the papers in her bag instead – it was easier. She could tell Biddy-Brigitte later that she hadn't managed to do it. She wanted to giggle – it felt like the time she had ripped off a t-shirt from Arnotts for a dare –

and, when she was successful, Maeve had dared her to go inside and put it back on the rail again. Typical Maeve.

The aunt turned round and Aisling stopped fiddling with the satin stuff; nodded, blessed herself and went to stand by the chair. No lie intended. Brigitte wouldn't like a fuss. The aunt took her arm when she went to get up and Aisling felt her lean into her. The undertaker's assistant escorted them back to reception and checked for the taxi. Aisling looked at her watch. It seemed like they had been there for ages but the whole business had only taken twenty minutes. Luckily the taxi was already waiting outside. Aisling saw nothing interesting from the taxi this time either. If this were Berlin, a couple of days would be enough.

When they got back into the house, she didn't take her jacket off in the hope of making an escape into the city to have a better look. But the aunt took out two small glasses and put them on the table with a bottle.

'Schnaps? I need one now.' Still no sign of tears or distress.

The glasses emptied, the spirit burning its way down inside Aisling. She didn't usually drink straight spirit. It loosened the aunt's tongue.

'I'm glad I saw her and gave her the papers. Jules tried to put me off. She thinks she owns her, body and soul.'

'Jules? Who's Jules?'

The aunt looked surprised, 'Did I say Jules? I mean Monika. Jules was once our name for them because they look like men.'

Aisling did a quick bit of mental addition. So Katharina and Monika were an item.

'Monika doesn't though – look like a man, I mean.' She should have guessed there was more than friendship there. Not that Monika or Katharina looked unfeminine. Monika just looked German and Katharina too from the pictures she had seen. The aunt was more masculine than Monika could ever be.

'Is Jules a term for lesbian?' she added. Aisling couldn't imagine using that word to her gran but it was the aunt, so different rules. If she said no she could just drop it.

'Lesbian – you use such a word now in Ireland?' The aunt's tone was softer. 'I shouldn't be surprised. For you young people to-day, nothing is shocking. I've heard them here too. Getting married in the town hall. Now they make it out to be something clean and good.'

Aisling shrugged.

'Jules was what they called them in the Lager.'

'Lager?'

'The camp.'

As if that said it all. Was there a camp for lezzies – or Jules as she called them. If so was the aunt a closet? She poured more Schnaps into both glasses.

'In the Lager, there were many of them but I thought it was the dirt and evil in that place that made them do what they did.'

'Lager? The only lager I know, you drink it out of a glass,' Aisling wanted to laugh again – this time at her own stupid joke. This Schnaps must be strong stuff.

'So does Lager mean work camp then?' Aisling prompted but the aunt was on her own thought tramlines.

'The first time I saw them, I thought they were men, because they looked just like men. Maybe because there were no men, they needed to lean on somebody. It was in the half-light of an Indian summer night in September. At first I saw only the turquoise light coming through the cloudy sunset.

Then I spotted them behind the other block. I was on the way there to take a message from Anna to her friend. At first I wondered where did these men come from and where did they go? There were no blocks for male prisoners in the main camp though Anna said there were men in the prison block.

When I went back I asked Anna. Who are these men? She looked at me. 'Kein Mann, ein Jules', and said nothing more. I was no wiser. No man I understood but Jules was a man's name. At first there were none in the block where I was, I was with 'Bibelki. Then they put some in our block too and I knew then. The other women would read and pray aloud pretending not to hear the noises of those two in the bottom bunk near the door. The Blockälteste put them there as a punishment. She knew it would hurt the Bibelki.'

'Come again, the Bibel-ikies?'

'Bibelki? That was what they called them in that place. I only knew later they are called Jehovah's Witnesses in English.'

Bible thumpers and lezzies. What a mix! The aunt was silent again but Aisling couldn't really ask 'How did you end up in a camp with bible thumpers and lezzies or how come the lezzies ended up in a camp with you?' She had heard somewhere that homosexuals were sent to camps in the war but she didn't think there were so many lezzies in those days. Her parents acted like lesbians were invented in the sixties along with marijuana. No need to make a big fuss about it as it was probably a passing phase and, if it wasn't, it was grand as long as they made respectable couples with tidy gardens and invited heterosexuals to dinner.

Maybe the aunt was exaggerating or doting or mixing it up with her daughter. Did Gran know her niece was a 60-year-old lesbian who had been in a couple for a long time? Her aunt had seemed to drift off into herself. Aisling wanted to bring her back but didn't know how to ask or what to ask even. The voile curtain carried the smell of the freesia from Katharina's 'altar' towards her, and withdrew with a mock bow.

'So how long were you there – in that camp?' She tried for cool and casual.

'How long was I there?' the aunt repeated, 'I was one of the lucky ones – it was seven months – but the longest seven months in my life. Maybe it is because of me, she became a Jules. To punish me.'

Aisling stayed silent. She knew from listening to her Gran reminisce that you could easily cut the flow and she would suddenly remember there were things that weren't for Aisling's ears. Better to go for a safe question.

'Where did you say it was?'

'That place.' The word came out in a spray of dust motes lit by the light from the street lamp.

'It wasn't Auschwitz? That's in Poland, isn't it?'

'That place is not so far; it is near Fürstenberg – not far from Berlin – in Brandenburg.'

Brandenburg Gate rang some bell. Earmarked for a visit.

'Katharina wanted me to tell her all but I couldn't. Now it is too late.' There was finality in the dry mouth and eyes that made her seem as transparent as the light from the street lamp behind her. With her back to the curtain she was enough to spook anyone.

Time to change the subject. 'So what did Katharina do as a job?'

'Teacher, professor. She taught in the university. She wanted me to write about my life. She gave me her computer and said she would show me how to use it for the Internet to keep in touch with my family in Ireland.' Brigitte spoke with scorn in her voice. 'What would I have to do with the Internet at my age?'

'Why not? You can do your shopping on the Internet – get the news, all sorts.' Aisling heard her own voice but it sounded different – bright, insincere and unfamiliar – she sounded like her own mother.

'She never showed me how to use it.'

'I could show you how to use the computer if you like.'

'All you young people know about computers, I'm too old to learn. '

A piece of good news – a computer in the house and set up for the Internet. Aisling looked around her. Where was it? She could imagine these two old women fighting it out – both of them probably blaming each other for something or other.

'I don't want any computer. If *you* want it, you can have it.'

'I could take a look?' Aisling hadn't spotted it yet. 'I could type some things for you if you want. I have time.'

'If you want the computer, it is there in the drawer,' the aunt shrugged, 'I have no use for it.'

A laptop would be very handy. Aisling felt like a thief or a grave robber when she looked in Katharina's room for the computer. She brought it back to the table. It was a bit heavier than her own but with the same software so she could navigate around it no bother in spite of the German. There was some stuff still on it too – mostly in German. She'd find a way to delete it after she had a chance to read it.

Shame there was no wifi. Maybe she could buy a dongle. Time for the old-fashioned guide book to come in handy for the escape plan while the aunt dozed. Where to first?

Brandeburg Gate of course. The core of Berlin and of

Europe. Well why not? Dominating and big. Symbol of peace for over 200 years. Looks more like the triumph of war. Kinging it over the square and the linden avenue. How did the bombers miss it in the war? It's big enough. Why does Greece come to mind? Good marks for observation, Aisling. Guide says architect creating "Athens on the River Spree". What else does the book say? Willie Brandt arriving in 1961 when they closed the gate. Great man, great speaker, one of Dad's heros with photo on his study wall. Could have listened to him hold forth. No more traffic between East and West. Communism one side of the gate and capitalism the other. Need Dad now for detail. Or Katharina. What was it like being 16 years old and they cut your city in two. Wall going up a few streets away from where she lived.

Was she political? What was the story between 1945 and 1961? Something to do with the occupation of Berlin in 1945 and how they divided it up. Soviets got as far as Brandenburg Gate. Brits, Americans and French on the other side. Brigitte in the middle of all that making me take more notice of history than ever before. Maybe because she doesn't want to talk about it. More to history than the history books, Gran would say but then say no more. Why did they take so long before deciding to build a wall – sixteen years? Dad would have plenty to say and go on and on about the Cold War and the Iron Curtain. Family photo with bit of wall we saw in the states. Reagan challenging Gorbachev in 1987. Wonder what Katharina thought then? Was she one of the people climbing Brandenburg Gate in November 1989 or in the crowds at the official opening in December 1989? Who really took it down? Why did they not shoot the people in 1989 when they shot them in 1961? The spotlight of the TV cameras or Soviets giving up the ghost?

And Brigitte? Was she right here in 1945 with her brick-rebuilding from the ruins? Meeting American soldiers? What was she doing in 1989? Somebody said something about her early retirement at sixty. Or was she still working? Could ask her. More interesting history here. Things happen at the centre to real people.

Chapter Nine

# Left to Jules

Aisling sat with her earphones on, pretending that she didn't hear Yola open the door to Monika but she couldn't ignore the tap on her room door and mumbled, 'Come in.'

Monika's face was so tight she looked worse than Katharina in the coffin. So what had the aunt said to her this time? Distracted, Monika looked around the room – of course it was Katharina's room and she was Katharina's partner. Aisling felt herself blush and swung her legs off the bed.

'I'm sorry to disturb you. I came to talk about the… ' she paused then restarted, 'I came to tell Brigitte it will take three weeks to arrange the cremation.'

'Three weeks!' When she had first realised that this trip was more than a few days she had been pleased. But three weeks was way over the top.

'Yes, I know it is rather long. In Ireland it is much quicker.'

'Three days.'

Aisling felt like telling Monika she'd arrange a funeral pyre herself rather than wait three weeks.

'It is possible to make it a little bit sooner with a special arrangement in Poland. I would like Brigitte to tell me what she wants. Should we wait three weeks for a cremation in Germany or should we have the cremation in Poland sooner but…,' Monika sighed and stopped – her face a question mark. 'Maybe you could find out? I know she likes you. You are good to her.'

She hesitated again, ' I could ring back later this evening. Or you could ring me. You have my handy number?'

'Handy?'

'My mobile telephone.'

'Very handy, I'm sure,' Aisling muttered, she could see why this 'Jules' and Brigitte would find it difficult to communicate. Both created a sense of expectation that other people would fit into their plan. She pitied Katharina stuck somewhere between the two of them.

'Sorry, I didn't hear what you said,' Monika's voice had the echo of defeat.

'Nothing. No I don't have your mobile number. Maybe Brigitte has it,' Aisling shrugged, 'I've only known her a few days. But if she talks about it I'll let you know. Would we all have to go to Poland?'

'No, the cremation is arranged by the… Bestattungsunternehmer, sorry I don't know this word in English – the people who make the funeral arrangements.'

'Undertakers,' Aisling inserted.

'The undertakers bring the urn to the cemetery.'

'Whatever,' Aisling replied, promising herself that she would be long gone if the funeral wasn't for another three weeks. It would be someone else's problem. She waited a while after Monika and Yola had both gone before going into the living room. She changed out of her lounging – about pants and into some jeans so that she could make a quick exit if she felt like it.

Brigitte looked at her suspiciously, 'Monika was here earlier.'

'I know. She popped in to say hello. She said there may be a bit of a wait for the cremation,' Aisling replied.

'So she drags you into this now too.'

In spite of the words of disapproval, Brigitte looked pleased at Aisling's surly tone. 'I suppose she told you that she wants to send my daughter to an oven in Poland. To think that I carried her away from the camp and fought for us to live through the end of the war to have such a death. I asked her was it done in Auschwitz still or did they have a new place now?'

Aisling couldn't help smiling and turned away before the aunt could see it. There was no longer any doubt in her mind now about the wicked strain in the aunt. She could certainly pick something that was bound to make Monika suffer more. She took a matter-of-fact tone for her reply, 'Apparently it could take three weeks at least here in Berlin and it would be quicker in Poland.'

'Yes and cheaper too.'

Aisling decided to ignore the Monika wind-ups and do a side kick of her own. 'I suppose she could have done it without asking you. You'd never have known,' she paused before adding, 'I wonder what Katharina would think about it?'

The aunt's mouth worked in silence like she was chewing her tongue.

Aisling persisted, 'If the funeral is not for another three weeks, I'm sorry but I'll have to go back. I have to start back at Uni.'

'Uni?'

'University. I could manage two weeks maximum. Maybe Dad would come over for it.'

Brigitte was silent for a while. Aisling helped herself to some juice from the fridge. She'd buy herself an energy drink when she went out. When she went back into the living room, the aunt muttered in her direction, 'That Jules should never have asked me about Poland. Why is she waiting? Katharina told her to make the arrangements, so that I wouldn't have to suffer: still she comes round here with her questions that have no answers.'

'Why don't we ring her and tell her to go ahead and arrange the cremation as best she can and just let us know when the funeral is arranged for. I'll do it if you like.' A nod was enough for Aisling to lift the phone and dial the number before the aunt changed her mind.

She struggled with how to name her but it came out before her mind engaged, 'Aunt Bridget has decided that you should go ahead with the cremation wherever you think. Oh, and could you let us know what is happening when.' The aunt nodded her approval at this last request.

'Enough of this,' Aisling told herself. She could hear the escape, escape, escape alarm in her head. She mumbled about fresh air and headed out before the aunt could ask her when she would be back. She would try out the S-Bahn. Just hop on and see where one stop would lead her. No ticket to give her a buzz. Maybe here they fined you on the spot. Maybe she could get away with playing innocent tourist.

She got out at Oranienburger Tor and let Oranienburger Strasse roll on her tongue. Seedy and smart intermingled with the smell of fried onions and spices and a dream beer under a palm tree. She licked the edginess of the street from her lips when she reached the entrance to a little courtyard with delicate brickwork that reminded her of marquetry. She'd seen pictures of the courtyard at Hackesche Höfe – and examples of tasteful restoration of Berlin after the Wall – was it from an Internet search or her guidebook or was it somewhere else? She was impatient because she couldn't work out where the boundaries were before and after the Wall came down. There was less of a contrast than you would find north and south of the Liffey.

Wandering in a confusion of streets Sophienstrasse and big hamburger street with OMG an Irish shop! Window of icons, tweed caps, whiskey, Barry's tea. Tempation to go in and get something for Brigitte. Resist, resist turning into Mum or worse still Gran. Sharp steps down the street, round again and circling back around the arches under the S-Bahn. An Irish pub too. Resist. Roasty summer so now a beer would be welcome. Try German Weihenstephaner. Cooler. Stylish. Tall wooden tables. Here's a lesson in marketing history. "Oldest still-existing brewery in the world". How old? 1000 years. Beat that! Good beer too. Imagine Matt here to take Michael's screwed up face from the blank wall as he chokes on the beer she dares him to put down his neck. Aisling the winner. Thanks to him she developed a taste in beer. Wishing for Matt's address to send him a postcard. Maybe Dad with 1000 years of history in a gulp. Weihenstephan in Mitte so in the former East. Hardly here in GDR days so what was here? Duck into Hackeche Höfe arching a way through designer goodies, finding postcard and coffee to sober up.

Out to find U-Bahn and realised it was her U8. Easy to go 'home'. The aunt was still sitting in the same place she'd left her in. She made polite enquiries about Aisling's trip out but there was something else on her mind. Aisling sat down after getting the aunt some water and herself some juice. Damn, she'd forgotten the energy drink. She was about to head out again when the aunt asked, 'Aisling, will you be there in case I need help this evening? '

Help? Aisling recoiled: she didn't want the old dear beginning to depend on her. Brigitte saw the unspoken response and fumbled with her cardigan – an uncharacteristic gesture – and spoke with her head down, 'I want to take a shower to-night. I don't think that I will need help but I am a bit shaky and I'm afraid of falling at this time. I know I will be all right if someone is nearby. If it was after the funeral, I wouldn't care.'

Aisling's reflex action was to say no, sorry, I'm going out but she fancied just staying in and plugging herself into her I-pod.

'Don't you have a shower in the morning?'

'I do but I like to take one sometimes in the evening. It's easier. I sleep better after a shower and I haven't slept much this last night. I would just like it if you were there. I don't need you to do anything.'

Better to stay than come back to find her on the floor. Avoid complications: lesser of the two evils before a grudging acquiescence. 'Well, I was just going out for a few minutes but after that I'll be in.'

When she came back in, the aunt was already in the bathroom so she left her to it.

It was nearly 10 o'clock. Aisling came into the living room feeling guilty. She should have given her a shout or something. At first she thought that Brigitte was already in bed. There was no light – just the curtain billowing out with the draught. She jumped when Brigitte spoke from her chair where she sat in a long cotton bathrobe that was a sort of puce pink. Gross.

'Would you like something to drink?' the aunt asked.

'Water would be good. I'll get a glass.'

They sat in brittle silence for a while.

'You've been in Berlin a long time?'

'Delia and Dieter brought me back to Berlin with them when they were visiting Delia's parents in Manorhamilton. To look after the children.'

'So you were a nanny?'

'More like a member of the family."

'So didn't you want to go home when the war broke out?'

'Go home! That was my worst fear at first – greater than my fear of war. I loved this city. It was beautiful and modern. There were shops and stores and people lived in apartments with running water and bathrooms. There were more buses, trams and cars than horses – and even then they had bags to collect the horseshit so that it didn't fall in the street. At first I thought that because the war wasn't anything to do with me, it couldn't touch me. It's great to be young and foolish. I had no idea how quickly that would be taken from me. By the time that I might have been glad to go home, it was too late.'

'So after it was over, why didn't you go home then?'

'I stayed then because Katharina belonged here. In Ireland they had no time for unwed mothers. I didn't want to give Katharina up for adoption. After the hell I went through, Katharina was all I had left. She was my reason for living.' Brigitte paused, 'And now that I have lost her, I have no more reason for living. Katharina hated that. She hated to know that I had to struggle for her when I would rather have died. Maybe that's why she died before me so that I could die in peace now. And what if this is all there is? No-one has ever come back to tell us that there is something more, something better. So what was the point in any of it?'

The matter-of-fact way Brigitte talked about death was out of sync with Gran.

'Don't you believe in God and in heaven?'

'If there is a God with power to change things then he must be cruel. I'd just as soon go back to hell again.'

It felt odd for this gran-like person to be coming out with heresy, 'Well at least Katharina had a good long life. It's not like she died young.'

'I suppose sixty seems old to you but she was my child and I could never think of her as old.'

'So what did Katharina do before… ?' Aisling couldn't say the words 'she died' but she refused to say 'passed away. Brigitte didn't deserve euphemisms.

Brigitte didn't need her to fill in the blank, 'She did what she always did all her life – reading, studying, writing – even after she left work because of the illness, she kept it up. She taught at the University. They paid her for doing what she loved most. She used to laugh and say that one day they would catch her out and she would be out on her ear. A good job with a pension that she didn't live to see. "Mama, you'll get my pension if I die before you, you know. At least you won't be short of money." I laughed then at the thought of my daughter dying before me. She said that before she told me about the first lump. What do I want with her money when I hope that I won't be long after her?'

Aisling sat silent. She wished she'd put on the light when she came in. The streetlights and the open window were deathly. She couldn't disagree. What was there now for this old woman to live for? For a moment she had some sympathy for the way that her own mother had clung to her since Michael died. For a moment she forgave Michael for topping himself. He was the sensitive one. It was like he felt everything for everybody not just himself. There were times she thought him stupid or even selfish for taking it all onto himself but maybe he couldn't stop himself.

'I will have some Schnaps,' the aunt announced into the silence.

Aisling leapt up to put on the light before rooting in the sideboard that stretched along one wall. 'Would whiskey do?' She pulled out a bottle of Jameson's

'Yes, Katharina got it last Christmas for me.'

Time for a change of topic. She had spotted an ancient record player in the cupboard and a collection of vinyls – antique or what? 'Can I put on some music?'

"Flesh and Blood". Johhny Cash was top of the pile. It took the aunt on another beautiful Berlin trip. Coffee and cake with Katharina on the Spree. Look now at this calendar, Katharina got me – photos of old Berlin before they bombed it to bits. The joy of Museum island still there, to see the Reichstag being built again, to feel Friedrichstraße back to life again and remember weaving a way between the trams, the cars and the double decker buses to meet Delia in Loeser and Wolff's. So many brands of cigarettes in Berlin but no Sweet Afton! But now even in Ireland she didn't manage to find Sweet Afton. The tumbler-full of unfamiliar whiskey burned its way inside. She should have put some coke in it to drown the taste.

'And the dancing we did the first year after I arrived – usually at parties. Herr Goldmann lost his job in the orchestra then and Frau Goldmann was free to sit with the boys so I could go too. Delia would teach me to waltz in the living room to the Blue Danube. I used to play it every Friday night after I did the ironing. I would have a little Schnaps and sometimes dance too.'

The aunt rose to look for it but Aisling found it first. Both on their feet and several steps beyond tipsy moving now to the music – the aunt in the arms of Delia or some dream lover and Aisling holding her at arms length moving with her to make sure that the old bat didn't fall over. If any of her friends could see her now. Steering her finally to fall back into the chair. Aisling laughed a whiskey laugh. Brigitte's head sank onto her chest and she roused her and shuffled her off to bed.

She heard her after that in the bathroom – just as well. Aisling hadn't thought about that. Well she wasn't here to baby-sit. Whiskey sleep with no dreams this night.

## Chapter Ten

# Past and Present

Aisling was bored and hungry. The aunt was sitting dozing but she'd be sure to wake up if Aisling started rooting around in the kitchen. She lay on the bed, plugged into her music. The bookshelves in Katharina's room held mostly history text books. Those in English were mostly about Ravensbrück concentration camp. The aunt hadn't given her the name but a quick flick through one of Katharina's books in English told her Ravensbrück was near the place called Fürstenberg, mentioned by Brigitte. The sample of drawing from prisoners fascinated her. Violette Le Coq drew stick figures reminiscent of Lowry, one of her favourite painters. The contrast between her drawings and one by another prisoner which was all buxom women with rounded buttocks was curious. Which was more honest? Or were they both true? Reading some excerpts whetted her curiosity. No wonder Katharina felt a bit cheated if Brigitte kept the shutters down.

The comic-strip story of Berlin was another good find. Effortless German but a bit too childish. The last days of the war and the first Spring of liberation. But she was too restless to read about goodie-two-shoes with blond plaits for long. Still, it would be good for her German and gave her ideas for writing her own comic strips. If she really had to wait three weeks, there would be enough time to go home and come back again. If she didn't she'd have to find ways to fend off boredom. She retrieved the sheaf of old paper. What was so important that it should go in the coffin? Maybe it was the aunt's will or something. Why not tear it up or burn it? She took the bits carefully out of the envelope. The pages were pinned together with an ordinary pin in the top corner that had rusted into place. On top there was what looked like a letter in neat writing.

> *Berlin*
> *18th August 1939*
> *Dear Mammy,*
> *I can't come home yet. I'm writing to tell you that you mustn't worry. I'm fine here with Delia and Dieter. I'll be home soon DV. I hope everyone is well.*
> *Yours,*
> *Biddy*

Aisling ignored the twinge of guilt. It wasn't really like reading someone's letters. It was never sent anyway. Biddy must be what her family called her. Dad called her Aunt Bridget but now she called herself Brigitte – of course that was the German for Bridget. No wonder she changed it. Who'd want to invite 'oul Biddy' as a name? It was more like a diary than a letter after the first page.

> *Berlin 20th August 1939*
> *Dear Mary,*
> *I decided not to post my last letter to Mammy but to send a telegram instead. Now I'm worried that she will take fright*

*when she sees the telegram. I just hope that Mickie brings it to the house as if he was bringing the usual letter. He'll know what it says anyway so there is no need to rush up with it as if there was something wrong. I don't want to tell her the reason I don't want to leave is because I'm afraid that they might never let me back again. It would break my heart to leave. I love the life here. I want to stay here forever. To live in an apartment like this one – big high ceilings and strong wooden doors – a tiled bathroom with hot and cold running water in the bathtub. A dining room to eat in. My own room to sleep in. But it's more than that. It's the feel of the place – the sunshine through the open window and the sound of the pump station and sometimes the voices of the children in the schoolyard.*

*When I go out in the streets I love the smells of different food, the sound of trucks and trams, the wide streets and high buildings and trees too. Even the horses and wagons are smarter than the country horse and cart and there are more motorcars too. In our street it's so neat the way that the apartments all face the street in front and behind there is the big open space with the school at the back. And people, so many different people all going somewhere doing something. People that I don't know and who don't know me.*

*My favourite thing is to go to Karstadt with Delia. The store is mighty and we go up to the café at the top for coffee and cake – Kaffee und Kuchen. Tell Mammy and Daddy everything is fine here.*

*Yours,*

*Biddy*

*26th August 1939*

*Dear Mary,*

*I miss you. I have no-one to talk to here. I haven't posted my last letter so maybe I will send them together. If you get this letter, tell them all at home I'm grand. There is nothing to tell you. All they talk about is whether there will be a war. Delia listens to everything on the radio. There is a new programme in English — Germany calling. He's Irish but calls himself Lord Haw-Haw. Sounds more English.*

*Write back.*

*Yours Biddy*


*2nd September 1939*

*Dear Mary,*

*I still don't understand enough German to follow the news. Delia listened again to that stupid Lord Haw-Haw but I can't stand the sound of his voice. Do you listen listen to him in Ireland too?. I imagine you going over toMickie's house, as he's the only one with a radio. They call him Joyce but he doesn't sound Irish. He sounds like his name, Lord Haw-Haw, a donkey who took elocution lessons. I only want to hear that the war will be over soon. Most days I am too fed up to write letters.*

*Yours Biddy.*


*September 1939*

*Dear Mary*

*No letters this week. Britain declared war on Germany yesterday. Delia says Ireland is neutral and Dieter works at the hospital so there is no reason for us to be afraid. I've seen the uniform hanging in the wardrobe but I have never seen* him wear it. *Mammy wrote saying that she got a fright when the telegram arrived. I wrote back telling her that I'm fine and everything is calm here and that it's safer for me to stay here than to travel to Ireland. I've made the decision to stay no matter what.*

*You'll have to visit after the war.*

*Yours Biddy*


*New Year 1940*

*Dear Mary,*

*My first New Year in Germany was a bit of a let-down. Delia spent the evening complaining because Dieter has to work more and more. They don't go out very much anymore. Dieter says he doesn't like to go to the film theatre any more. I don't mind because now Delia takes me. I love to go to Palasttheater am Zoo and enter another world away from this stupid war. I don't mind that I don't really understand it all because it is all in German of course.*

*Dieter wants Delia to go to stay with his parents in Bavaria. He says Berlin is sure to be a target for bombing. Delia wants to stay with him. I am tired of listening to them arguing and I'm glad it's in German so I pretend not to understand. Delia says that if she leaves then she will take me with her or find a way to get me home. She needs me at the moment so there is no question of me leaving. I get up early with the children and one of us goes to the bakery for bread. Now there are queues and everything takes longer. When they have their nap in the afternoon after school I queue again for bread and anything else I can get. I don't mind it anyway. I like to be among people.*

*There's a lot of snow and I had to stamp hard to get*

*enough feeling into my feet to take a step. The snow makes everything look special again. I like to walk around the streets and look at the people – even the trucks of soldiers. When I get on the tram or stand in the queue at the bakers. I dream of the day the war will end. I could spend all day admiring the tall elegant buildings around me. I love the way the tram goes around the little garden area in the centre. I see myself getting off at Karstadt and having Kaffee und Kuchen on the terrace there. I pray for the day that everything is normal again.*

*I found out that Backpulver will do instead of baking soda to bake a scone of bread. Buttermilk is easy to get. Now I often bake soda bread for Delia. I'm not sure if I am doing the right thing. To-day she said the smell made her homesick. I talked about the hardship of living on the farm just to make sure that she didn't get too romantic about going back to Leitrim. Dieter doesn't like scone bread so I still have to queue for bread. Sometimes his favourite Roggenbrot is gone and I have to decide quickly which other to get. We hardly ever have bread rolls for breakfast now. I wonder if Delia is more homesick now it is too late to go back to Ireland until the war is over.*

*Hope all is well with you.*
*Yours Biddy*


Aisling heard the aunt in the bathroom and jumped guiltily. She shoved the pages in the drawer where the laptop had been. How come the letters are from Biddy to this Mary? Did Mary send them back or did Biddy never post them? Biddy certainly made living in Berlin sound a lot better than Leitrim. No wonder she was afraid that she'd be sent back home. Aisling couldn't imagine being stuck in that little house in Leitrim for any length of time. Her Granny had told her about going to the well for water and about the bathroom in the barn.

She heard Yola calling her, 'Kaffee und Kuchen'. She must have been at the bakery. At least the aunt could still have her Coffee and Cake. The aunt insisted Yola sit with them for coffee and cake but you could see neither of them was comfortable.

'Do you like Berlin?' Aisling asked Yola to cover up the awkwardness.

'Yes. I do like it,' Yola looked delighted with herself. 'Do you like the Pflaumenkuchen?'

'Yes but our plum cake is different. Do you have family still in Poland?'

'Yes. My mother lives there. My brother too.'

'Do you miss Poland?'

'Not Poland. My mother yes but not Poland. I like live in Berlin. My son has work here.'

There was a silence then and Aisling accepted another helping of cake to help fill it. She had barely cleared her plate before Yola was clearing the table. The aunt made no effort to make conversation.

'Do you ever miss living in Leitrim?' Aisling threw the question into a silence and felt her blush rise from the image of the young Biddy leaving Leitrim for Berlin coming through the letters. The aunt didn't seem to notice anything odd.

'I went back a few times. Not many. The last time was before my mother died in 1987.'

'She lived in the old house until she died, didn't she?' Death again. Tactless she could hear her father saying, talk house not people; 'We go down there for weekends, quite a lot. Dad made a few changes.'

'Yes, Peggy told me Diarmuid has renovated the old house.'

It made Gran sound younger somehow to be called by her pet name – though Aisling knew she hated it. Probably because it sounded country and old-fashioned though Gran's line was that Peggy wasn't the name she had been given at Baptism. Did Brigitte know that Granny hated to be called Peggy?

Babbling to fill the silence. 'He didn't really change the house that much. Not enough for Gran anyway. She came down with us for a weekend once and wouldn't come back. Daddy wanted to restore the house rather than modernise it except for a new bathroom and the kitchen in the extension at the back. He took off all the layers of lino and the wood underneath that was beginning to rot and found the old flagstones underneath. He took down all the boards off the ceiling and you can see the old beams in the kitchen now. The big range in the kitchen, with an oven and plates for cooking on, is still there. Mum won't use it for cooking though. She uses a camping stove and Dad has to do most of the cooking when we're there. He bakes soda bread in it when we go there for weekends. But we haven't been back since… '

'Since… ?' Brigitte's eyes stared black at her. 'Since your brother died?'

Aisling winced. I'm not the only one who can be tactless here. Sometimes she wanted to rewind it like a video but she knew that no matter what the story would be the same. That was the way it was.

Brigitte spoke into their separate silence, 'They say it takes a year to get over the death of someone close – I don't believe it. Some deaths you never get over even if it is not someone close.' She paused and abruptly changed tack. 'You don't mean to tell me Diarmuid bakes soda bread?'

'Oh not real bread. He found some ready-mix soda bread where you just have to add water. He says it is just as good as what your mother used to bake and far better than anything you get in the shop.'

Aisling wondered now if they would ever go back to those rituals. Her father would get up early to feed the range that was still hot from the night before. She could hear him below raking out the ashes. She pretended to hate those trips to the country but breakfast always tasted better there. She liked her father's ritual. He took a cup of tea in bed to her mother after he fed the range, and then he would go downstairs again and have a shower in the new bathroom and marvel at how there was always hot water from the range at the kitchen sink. If she closed her eyes now she could taste the smell of turf, bacon and brown soda bread baked the night before and rolled in a tea towel. He would have a late night whiskey while it was baking and chat about his childhood. Aisling liked to mock him – especially the bit about the first time he got a ten-shilling note and everything he bought with it, 'At least his soda bread looked like the real thing,' Aisling added.

Brigitte's voice took on a new energy and edge, 'Well I can believe bread from a packet would taste better than anything from that shop. When I went there, I thought maybe with that Celtic tiger now, it would be possible to find some decent bread in Leitrim but the main thing they sell is packaging. Inside there is damp soda bread or sliced pan. For fresh bread, it's those imitation French sticks – and croissants. But they have no idea of fresh bread to start the day. The Germans could teach them a thing or two. And the Irish idea of a cake is something with so much sugar and food colouring, it's just as well there's no fruit near it.'

'Sliced pan – that's the sliced white loaf isn't it? Gran makes me laugh about that. Sliced white loaf was a treat when she was young.'

'And so it was. White bread was almost a delicacy when we were growing up. We even preferred white soda bread to brown because it was Sunday bread. When I went back, I couldn't eat any of it. I lived on oatcakes. I had been away too long maybe. Soda bread reminded me too much of hunger.'

'So how many of you lived in the old house?' Aisling heard their names reeled off by her Gran often enough but she had usually switched off her brain by that stage and never remembered them. Luckily Gran would repeat it all again as a preliminary to some bit of news or story of the past.

'John-Joe, Liam, James, Mick and Peggy of course.'

'So there was six of you and your parents in that little house.'

'And it wasn't a small house compared to some – or a large family for that matter. We had three bedrooms upstairs. Peggy and myself shared the smallest room – the one on the right at the head of the stairs. And of course there was my grandmother in the good room downstairs.'

'I always sleep in the little room upstairs. Maybe I even slept in the same bed as you. My father found some old iron beds in one of the sheds. He had them done up and put back with new mattresses. My mother was disgusted: she said he could have got some brand new pine beds for half the price he paid for getting the old beds restored.'

'I hope he didn't put the springs on it again. I don't know whether it was the mattress or the springs but we always ended up in the dip in the centre fighting for blankets or the blanket with sleeves as Peggy used to say.'

'Blanket with sleeves?'

'Yes an old coat of my grandfather's – the wool in it was thicker than any blanket and warmer.'

Aisling grinned at the picture of Granny curled up in bed under an old coat. It was a long way from the image that she created of a quaint old farmhouse, good wholesome food, and a maid. The bathroom in the barn was always the bit that intrigued Aisling after the first time she stayed there. When they went there first, before they had the extension with the proper bathroom built on, the bathroom was a toilet and hand basin with a makeshift shower that either scalded you or doused you in cold water. You had to go out the back door to get to it. She hated using it. Once she asked her father what happened to the bathroom in the barn because she saw no sign of it. Wouldn't it have been easier to modernise it than to build on a toilet to the house, she asked.

Her father laughed, 'Bathroom! What bathroom?'

'Granny said something about the bathroom in the barn.'

'That's my mother for you. If there is anybody who could make a silk purse out of a sow's ear, it's her. You may think that stepping out into the flush toilet that's two steps from the back door is hard going for you. Do you know what toilet your Granny used all the time that she lived here?'

Aisling shook her head, puzzled.

'There was a bit of wood with a big hole in it in the barn above. The shit fell down through the hole into a pit below which they came to empty once a month. To be fair there might have been a pitcher full of water and a basin up there too. The big aluminium bath that was used for washing sheets and for Saturday night bath was kept there too. I love my mother sometimes – at least she's not one of these whingeing old people that spend half their time crying about the poverty of their youth and the other half complaining about the lack of religion now that people are better off. Bathroom indeed!' He laughed again, 'They were still using that earth closet when I visited here first but my mother made sure I didn't have to use it. She carried a potty with her the whole way from Dublin on the bus. I know that story because of the jokes of Uncle Liam. It might even have been the potty that persuaded my grandfather to finally part with the money for the toilet and hand basin and the shower that never worked properly.'

'Is it true that you didn't have running water or a bathroom when you were little?' Aisling asked Brigitte.

'Indeed it is and we weren't the only ones – in the country anyway. When I came to Berlin, I couldn't believe the bathroom in the apartment. Believe me it was as good as anything you'd see to-day. It wasn't just the running water, the flush toilet, and the big bath. It was beautifully tiled too – so easy to clean and a long way from peeing into a bucket and then having to empty it or dragging yourself off to the barn for the obligatory Number 2. In Berlin the whole apartment was so modern – with electric lamps everywhere – inside and out. But more than anything else it was the life of the city that I loved. I hated the farm. The only time I ever missed it was when I came back to Berlin after my mother died. Then I missed the view out over the lake and the hills beyond. You know I never remember remarking on that view when I was young. The first time I even noticed it was when I went back for my father's funeral. I did appreciate it when I went back there for a week to look after my mother. A week that turned into nine weeks. Then I liked the peace and quiet too. I missed that when I came back here again.'

Brigitte was silent again. There were no words for the view over the lake from the front of the house. The sensation of light filled her whole being. Every night during those weeks, she stepped out into the night air; air that smelt and felt like a tangible presence, taking the loneliness out of being alone. She learnt to love the shades of moonlight on the fields and answering light on the lake —usually silver or grey but sometimes passionate red, swooping stories back across the fields. Stories of placid water turned to a stream of blood when neighbour turned on neighbour. Stories of the skirt of a married woman lifted for love and exiled forever; leaving the children confused and motherless. When she spoke her tone was matter-of-fact, 'I loved to stand at the front door and look across the lake – especially on good summer evenings with the swallows out.'

'Yeah – it's a good view all right. But would you think of going back there to live?'

Brigitte laughed, 'Not now – what would I do there now?'

Aisling felt relieved somehow. The cottage as they called it now was all right maybe for a weekend but imagine being stuck in the country living like that with maybe the odd trip to Manorhamilton. You'd have to be off your head. The very thought of it made her restless to get out again and see a bit of Berlin.

'I'm going out now for a bit of air. I thought I'd go and look at this famous Berlin wall. I saw a bit of it when we went to the States a couple of years ago.

Brigitte laughed, 'So we sent if off round the world, did we? Here it's well hidden in memorials and museums. There's one bit they turned into a big art gallery – the East-side Art Gallery. Wall paintings near Warschauer Strasse. I've never been. Or some crosses by the Spree. Youngsters sitting in the steps in the sun. They have no idea of what it was like. Even Katharina agrees with me on that. I'd rather go to any graveyard if I want to remember the dead. Better to go to Bernauer Strasse. They built a small museum and a new church too. The old Church was on the wall. I remember the day they blew it up. Now there is a new one there.'

'Yeah, yeah, maybe I'll go there.'

'You can walk, if you want. It's not far and there's plenty of information and photos too according to Katharina.'

'I'm not much of a one for museums but I'll pop in.'

The aunt was right. Armed with her directions, Aisling was there in no time. The place wasn't a bit like a museum. It helped make some sense of the bit of the wall that you could see from the viewpoint on top. When she went down again, she played a while in the documentation centre on their computers to get some pictures of what had happened there over the years. It was weird to think of going through cellars to get from one side to the next. The bit she liked best was the old newsreels with people jumping from windows. She couldn't help laughing at the guy trying to help a woman who looked a bit like the aunt – he had his hand up her skirt – then she fell. It wasn't clear what happened to her even though there were people waiting with blankets and things for people to jump onto. She was surprised to learn the wall went up around the same time as the Beatles– her father was already a student at UCD, growing his hair long. Embarassed now to remember that she thought the Berlin Wall went up right after the war. Glad her father wasn't with her to mock her lack of knowledge of history. Looking at the pictures of a young guy – about the age her father was at the time – swimming across the river and being shot.

The sense of desolation around the new church attracted her in spite of her tendency to avoid anything holy. There was a photo exhibition of the old church which had been slap bang in the middle of the wall. The people who had designed the new one to replace it were obviously not the usual religious hypocrites. This was surely a case of 'less is more'. She'd tried to persuade her mother of that when they were doing up the living room but her mother was such a kitsch freak with traces of the hippy she once was and she would always add some Indian patterned cushions or a little shelf for photos which became a place of clutter and another opportunity to have an altar of candles and flowers for Michael.

Here, there was only the stark wood and cement structure – a never-ending circle of something. Of secret suffering maybe. No window on the world outside. The bits of the old church as a reminder of what happened. She had to admit that she preferred this new church to the old one that the Commies had torn down. It was a far better symbol of religion than any other church she had been in. 'If I ever got married, I would get married here,' she told herself. 'I would dress up Gothic style for it.'

Potsdamer Platz next on the list. The empty space overlooked by surveillance towers well filled up according to the aunt. By all accounts, as she said, never having been there herself. Coffee in the shopping centre, trying to work out where she was sitting in relation to the old Berlin. Walking around, Aisling found it impossible to tell what had been east and what had been west. Piecing together the bits from the Bernauer Strasse museum. Glitzy domes were apparently all the rage with the architects doing the makeover after the wall came down. Glamour and glitz for the plebs in the Sony

Centre. Glassy stars and big screens. One big thing in favour of Berlin — no sense of snobbery. Scruffs and designer dolls rubbing shoulders. Moving on to the Reichstag. Dome for the people, making the polarities of east and west irrelevant. Does it really? Check out Checkpoint Charlie. More touristy than Bernauer Strasse: so glad to have been there first.

Chapter Eleven

# War years

No sleep again. Aisling doodled as she leafed a few more pages from the sheaf. Was it all unposted letters of loneliness? Was the friend Mary in Ireland dead or alive? The letters gave the Second World War an original slant. Shapes forming for her own graphics. The old photo images of Berlin merging with the images in her guide book, merging with the photos she took. Could she reproduce a mix of old and new? Make Brigitte's story her story too? They would all laugh at her for wanting to write a comic book. Even Maeve had laughed at her for reading comic books. 'What about Asterix comics?' she reminded her.

'That's different. Those comic books are all about superheros, fantasy and weirdoes'.

'And what's so different about the novels you read, Maeve?'

'You can't compare adult literature with those comics – they're for children, Aisling. Time you grew up.' Time to tell Maeve there is a developing genre of graphic novels? No Maeve to tell and too soon to tell anyone anyway.

The anti-heroine Brigitte – two-faced young and old. Would it be possible to get hold of the film she mentioned in one letter, "Mein Leben für Irland". Nazi propaganda using the

Irish hero giving up his life in the struggle against British Imperialism. Excitement stirring. No-one to douse it. Material here for a comic-strip in book form to poke fun at nationalism by mixing the stereotypes. Using montage to merge image and experience. Ambition bites life into the crackling paper. No-one to ridicule her dreams of making her living with her comic-strips and cartoons. A sci-fi reality perspective on the past and present. Using a mix of styles of comic-strips and cartoons. Mixing the "Troubles" in the North, the border in Ireland and the Berlin wall. Forget the marketing and iconic images for sales pitch. Of course it could be hard to persuade her parents to give her an allowance if she quit her university course. How to survive? Worry about that later. Now for dipping into real history.

*January 1941*
*Dear Mary,*
*Another new year and still this blasted war. I'm fed up waiting for it to be over. I didn't even think to write to you this past year. This letter is my only New Year's resolution. I can't be bothered even to check to-day's date on the calendar — every day is much like another. They call New Year's Eve Sylvester here. On my first one we had a party but the partying days are over for now. I like the sound of Sylvester rather than New Year's Eve. I wonder why it is Sylvester, I must ask Delia. It's hard to believe that another year of waiting is over and we're on our way to the end of this one. All I know is that it's Sunday and the nights are still long and dark. Even after Mass there are people doing the Heil Hitler at each other. We stick together in a group and rush home to finish preparing Sunday dinner. I have to do most of it now as Maria has gone to work in a*

*factory. I don't really mind but by the time it is over I am ready for an afternoon nap and then it is nearly dark again.*

*We still have coffee in the afternoon on Sundays but now it is later and we have bread and jam not cake. Then we have cocoa and more bread and jam for 'Abendbrot'. We are lucky to have that. Cocoa is a rare treat this winter. I don't ask where Delia got it. To-day I am tired but too restless for a nap so I write here for the first time in a long time. It's good to have my own tongue in my head for a change. I've got very used to German now. Delia and I speak it together sometimes to give me practice. The strangeness of it makes me feel like I am someone else.*

*The best night so far this year was the outing to the pictures with Delia. After our bread and cocoa, Dieter was falling asleep on the sofa and Delia put him to bed. I heard them laughing in the bedroom so thought Delia would go to bed too. Then she came back in with her hat and gloves in her hand.*

*'Get your coat on. We are going to leave all the boys sleeping and go out,' she said to me, 'There's a film on about Ireland.'*

*It was like old times when we linked arms together and laughed our way onto the tram. We are more like sisters now. I thought she was joking when she said the film was about Ireland but she wasn't, 'Mein Leben für Irland – My life for Ireland.' In the cinema she laughed and cried a lot. I cried mostly because it was such a sad story. I couldn't see what Delia found so funny especially as she was the only one to laugh. Maybe it was the way that they presented Ireland. I found that odd too. For me it hard to believe that the story really was about Ireland, it could have been anywhere really.*

Delia told me that they made it in Germany of course and the school was a real school. Many of the young actors were from the Hitler Youth. I could believe that because of all that stamping of shiny boots.

The fire where they burnt the books was meant to be a symbol of rejecting British rule and becoming Irish but it made me feel uncomfortable. It reminded me of the burning of the books in Berlin more than about anything in Ireland. When Delia and Dieter spoke about it, they said that it marked the end of any freedom of expression. It must be true because they never spoke of it again even to each other and now everybody is careful what they say and who they say it too. There are so many things that are forbidden, like tuning in to any broadcast from abroad. We miss that. Sometimes I catch Delia with her ear right up to the wireless and wonder what she is listening to but I don't ask. Sometimes in the film, Delia gripped my arm tight. I liked the boy who gave his life for Ireland. I could believe in him. He looked manlier than the other boys. I could fall for him all right. He was a good actor too. You could see how he was torn between some sense of loyalty to the British and support for the Irish cause. But the strongest feeling he had was for his friend's mother that was clear. He really did love her and it was really sad to see him dying in her arms. He wanted her to believe in him and he got his wish. I think he gave his life for her and not for Ireland.

Afterwards we talked about it on the way home and I wondered if Delia saw a different film. She said it was all a way of persuading people to die for their country. It was to convince Germans they should be ready to give up their lives in the fight against the British. She told me the man in charge of making the film was the brother-in-law of Goebbels. She spoke lowly into my ear and in rapid English with a strong Leitrim accent when she was telling me this. She switched to German if she saw anybody coming within earshot. I was surprised because I thought it was a film about love when love is hopeless. It wasn't just the difference in their ages. The woman he loved was married. You could tell the filmmakers had a simple view of the struggle against the British. It made it look like a clear-cut fight between the British and the Irish and it wasn't always like that. I'd love to watch it with you one day in English.

Yours Biddy


17<sup>th</sup> March 1942

Dear Mary,

To-day I'm homesick. Really homesick for the first time since I came here. Saint Patrick's Day isn't celebrated here so I'd miss it anyway but it made me realise what a sorry state we are in here. In Ireland St. Patrick's day was a chance to let your hair down in the middle of Lent. Now it feels like Lent the whole year only worse. We never have visitors now and hardly even dare speak to people in the street. I feel embarrassed now when I see Frau Goldman in the street. She and her husband used to be regular dinner guests before this horrible time started. I don't bump into her often, as she doesn't go out. I see the children set off very early in the morning. Dieter says they have to walk to a Jewish school because they aren't allowed to go to the nearby school anymore. Herr Goldman was sent away to a labour camp leaving his wife and the children alone. I expect Frau Goldman is glad now that her mother lives with them — unless she feels that she has to look after her too. She used to complain about her mother trying to organise everyone but it must be better to have her there than not. More rations for one thing. Delia was furious when Herr Goldman was sent away. He is a violinist in the orchestra — a labour camp could destroy his hands and maybe his health. Apparently some musicians are forced to do manual labour. Delia says that she also heard that they have orchestras in the camps for the German SS so maybe they took him because he is such a good violinist and he'll be looked after because of that. Dieter doesn't say much. He just shakes his head.

I'm glad Ireland is not in the war. Do you have rations too?

Yours, Biddy


*8th September 1942:*

Dear Mary,

It's strange to remember times when things were still normal. I see the Goldman children at the window sometimes — staring out into the street and stepping back when they see me look up. They are not allowed to go to any school now and I'm afraid for them. It's not safe on the streets for anyone with a yellow star and they say that even women and children are sent to camps now. I don't understand politics — or religion either for that matter. I've got used to the war now but I still spend every spare moment hoping it will be over soon. I don't care who wins as long as it's over. Everybody complains but the curfews and the shortages can't last forever. Don't tell Mammy but I'm still not sorry I stayed in Berlin. This can't last forever. One day we'll be jumping on a tram here together.

Yours, Biddy

*15th September 1942*

*Dear Mary,*

*Twice in one month even though I am dropping with tiredness!
I was too tired to write you my news. I am no longer a nanny!
Klaus started school now too. The school is the one that is just
behind the house so the two older boys can go there together.
They don't need me to take them or fetch them. Josef, the
youngest has a place in the crèche where I work. Dieter
arranged it for me. The crèche is for hospital staff and I can
take Josef with me every day on the tram.
How are things in Ireland?
Yours, Biddy*

*4th October 1942*
*Dear Mary,*

*I'm too tired to write really but I wish I had someone to
talk to. Now I have got used to speaking German all the time
and I've almost forgotten my own tongue. The work at the
crèche is harder than being at home. I get all the heavy work
but I won't complain. At least we are still here. Dieter and
Delia don't talk about leaving, not even to me. Dieter can't
leave and Delia won't leave without him. They don't want to
fight and they can't talk about it without fighting. I don't
know how long the truce will last. Delia also has to work now.
She translates from German to English in some office but she
only works until 2 o clock and she comes back to be there when
the two older boys get out of school. She hates her work but
she says she has to do it and it means we are all safe.*

*She asked me to-day about my work and if they ask me
about where I come from. She tells me to make sure that I tell*

everyone that I am Irish and that Ireland is neutral in the war. I should make sure to put in that the Irish hate the British and fought against the British for their freedom. We speak about this in German and she makes me repeat it to her several times. I don't tell her that I hardly ever get a chance to talk to anybody at work but they all know I am Irish. Tonight I can't sleep even though I can feel the tiredness go through to my bones.

    Yours, Biddy


November 20<sup>th</sup> 1942

Dear Mary,

I'm afraid that they will send me home. Delia and Dieter have been talking late at night and I try to listen through the wall. Apparently the German army is not doing well on the Eastern Front. It's funny to think of the British, the Russians and the Americans all fighting Germany. I can't hear any words through the wall but I know they are talking about Delia moving to Bavaria. They are not fighting about it anymore so they are planning something. Delia doesn't want to stay with Dieter's parents but Dieter has other relatives there. When we eat together now, they often speak German very quickly. I know it's because they don't want me to understand everything. Delia only tells me what they want me to know. Sometimes she says that Dieter might have to move into the hospital. Sometimes that he might be transferred to Bavaria. When we were taking soup this evening, Dieter said he was sorry that he didn't send Delia and me back to Ireland when he had the chance. Delia was angry then. I'm glad he didn't because if she had gone back to Ireland, she would have taken me for sure and I would never have got back here again. I still want

113

*to live here even though I am homesick sometimes. Without the war, of course!*

*Yours, Biddy*


*November 23rd 1942*

*Dear Mary,*

*I still haven't posted the letters but I want to tell you I was right. Delia told me to-day that she is leaving with the children to live in Bavaria. She insists that I go with them. When I said no that I would stay in Berlin, Delia was shocked. Then I told them I would wait for a chance to go back to Ireland. They both looked at each other and said nothing. I told them I know I can't leave now. The truth is that I really want to stay here. The war can't last forever. Dieter kept saying how sorry he is that he missed the chance. At one time he could have arranged for me to get back to Ireland by going through France to Cherbourg by train and then the ferry direct to Cork but not now. He could have arranged all the German papers. Delia shakes her head, 'Not on her own — even then,' and insists again that I come with them to Bavaria and wait until the war is over. I say little as I am determined to stay. They can't make me go to Bavaria. I am old enough to make my own decisions. They say Bavaria is more like Ireland. It gives me another reason not to go.*

*I still have my work. I think Dieter suspects that I have some other reason to stay that I don't want to tell them. He just shakes his head and looks worried. It's too late to worry now. I'm looking forward to the day the two of us can laugh away our worries.*

*Yours, Biddy.*

*29ᵗʰ December 1942*

*Dear Mary,*

*December has been a long month. We seemed to spend a lot of time sorting things into boxes to put them in the cellar for storage or into the trunk that Delia took with her. Delia would put something in one, then take it out and put it in the other. She gave a running commentary on why the tablecloth or the set of cutlery or the china or whatever was important to her. It feels strange now with the apartment empty. Every room rattles. Dieter's study is the only room that feels the same. There are spaces on the shelves where he took away many of the books. Most of what remains is in German and medical by the looks of them. I like to sit in there. If he does move to the hospital I will bring a bed in here. Dieter wanted Delia to leave earlier but she insisted on staying for Christmas and he gave in. I said that if I changed my mind I would join them later.*

*They went today.*

*Yours, Biddy*


*30ᵗʰ December 1942*

*Dear Mary,*

*I went back to the kindergarten yesterday and told them that I will stay on but Josef will not be coming any more. The leader says she will soon leave anyway. She doesn't say why. At least I still have a job of sorts and a rations book.*

*Your Biddy*


*31ˢᵗ December 1942*

*Dear Mary,*

*Sylvester again. What a way to welcome the New Year! I hope we all have a better year this year.*

The day after Delia left, Dieter said that he will not stay here very much and I could sleep in his study. He told me some nurses would move into their apartment.

Yours, Biddy


*30<sup>th</sup> January 1943*

Dear Mary,

I missed Dieter when he came to pick up some clothes not long after New Year. He left a note saying that he will come to see me in the kindergarten.

Every day now there is talk of the Eastern front. Nobody dares say how many lives have been lost already in the Battle of Stalingrad. There's a lot of low murmuring when the new matron is not listening. She is the only one with any enthusiasm left for the führer. I thought I heard someone say millions were dead already in the Battle of Stalingrad. Surely there could not be millions of people killed, even if they were not all soldiers. I must have been mistaken. Adelheid, one of the women who work at the crèche, has two sons in the 6<sup>th</sup> army. She shakes her head and cries when the children cry. I hope the new matron doesn't catch her. I worry about her. She has been kind to me. She's my only friend here. The work is harder than ever but I am glad of it. When I get home I fall into bed. It passes the time but I feel like my life is stuck in a station waiting room, just waiting for the war to be over so I can really start my life in Berlin.

I miss you, Mary. If you get this tell me some news about my family. My mother doesn't write much. Give me news of your crowd too.

Yours, Biddy

*2nd February 1943*

*Dear Mary,*

*My wish might be coming true at last. Everybody is talking about the surrender of the 6th army in Stalingrad. There is more low murmuring. I don't catch the words but I can tell from the way people shake their heads and the expressions on their faces that they would criticise Hitler now if they dared. Adelheid got word the other day that one of her sons was already killed in the Battle of Stalingrad but now she has hope that the other has survived as a Prisoner of War. Apparently the leader of the 6th Army, someone called Friedrich Paulus, disobeyed Hitler because he surrendered instead of fighting to the last man. Though I think she is afraid that the Red Army would kill the survivors instead of taking them prisoner. Nobody dares say it but I think the defeat means that Stalin and his Red Army have a chance of winning the war now. I hope, whatever happens, it means the war will be over soon.*

*I spend less time with the children with this new matron. I'm all day up to my armpits in nappies, children's clothes, towels and the covers of the small beds — soaked with pee of course. All these have to be passed through a monstrous wringer and hung to dry. The wringer is electric and when it breaks down it is even worse as I have to use the hand one. At least it is work of a sort and without it I would be in a worse state. I pity the poor children who are subjected to a strict regime of food, change, sleep, crawling or walking. It has become a joyless place but still they manage to play and smile. That keeps me going. I soon realised that the new matron doesn't do the Hitler salute just to stay out of trouble like the last one. She is clearly a committed supporter and she trains the children to march and salute. I wait to get home before I laugh at the*

117

ridiculous scene. She like a Sergeant Major and the little ones stamping their feet to the music and then stopping for the Hitler salute. She stands in front of the picture of the Führer. I am sure she means the children to salute her. I hope she doesn't want to check my papers. They got me this job all right but now maybe they want more. I live in terror of anyone asking to see my papers in case there is something wrong. I do the Heil Hitler salute in an orderly and serious fashion but I feel sure they will see through me someday. At the moment there is more talk about the Red Army than the British. Even so I make sure everyone knows that I am Irish and Ireland is against the British and against the Communists too. On the walk to and from work each day I try to look as dowdy and dull as every other woman who walks to work. That's not too difficult, I'm sorry to say.

Yours, Biddy

*26ᵗʰ December 1943*

*Dear Mary,*

The year has dragged on dismally. I spent Christmas day alone and a good part of the day huddled in bed for heat. My Christmas dinner was bacon from home with spuds and onions from Herr Schmitt. It makes a change from soup. When this is over, I never want to see soup again in my life. I haven't had the heart to write here. Now I really am homesick and lonely. I wish every day that I had gone home when I could – Dieter came by today and brought a tiny morsel of sausage and bread. He doesn't call often now and his uniform no longer hangs in the wardrobe. He would try to get me home if I want but he may be just saying it. I know it will be hard for him to do it now. He says Delia is OK and is working. But I know that *already because I still write to her and she writes back. Dieter says it would be easier to send me to Bavaria. I said yes I will go soon but I haven't the heart to do anything about that either. Maybe the war will soon be over now that they are really fighting.*

*Dieter found the remains of a bottle of Schnaps in the sideboard and we finished the bottle together. This war turns everything topsy-turvy even my feelings. Dieter kissed me goodnight and I felt funny. I do love him but I think for both of us it was only because of the Schnaps and missing Delia. I just laughed and pushed him away from me to his own bedroom. It makes me restless so I write this by candlelight like at home. I don't want the brightness of electric tonight even though the blackout curtains are well fixed.*

*New Year's Eve 1943.*

*Another Sylvester and I forgot to ask Dieter why they call it Sylvester — is it a saint? We would need a saint to help us welcome in the New Year. I thought the war would be long over by now. I lie awake every night now listening to the sirens. We are lucky that we allowed to use our cellar as an air-raid shelter. In the public air-raid shelters, people are just huddled together like cattle. Herr Schmidt insists on coming round to check that everyone goes down to their cellar. He takes his role very seriously and becomes more military every day. When there were raids every night I decided to make my bed in our cellar but he still comes to check that I am there. He stayed yesterday to chat. I am glad of the chance to keep practising my German and he makes me do the salute several times so that I do it correctly. It is a small price to pay. I rarely get chance now to* speak much in work and hardly dare buy a newspaper. I am glad that Dieter and Delia befriended him. Maybe they did it for my sake.

There's a pump in the cellar for ground water. Delia said that I should never drink it but sometimes I have tried it and I have had no ill effects so I don't always climb the stairs with a bucket. There is an old boiler that was used for heating water for washing. I use the boiler to keep warm if I am not too tired to make sure there is water in it. I have a good selection of scraps of wood. I gather them on my way home from work. I have made the cellar quite cosy. All the cellars have their own door and I have ours to myself most of the time as the nurses are hardly ever here at night. I have made it into my own private waiting room. I dream of the things that are stored in the boxes and of the day that we will unpack them again. I have taken up reading by candlelight. I moved some of Dieter's books down here but I can't read the books in German. I feel guilty when I burn some of them but I tell myself that he won't notice they are gone. I read the children's books in German and am happy when I can understand them.

I've taught myself a sort of wide-awake daydreaming to pass the time and fill the space of my longings. I long for the feeling of glamour that I had when I came here first. I want to ride on the trams again and swing around the corner with a light heart looking at shops and bits of sky. I long for people who can look you in the eye again. I long for cafés with bowls of hot milky coffee where you pay with real money. I long for a trip home to Ireland too. I packed my things. It was easy to put everything I owned back into the small cream pigskin suitcase I love so much. I keep it in the cellar now and stroke the label on it for Berlin. The label on it reminds me of *something from a film. I've only ever seen one film in Ireland. I can see Rudolf Valentino saying goodbye at the station and holding onto the hand of his loved one until the train pulled away. It would be lovely to go to Manorhamilton to see a film with you. I will come for a visit when this nonsense is over. Writing to you makes me less lonely. One day soon we will read these letters together to remind us of hard times.*

*Yours, Biddy*

The date on the next letter was 30th May 1945 but the writing was hard to read. Aisling wondered about the gap. The time in the camp? She had heard the aunt call out, 'Supper's ready' about 10 minutes before but had pretended not to hear. Now she decided to risk an evening with the aunt rather than escape into the city. She would find a way to ask her about the war. Time to gather more ideas for her sketches. She waited for the deadly lull after 'Abendbrot' when they both looked for something to talk about.

'So how long have you lived here in Berlin?' Asking for a response to a question already answered by the letters.

'It feels like a whole lifetime,' Brigitte sighed, 'I was only eighteen when I came to be a nanny for Delia and Dieter's children.'

'So you came for work?' Questions looking to connect the letters to the person then and now.

'Yes work, although you'd think from my parents it was a finishing school I was headed off to. Delia was from Manorhamilton – her father was a tailor and her family had a draper's shop there. My parents ran up a mighty bill with a suit, hat, gloves, coat and suitcase. No daughter of theirs would let the family down. Delia met Dieter in the Mater hospital in

Dublin when she was training to be a nurse.' Brigitte whistled a deep sigh from her chest, 'It was the happiest day of my life, the day I arrived in Berlin.

'And you've been here ever since.' A lifetime, Aisling conceded to herself.

'Ever since.' Like an echo.

'Were you a nanny during the War too?'

'When the children were old enough, I worked in a crèche.'

'What about Delia's husband, was he a German soldier?'

'He was a doctor and an important one. He stayed in Berlin for a long time but then he was posted to the Eastern Front.'

'And you stayed in Berlin when Delia went to Bavaria?' Aisling enjoyed seeing a bit of fluster in the aunt. The memory of the Schnaps and snuggle? Maybe there was more to it than she told Mary. Could be she had an affair with him and Katharina was his daughter – that would be real news in Manorhamilton. It was worth a bit more interrogation.

'Well, he was hardly ever there. And the nurses who moved in were hardly ever there either.'

'So you were on your own most of the time?'

'Well, I was in the apartment on my own but there were other families in the building.'

'Were there bombs?'

'Oh, there were bombs all right.'

'Weren't you afraid?'

'At first, I wasn't afraid of anything – that's why I stayed when I had the chance to go. Maybe I didn't know enough about anything to be afraid. Then it was too late to go home anyway. I did not think of it as my war – it would be something settled one way or another by the powers that be – nothing to do with me.'

Aisling closed her eyes, mentally trying a sketch of the aunt.

'What about the bombs?'

'Bombs fell on guilty and innocent. Some of the houses in our street were hit. Our neighbours, the Goldmanns, were long gone. Vanished one day. I hoped they managed to get out of the country and I was relieved for them. I still don't know what happened to them.'

'But the house you were living in was hit?'

'Yes, I came back from work one day to find it gone. It was after one of the raids in the middle of an afternoon. The Allies took greater and greater risks – maybe to convince us they were winning. The kindergarten took all the children to the air-raid shelter and the matron told me to go on home. I saw one of the bombs burst as I made my way home.'

'You saw an actual bomb?' Aisling was impressed.

'It didn't look like a bomb or what I thought a bomb should look like. I was running but there was no-one left on the street. It seemed like the planes above my head were looking to drop their bomb directly on me. I decided it was all over and stopped. Then I saw it in front of me – a glorious green glow that looked like something alive – like some creature with a message from heaven. I was mesmerised by it and watched it hit the wall. My feet were still on the ground but I was in a cloud of dust and could see nothing except that the heavenly creature had vanished inside a heap of green dung. Then the dung turned into a giant brush of fire sweeping down the street setting everything in its path alight down to the cellar steps. When it settled I could hear screams so I knew I was still alive.

Every cellar was full of people. Like ours their cellar was an air raid shelter. I didn't stop to see what happened next. My legs felt wobbly and strange as if they were not really part of me but they carried me down another street and another and then I realised I was running away from home. Nowhere was safe so I thought I might as well turn and go back. I got lost avoiding the street of the bomb and around another corner I overheard bits of German – eine alte Frau. They were looking for an old woman: I don't know if they found her: lots of familiar places had melted into the thick smoky air. Sometimes later there were whispers in a queue for water or soup, or reading out the names chalked on the doorway of the building where they used to live. You might hear then of a missing name – some neighbour burnt alive.'

'Did you ever think of telling your story? Oral history or something similar?'

Brigitte looked suspicious.

'Why not tell your story, Mama?' she mimicked. Must be Katharina.

'My story for Katharina and Monika. Now you too. Everybody wants the story with the angels and the devils. They say they want the truth but the truth is too ugly to tell. Easier to pretend those things did not happen or take memories out and look at them secretly. No-one can put words onto it. Maybe no-one can hold such horror in their head for very long. It is better forgotten. There is no point admitting that such things can happen when they should never happen. It's too hard to think that someone was responsible. Even after the war when it was over, then it was too hard to face that someone British or American had bombed houses full of people. In order to be able to eat, we had to accept them as our liberators.

Sometimes people looked at me in envy because I was one of them in a way – almost British. Sometimes they looked at me with hatred. Either way, I don't blame them.'

Aisling felt the adrenalin rush again. She would check the aunt's story but truth or fiction, it kept making great images in her head. Her colour scheme was now green and red on top of black and white, not a whole palette of colour.

'Do you know if there is any film or photos of the green bombs?'

'Those fire bombs were better forgotten. The Allies did not want them remembered. We did not want our shame remembered. There were whispers telling how Hamburg was even worse than Berlin. There was a bookshop here in Berlin, where the owner had photos but he kept them hidden. Only people who asked had the chance to see them. He let me look at them and I knew why he did not want them on display – the suffering of so much pain is not for spreading around. Only people like me needed to see those images to be glad it was over. It was as if I was taking a secret look at something dirty from my past. When he saw me he would get them out and leave me there in silence for a while. Later we would talk about the weather. Surely for someone who had no memories, such pictures would be even more of an obscenity.'

'So the photos might still exist?' The aunt looked at her with vacant eyes and said nothing.

'Why did you feel ashamed? You didn't do anything?' Any question to stop her clamming up.

'Why did I feel ashamed? My own daughter thought I must have done something so bad I couldn't talk about it. Maybe I did. Maybe we all did. Maybe we all do.'

'Yes, but you didn't blow up your own house, did you? I

expect the British and Americans were proud of what they did. They stopped Hitler. It was Hitler they were trying to bomb. You just happened to be in the wrong place at the wrong time.'

'But shame is not for what you do or don't do. Shame is what you feel in front of others. Would you like someone to know that your wife carried your dead baby in a suitcase all the way from Hamburg to Berlin and then committed suicide in front of her remaining two children? Would you be proud of that or ashamed?'

'Well, I suppose I wouldn't go around boasting about it but I would expect people to understand that it was a war and strange things happen and people do strange things. I wouldn't feel ashamed of it or guilty.'

'Ach so. Maybe for young people to-day it is different. They have grown up with Television and they see wars and bombs every day. Maybe you would not feel ashamed and dirty if it touched your life. But you don't know.'

'But I do know,' It was out before Aisling knew the words were there. The aunt looked at her strangely.

'Maybe it is not the same but I felt like that when Michael died. Ashamed and dirty. Not guilty, but it was as if it was something that I had done. Something I couldn't talk about. But I didn't even know what it was.'

The aunt looked at her. Aisling shrugged. She wished she hadn't said anything about Michael. The aunt was a wily old bitch and could corner her if she wasn't careful. How to get this back to bombs in Berlin without it being too noticeable?

'So where was this apartment that was bombed? Is it far from here, maybe I'll go take a look? And where did you live if it was bombed?'

The aunt looked at her again. Clearly she sussed these last

questions were a smokescreen but she answered anyway, 'I was one of the lucky ones. It wasn't a firebomb that hit our street – only an ordinary one. Nobody was killed and the cellar was still there. A few of the people and the local blockwart cleared a way down the steps. The rest were still in there – more dazed and shocked than I was. We stayed there. I didn't go back to work after that. I couldn't face them. No work meant no ration book.'

'So what did you eat?'

'I had hoarded some flour and potatoes in our cellar. The flour was alive with little small black creatures but I mixed it with bicarbonate of soda and water and made griddle scones on the boiler. I had hidden a jar of bottled beans, jars of pickled gherkins and some large jars of bottled red cabbage – buried in sand in buckets. I was lucky they were still there too. Bottled fruit. The jars came from Delia's mother-in-law in Bavaria. She would bring a great suitcase full of jars of stuff when she visited. Delia wouldn't touch most of it before the war and even on rations, she would rather go hungry than eat it.

'When I ran out of tea leaves, I used to make tea with nettles that I gathered. I always had some dried stalks hanging in the cellar. I kept a store of the ration coffee to swap for something. I couldn't drink the stuff. In daylight I would scrabble through the rubble for anything I could find. The skin on my hands was raw and bleeding from scrabbling there but it was worth it when I found something. Like the cooking pots. I brought them to the cellar and used them to heat the cabbage or beans. The memory of putting them away carefully after Sunday lunch of goulash or rouladen gave me appetite. I stored anything useful I could find in the cellar.

'The strangest thing of all was that, one day, when I was

huddled in the cellar, a parcel came from home. Would you believe it – a postman delivering to a street that had been bombed! He pushed his cart up the street and people would appear from nowhere waving their papers. My surprise made me realise that I was still a foreigner. In my parcel there was tea and bacon and two of my mother's griddle scones. Only two because they had to be eaten fresh and she didn't know how long the parcel would take. I swapped some bacon for some more potatoes and a few onions from Herr Schmidt's garden. I ate the best meal of my life that day and then huddled up beside the boiler and pictured myself beside the range at home. When they came for me some days later, I still had one piece of bacon from that parcel and some tea. One of the hardest things, when I was in the Lager, was the thought of bacon slowly rotting away while we were so hungry. Many nights before I fell asleep I wondered if some hungry rat would get through the defences I had created to protect it or would someone else have taken over my little cellar to live there. I missed my little cellar.'

'How do you mean when they came for you? Who came for you?'

The aunt sighed, 'I told you I don't want to tell fairy stories.'

Clammed shut. Aisling yawned her exit with excuses of tiredness.

Brigitte turned her eyes now from the voile blind, which had found a partner in the light evening breeze. It wasn't important now. To tell or not to tell. What did it matter? She took out a cigarette and lit it. 'Cancer sticks', Katharina had said when she was a teenager. She had never smoked and was always trying to persuade her mother to give them up.

Chapter Twelve

# Ferienlager

Looking for a history book to settle the uncomfortable restless sensation. Hangover from the whiskey? Hitting on the website for the bookshop fed her restlessness. She needed some more visuals of Berlin in the war years. Flicking through Katharina's collection on Ravensbrück, she wondered why these books stayed here. If Katharina taught history she must have had lots more books somewhere. The books on this shelf were not academic thankfully and a few were even in English. Probably bought with Brigitte in mind. In the graphic novel of Spring in 1945, the face of a young woman, with a square set jaw and high forehead, looked familiar – it reminded her of her cousin Celia who was supposed to be the image of Gran when she was young. She looked at the pictures of ruined buildings, rolled up bedding in the street and people sitting, standing or walking. Ideas formed. She needed a scanner now. She could scan the images from the "Everyday Life in a Women's Concentration Camp 1939-1945". She could scan the images, zoom in on some and use them as a basis for her drawings. This would be a major project.

The feeling fluttered still – somewhere between uncertainty and fear. The old photos brought her back to the days when her dad gave her his old Canon. He ditched it when he got his digital camera. Aisling enjoyed playing around with the Canon. Anyone could take a good photo with a decent digital camera but there was none of the magic of capturing an image in the old-fashioned way. For a while Aisling enjoyed the perverse eyeball to lens, seeking out the perfect match for a single moment of being. It didn't last and the camera was gathering dust now on a shelf in the cottage in Leitrim.

Back on the bed again and looking at the yellow and brown stained pages. The unspoken battle between Brigitte and Katharina; between Leitrim and Berlin; between memory and the desire to forget. She could feel the pages crackle with stories the aunt wanted to tell and wanted to hide. It made her want to know more – to know more of the unspeakable things. A story of people who could be cruel for no good reason. She'd have to worm more out of Brigitte. She watched and waited for her chance after 'Abendbrot'.

"Would you tell me a bit about the camp?"

Brigitte looked at her through blank eyes which had lost their usual stern sky-blue. She was probably somewhere in the past with Katharina. She hadn't mentioned anything about the whiskey of the night before. Just as well. Aisling would stay away from that, even if the aunt went on it to-night.

'Camp?' Brigitte asked her from a face that had crumpled in on itself.

'Yes you know the Lager, *that place* you told me about.' Aisling switched her tone and put the emphasis on 'that place'. Said in the right way, it should be guaranteed to tune her into a certain wavelength.

'So you want to know more about my days in the Ferienlager?

'Ferienlager? Holiday camp?

'Anna and me – we called it that. Some called them 'Arbeitslager'.

'Workcamp?'

Aisling sighed. Brigitte was doing a wind up. Get her talking and find a way in through the contradictions.

'Ferienlager?'

'To survive as long as I have, you need to learn to see with other eyes than your own. Anna was taken to the camp in 1940. To begin with it was only sixteen wooden blocks, and a building housing the kitchen, baths, and offices. Many of the houses – the villas and apartments on the outside of the camp for the women guards – were already finished. The women swept the sandy road into intricate patterns. There were still small trees and shrubs near the blocks. Even flowers and some salad leaves grown around the block in summer. They went to work building more blocks and more houses, or worked in factories in the town.

Each woman had a dish, knife, fork, spoon, glass, and a dishcloth. My can was just an old tin but Anna's was a proper enamel can, I have it still. In the days of the 'Ferienlager', each prisoner had a cupboard, one woman to a bunk with her own quilt. Showers with warm water; flushing toilets. Enough heat from the stove. Maybe the early days of the camp was how it was meant to be. Who knows?

'Anna taught me phrases and words in German for me to repeat during the day. Die Blumen wachsen – warmes Wasser. Alles in Ordnung. Another word was paradise. Paradise! Paradies! You can find paradise in comparison if you can believe in it still. Anna held onto her belief in God, in images of order with a full belly and cleanliness. She had a great laugh – like a hyena. On the worst days even days of punishment she only had to speak of planting flowers in the Ferienlager. Her laugh was as infectious as dysentery running rife. If the guards caught us laughing, she would make some remark about my German and they would join in. No-one could hate Anna. Laughter and kindness helped us keep the horror outside. Laughter and kindness are the only defence against prison. Knowing facts and history is not enough.

'Ferienlager – if I rolled the word on my tongue, I could taste the water of the lake where I went with Dieter, Delia and the boys on a sticky summer day and the fish lunch afterwards at the restaurant by the lake with my new family. I could feel the waters of the lake on my shoulders where I dipped in and out on my hunkers moving my arms as if I was swimming– too timid to admit that I did not swim but the children knew and laughed at me.'

'How did you meet Anna?' Aisling wanted her to focus.

'In the early days each category of prisoner was in a separate block but by the time I arrived, there was so much overcrowding nothing worked, they shoved women in everywhere. I had a red triangle even though I wasn't a political but they put me with the lavender triangles because I was on my own. I shared a bed with Anna and another lavender triangle. I was lucky.

'Sleepless nights, muddy days and watery soup but we were still expected to do a hard day's work. It killed many that winter.'

'What about Anna, how did she die?'

Brigitte sighed again, 'The end of the Ferienlager. I was afraid that when Anna died there would be no more laughter. No protection. So many rules and regulations; even when the place was falling to bits it was impossible to keep up.'

'Not exactly a holiday camp after all, then,' Aisling commented.

'You young people are all the same. "Mama, you and your Ferienlager and how cruel women can be to other women. You never speak of the Nazis who put you in there",' Brigitte mimicked, 'Inside or outside the camp, people hate each other for good reason or no good reason. Find the Nazi in yourself before you look for it in someone else, Katharina.'

Aisling flinched. Had Brigitte lost it? Did she really confuse her with Katharina or was it memory talking?

Brigitte took a tissue out of the packet sitting on the table beside her chair and carefully sealed the packet again. Beside it were her reading glasses in their case – never taken out as far as Aisling could see but they travelled every day from the bedside table to the little folding table by Brigitte's chair. Beside them the remote control for the TV – that stayed on the table always. Aisling had yet to see that in use either. Once she had asked to turn on the TV and put the remote on the chair beside her. Brigitte fidgeted so much it was impossible to watch anything anyway. Finally she asked Aisling to put the remote back in its place and then she settled again and dozed off. Aisling realised then what the fidgeting was about. The remote had to sit there in its place beside her tablet box.

Gran would like one of those boxes, Aisling thought: morning, afternoon, evening; three little boxes for every day of the week. Gran marked hers carefully every day on bits of old birthday cards ever since the day she had forgotten to take her blood pressure tablets and rang Mum in a panic because she had pains across her chest and couldn't move. Her Mum believed she was just attention-seeking and it was all in her imagination. Maybe, maybe not. She watched now as Brigitte put the tissues back in their place – beside the bar of chocolate. Aisling fetched a glass and filled both glasses from the bottle on the table. Sometimes she put ice cubes in her own but Brigitte always refused them no matter how hot it was.

She's a fine one to talk about rigid regulations in 'that place' – little rituals over nothing. Order had to be established in the midst of misery. Beds neatly made, inspections under the bed. Aisling grinned to herself – at least Brigitte wasn't into inspecting your knickers – not like Gran. You never know what will happen in the day. What if you had an accident and ended up in hospital? Clean decent knickers and none of this modern nonsense. An image of Gran holding up one of her own thongs from the wash came back. Not something to share with Brigitte.

## Chapter Thirteen

# Patrice at the Postbahnhof

Aisling turned over in the single bed to escape the light from the street. Not a bad idea to go to the Patrice concert, she thought. She had never even heard of him before she got the email from Alex but she couldn't spend all her time holed up with Brigitte, mourning. Nobody expected her to be grief-stricken. Katharina was sixty years old. Probably she had enough of being sick and was glad to die.

She was now in possession of a key so she could come and go as she pleased. Her task of the day was to find out if she could get a ticket to the concert. She hadn't worked out Internet access on the laptop yet, so she headed for the nearest internet café. A bit of surfing would give her the information that she needed. It wasn't the easiest of searches but she did find it in the end. Postbahnhof sounded like a sorting office near a station. If it was not too expensive she would go. It was near the Ostbahnhof or East Station so easy to get to. She debated whether to take her phone. It would be class to send back live photos to Alex – or even Andrew himself – but Alex would turn it into something to boast about. Better to wait and e-mail a 'By the way, I saw Patrice at the Postbahnhof,' dead casually. It would be worth going just for that even if she didn't like him. Free of bag, phone, and I-pod she felt light.

The venue looked a bit like one for a rave party rather than a concert but inside the atmosphere was good and the twenty-two euro ticket was comfortably inside her bargain zone. Without much of a queue! A much more civilised city than Dublin. The bar was big: most of the people were around her own age and she'd chosen the right clothes – her comfortable black Armani jeans and a black sleeveless top with a bit of stylish swirl design in discreet glitter. It was the sort of place where you could wear any style but she felt like she blended in. By the time she got a beer and had a wander around, there were sounds of something. He was on – no support group even and no hanging about for superstar tantrums.

Aisling had never been a fan of reggae music. She tried listening to it so that she could talk to Andrew. He liked the old stuff – the Bob Marley days. When she knew it was no go with Andrew, she stopped playing them. She hadn't even downloaded any reggae to her I-pod. This guy was better than any of the reggae that she had heard before. His name sounded French but he sang in English mostly and lived somewhere in Germany. He was dishy enough to rustle some feelings up in the pit of her stomach. That was the place to keep them she told herself.

It was a great feeling to be on the scene here, where nobody knew her and she knew nobody. She could dance and move as she liked. There was nobody to care about her pear shaped bum as she bumped around. Free to shift around and get more sightings of the tasty-looking Patrice. Enshultigung excuses from time to time to other good-humoured bum bouncers with camera phones above their heads. Light sweat on her lip – not enough to disturb her make-up.

Moving around and dancing on the spot made a bit of

flirting inevitable. Not too close – she didn't want to get into a conversation about what she was doing in Berlin. It was the best live concert ever and she resolved to search out some Patrice to download. That laptop was going to be really useful. To-night was a night of finding something for herself. She sang along, revelling in the anonymity of it, and laughed out loud at the thought of playing it for the aunt.

'Don't give up the fight, no no
Uh ya ya ya
Uh ya ya ya
Yes everyday good
Uh ya ya ya
Because of being alive
I say I say
Everyday is good because of being alive alive
Yeh yeh oh nana
From the day I was born till the day me gon die ya die
yeh yeh
Everyday is good because of being alive alive
Yeh yeh oh nana
From the day I was born till the day me gon die ya die
yeh yeh'

If she had any criticism of Patrice he was a bit too sweet maybe – but tough and hard enough at other times to make that palatable. The concert finished early enough to get home for about 12.30. She saw the light on in the aunt's room. Since Michael died, her mother would lie awake until she came home. Aisling would leave it as late as she could but at 2, 3 or even 4, the light would still be on. She would call out, 'I'm back, night-night,' but never waited to hear an answer. She did it now in automatic mode and heard an answering, 'Sleep well, my dear.' The voice sounded so like Gran, it was a bit spooky. The aunt in some ways was so unlike Gran and yet in others they were like different versions of the same person. Her Gran wasn't so bad when she was on her own but the minute she got talking to that narrow-minded Annie, she took off. At least there was no sign of an Annie equivalent here in Berlin.

She grinned to herself as she remembered the last episode she'd overheard. Annie had a son who had lived in England like forever. As soon as he could afford a one-way ticket probably. His daughter Lucy was planning to come over from England for Christmas in Dublin. All she wanted was a bed at her Gran's for God's sake. Listening to Annie, you would think that she had done something dire.

'So I said yes. Well I couldn't say no, could I? But would you believe it, she asks me, "Can I bring my partner?" Indeed, I soon saw her off – my partner indeed. The cheek of it – to think that I would have the two of them living in sin under my own roof and then I would be expected to cook Christmas dinner for them. It's enough work anyway for Mary and that husband of hers. They make me feel like they are doing me a favour to invite themselves round for Christmas dinner. Their two boys went off to spend Christmas in Spain and Aoife had to entertain the husband's parents. I've cooked Christmas Dinner long enough. At my age, I deserve to take a rest. Anyway Lucy went to Breege's in the end. You know what that means don't you – partners? Where Breege was going to put them, I don't know. Sleeping together of course and not only sleeping, you can be sure. These young people are no better than animals – lying down with whoever takes their fancy. It's the children that come out of it that I pity. Half of them don't know who their father is.'

Hypocrites! It was only because they never had the chance and now it was too late. Gran didn't mention any of her own grandchildren like Aisling's cousin in London, who was divorced and with a new partner. She toyed with the idea of finding a way to introduce that into the conversation. No. Better to laugh. She needed her Gran as a refuge and sometimes as a cover.

In bed she fingered her damp groin. Was there a chance of working her way to some relief? An image of her mother sitting her down at the kitchen table for the famous 'sex' talk made her wriggle. 'This experience should be a lesson to you Aisling.' All that stuff about saving yourself for a special someone. Too late. Never too late. Anyway she wouldn't fancy someone looking for a virgin bride. Her mum's version of sex was a bit like a recipe for a cake – where the love bit was the cake and the sex was the icing. She'd hate it if I told her that. For all her talk about sex, she never mentioned masturbation. Porno images didn't turn her on. Her own graphics were better. Images. Labia. Patrice's lips and tongue.

Michael's face floating into her consciousness was a turn-off she didn't need. With a look of pure fright on his face at her threat to reveal his big secret. It gave her a buzz to have power over him. Did Michael really like older men or did it just happen like that? You could see their eyes light up when they saw each other. Aisling wondered how anyone could miss it. She guessed right away. If only he knew – she was the one with the real secret. She hated her mother's combination of not saying anything along with the silent warning looks whenever there was a story of someone her age struggling along as a single parent.

Was Michael afraid their mother would treat his secret like a condition? Or was it the fear of being called a dirty pervert? Knowing Mum, she'd probably do both. First the hysterics, then a bit about how people give gay men such a hard time then after a bit of reflection, 'How can we put it right?' Like that time that she was convinced that Michael was traumatised by the suicide of his classmate. Not likely, relieved more like. Ronan was a real bully especially with Michael. Maybe Ronan fancied Michael but couldn't face up to it. Mum wanted to take Michael to see a psychologist. To go with him too for God's sake. As if you would tell a psychologist how you really feel with your mother sitting there. Luckily Dad persuaded her out of it. Then after Michael died she blamed Dad for not letting her take him. 'The trauma was there all the time under the surface.' It was one of the few times she showed any sign: Michael's death may not have been an accident after all.

Older men were a push-over for sex. Their eyes went right down your top if you were showing a bit of tit. Every time she went over to Maeve's she could see her Dad, Gerry, lick his lips like she was good enough to eat. She should've known Maeve would find out in the end. The sex wasn't worth the loss of her best friend but she'd been attracted by the maturity in him. He made her feel like a woman.

The BMW and the cocktails in fancy hotels were a turn-on too. She wore her sexiest clothes. The big turn-off was the way he grunted his way to relief with the beer belly weighing her down. Though to be fair to him, he did manage usually to wank her off first. But now no more rubbing off older men's paunches for her. Better someone she wouldn't mind waking up beside. Patrice won that round easily. She wished now she had taken her phone to get some sort of photo of Patrice. She'd got closer than she expected. It would have given her satisfaction to replace her sneaky photo of Andrew with his beautiful black shiny face.

She stood in front of the mirror in the light from the street outside getting her slimmest silhouette, one to make her hips slim and hide her saggy bottom inside the line of her briefs. She took off her bra but left her silky top on and lifted her breasts so that they showed over her top. She giggled at herself, emptying Ireland, her mother, Michael, Gran and the aunt in the other room from her head and filling it with Patrice.

She got into bed keeping her briefs and top on letting her hands go inside them first. She lay half on her side holding the firm pillow so that her nipples could rub against the silk and cotton contact. Which of them would she use for her DIY? Patrice or Andrew? Or maybe greasy-guts Gerry?

Not Gerry. She missed Maeve so much and those rows still hurt. At the time it wasn't such a big deal. Aisling hoped Maeve would get over it. It wasn't cool to make so much of a fuss about sex. You did it or you didn't – the virgins or the slags. Simple difference. But amongst the 'slags' there were some who just did it at the drop of a hat, some who had done it once when they had one too many so 'couldn't care less' and the rest were more like her: they just didn't want to be trapped, so they chose who they did it with. Her big mistake was expecting Gerry to have his own condoms.

Chapter Fourteen

# Letters

*Berlin 16ᵗʰ May 1945*

*Dear Mary*

*I found the letters I never posted to you where I hid them in the wall of the cellar. I'm lucky they were well hidden. I was more foolish than I could have dreamed to write those things then. Lucky too that I didn't post any of them. Maybe somewhere inside I knew that it would be dangerous but to even write them was foolish beyond measure. It would be strange to post those letters now. It is less than a year ago but seems like an eternity. Reading my account of those times is like reading the life of a stranger. I seem so young and even innocent. My need of someone to talk to then — even on paper — was more important than anything else. It is harder now to pick up a pen and write to you but I force myself. I want to wipe out the last months of the war so I think of you in Leitrim. I spent a hard winter and spring in a workcamp near Berlin, a living hell.*

*Now I know more about danger but I care less. The life stirring within me brings a burden of hope mixed with despair. To have a child with no father. I know as my good friend you won't tell the news until I am ready. I sent a few words to my mother to let her know I am OK but I haven't told her why I* can not even think of coming back to Leitrim. If Irma knew my thoughts of death, she would never have left me. She was a good friend to me these past months and if it wasn't for her I would be dead.

I lost another good friend in the camp — an old woman who helped me live through many cruel days. I could still see the grey wisp of her spirit long after in the smoke of the crematorium. Anna didn't approve of a woman who took her own life by throwing herself onto electric wires. The body was left on the wires for a couple of days to put fear into the rest of us. The first time I looked up and saw the woman there, it made me think of crucifixion. I admired her courage. I wished I could be so brave. God help me and forgive me for these thoughts, sent by the devil in hell himself.

Anna and I waged our war against the armies of lice and cockroaches brought into our lives by Hitler. At times I felt the lash of the cold shower take me back to Leitrim although even washing outdoors was never as cold as here and summers never as hot as this one.

Memories of Anna, of Irma and of Leitrim keep me going.

You can write to me at the same address.

Your very own, Biddy


Berlin 17<sup>th</sup> May 45

Dear Mary

Past and present meet as I write to you but they cannot wipe out the place where they took me for those months. I long for someone to talk to in my own tongue so I write again to you, Mary but I don't know when I will post it. Maybe never. I told my mother I am staying in Delia's apartment so she can still *send to the same address. I know she will tell you so I hope to get news of you soon.*

*I hope Irma arrives safely in Vienna. My mind travels with her now. Who knows what she will face in the chaos of these days? Somehow she made me come close to wanting to live again. She wanted me to go to Vienna with her but I feel sick every day now and I want to be here.*

*The jar of blackberry jam from my mother's parcel was in the same hiding place in the cellar. That felt like a miracle – a miracle of hedgerows to the lake with the sun on my back in August before going back to school. Sugar always so precious even then in Ireland. Stirring the precious stuff in the big pan and licking the spoon when Mammy turned her back. Peggy would tell, so I had to be careful of her eyes too. Now, there is not even a ration book between hunger and me. Irma left me the jar to lick clean. It is as clean as if it had been washed.*

*Someone has been in my cellar while I have been away but not long enough to find my hiding place. It was in a part of the cellar no-one could use any more. I made it look like another pile of rubble and put a bit of broken lavatory near it so that they would think it was a shit-pit nearby. Even the bit of broken lavatory was still there and my guest used it. He also lit the boiler and boiled it dry. It still boils water but there is a leak. I catch the water and put it in again. We managed to have a real homecoming feast before Irma left. I traded half a pot of my jam for a loaf of bread. We ate more bread for one meal than we ate in a week in that place, topped with the taste of Ireland that spilled from my tongue – a surprise of purple hills, green fields and the kitchen dominated by the hungry black range, I nearly spoilt our sweet feast with salty tears when I thought of the generous hands of my mother. I* even found a small screw of paper with some tea leaves I had saved from the same parcel – just enough to make some decent strength tea which we watered and watered again just for the pleasure of taking some more and keeping the taste of real tea in our mouths. Black of course, I doubt if I will ever drink tea with milk and sugar again.

From under another pile of bricks, I found Delia's china tea-set wrapped in newspaper and bound tight in a small box still untouched. A wedding present of Delia's – waiting for her return. Whoever was here, he was not a black marketeer or he would have torn the place to bits looking for treasures to trade. Maybe someone travelling onwards? Probably someone with the permission of Herr Schmidt, who is still here and maybe it is thanks to him that I have a home of sorts.

The tea-set brought back Delia, Dieter and the children. For the first time since I got out, I wondered how they fared. I also found two canteens of cutlery still intact and felt bad about opening one to use it. My blankets were damp and mouldy but they dried a bit in the sharp east wind and we were glad of their steamy heat for the three nights that Irma stayed. We huddled together out of habit and the need for warmth.

I never thought memories of Ireland would be like heaven compared to this. I was foolish not to leave Berlin when Delia told me too. Now I have to learn to live or die with what is.

Your friend, Biddy

24$^{th}$ May 1945

Dear Mary,

I am alone now most of the time. Not lonely. There when people were so close, I often felt lonely. Sometimes I don't care if I never see anyone ever again — even Irma. I'm not even glad to be alive. But I don't wish myself dead either — not any more. Sometimes I miss you and my life in Ireland. It helps to write to you so I will do it while I am waiting to see what happens next.

I said I am alone but in fact Herr Schmidt comes to talk and bring me a bunch of soup vegetables from time to time. He whispers stories about the Russians and the black market. He looks at me strangely. I wonder always was it him who told about the dinner parties. Poor Delia probably never found out that it was one of her dinner party guests who caused my arrest. I don't even remember what he looked like. I remembered his first name, Adam but they would not have believed me if I said I remembered nothing. I wonder if he is alive. When I am no longer hungry, I smile at the thought they took me for a member of the resistance against Hitler and maybe a communist! It is such a relief to be done with the ridiculous Heil Hitler salute. Sometimes I am tempted to do it to Herr Schmidt but I may need his help with my ration book if there are rations again. His warnings about Russians remind me to be careful of the fate worse than death.

My beautiful Berlin has been turned into a wilderness where I must forage, forever watchful of the Russian bears. Maybe I should have gone with Irma after all. I switch from thinking of the next bite and concentrate on how to stop the cold eating my bones. Maybe I can bake griddle bread if I can find flour and enough fuel for a fire. I will have to use the black market myself if Herr Schmidt doesn't help me. I have to find something to exchange for some flour and I have to find wood for cooking. My visitor burnt most of the broken bits of furniture. The days are warm and sticky now in Berlin. I cook on the fire at night when I find wood.

*I can't stand cold anymore. Purgatory for me will always be the memory of cold even the March cold on the march when winter is long over in Ireland. My dreams swing between being frozen to death in the snow and being burnt alive in an oven. Once in the Lager, I got a seat near the stove. It was too hot there for me — nearly as bad as the cold. It dried the raw meat of my hands making the red under skin so stiff that I could hardly bend them. I dream of some cool air — not too hot, not too cold. At least in purgatory there is promise of heaven. Maybe hope of heaven will help me endure. I have no wish to go back to hell where you think there is nothing worse and then you are pushed beyond your worst imaginings.*

*I dream of heaven still even if there is no God to take charge of it all. Heaven is a warm bed with clean white sheets after a meal of new potatoes, roast beef, gravy carrots and marrowfat peas soaked overnight and cooked until they are mushy — all eaten from a white tablecloth. Saving space for a warm apple tart and cream after. I will always remember the dishes I heard murmured from other bunks at night. Lessons in German specialities. I still have recipes in my head from Anna. One day I will cook them. I will start with her lentil soup. It should be possible to get hold of the ingredients and I won't miss the sausage she insists should be added. There I go now — hope comes back in spite of myself. You'd think that it would drive you crazy to think of good things to eat when the hunger was so strong but it was the opposite. Sometimes the feast that we created was almost real — just as long as there was something working in your belly — even the vile turnip water they called soup. With the help of your imagination, you could feel strangely full. Will I ever eat a meal to match those eaten in imagination or taste again morsels as tasty as those shared with Anna or Irma? Who knows? I long now for Gurke, those pickled vegetables. I was so glad Delia hated them so much that they sat in the cellar and I could live on them in the weeks before they came for me.*

*Not so long ago, I envied the woman who threw herself onto the electric fence. She wasn't the first they said. I couldn't help wondering if it counted as suicide. They say people who commit suicide shouldn't be buried in consecrated ground at home – taking away your own life takes the power from God's hands. Even if it were suicide, what sort of God would refuse that woman anything?*

*Mary, if I send this letter, you must excuse my meanderings. It would help to hear how things are in Ireland.*

*Your friend, Biddy.*

Aisling put down the sheaf of papers. It had become more of a diary and felt more intrusive than reading letters. She felt embarrassed and ashamed. She had told herself it wasn't personal, it was history but it felt personal now. She lifted her sketch book. Making graphic images of everyday detail made the war more real. Would the cellar be a thread through the story from the green bomb of the Allies to the Russian bears? What about images of Germans?

Matthias told her that he was fed up with people who seemed to think being German was something to be ashamed of. Even his father and mother blamed his grandparents for letting it happen. Finding other people to blame meant you could ignore the Nazi in yourself. Creating space for neo-Nazis in your own denial. Matthias was a bit of a drama-merchant but Aisling liked his style. She agreed. Why should you take responsibility for something just because it was your country?

She had never felt responsible for the IRA or their bombs in her lifetime. It didn't feel like it had anything to do with her. She didn't understand it.

Matthias was better company than Irish men of her age. She thought of him as her best friend. He wasn't bitchy like her new friends or self-righteous like Maeve. Some people thought they were going out together but there was no sex with Matthias. Matthias was the only one she could tell about the things she'd done to Michael. When he came back she would break her promise to her mother and tell him about the abortion and about Maeve's dad. She understood Brigitte wanting somebody she trusted to talk to.

The secrecy of the affair was so sexy at first. The freedom of being grown up, of wanting sex. The joking with him on the stairs. She didn't think he was really coming on to her. Horsing about a bit as they queued for the bathroom. At first it seemed like an accident when his hand went between her legs. She blushed and he knew. For days afterwards, an image of Gerry was enough to make her feel the wet wantonness in her knickers. Fuck me on the stairs please, please me. She denied all when Maeve teased her about being different. In love? Yes, Yes, Yes and No, No, No see-sawed internally with anticipation. She knew when he offered to give her a lift home there was a possibility.

Talking music, he was surprised she liked traditional Irish music. He parked up to reach over to the glove compartment to get his phone out to play Iarla Ó' Lionáird. Touched her knees as if by accident. A bit ridiculous like a B movie but better not giggle like a schoolgirl. She reached for his hand and put it between her legs. She felt his little finger on her clitoris through the damp knickers and squirmed in pleasure. 'We shouldn't,' he said taking his hand away. 'No we shouldn't,' she said and reached over to kiss him knowing her skirt would slide up. 'Delicious,' he said and his hand slid down her back over her left buttock to her upper thigh. 'You know how sexy you are, don't you?' he said. 'But we really shouldn't,' and pulled back again.

'You're a bit of a tease,' she said.

'I don't mean to tease you,' he said.

He said nothing.

She said, so don't. She took his right hand and put it between her thighs again. Just see it as a little gift to me. No strings. Nobody need know. She had planned her clothes in hope of this. Boots and over the knee socks. A skirt riding up her thighs when she sat in the car. Knickers which he could get his hand inside easily. The squirm was completely genuine. She wanted him. She helped him get her knickers off. So easy to come against his finger technique. Moments of being only there moving against his hand. Fresh new wave for fingers in the vagina and maintaining the clitoral climax. Moaning into it.

'Wowee,' she said when the wave subsided, 'Thanks for the gift. Finger fucking good.'

They laughed and she felt safe in the cocoon around them.

She reached over and slid the zip down on his hard on, loosening his trousers down to get at his balls. She felt his hand then on her neck, gentle pressure down. Oh God, she'd never given a blow job before. What do you do with your teeth? Surprising soft-hardness in her mouth and it was working for him as she sucked. No way was she going to have spunk in her mouth though. Using both hands for pressure. Good luck rather than judgement she grinned to herself as he came all over her hands.

And so it went on from there. She told herself she really did love him. She fantasised about their affair going on forever in secret. Or maybe he would leave Anne and they would live together. She brought condoms and got him into the back seat of the car. She felt triumph when he suggested a hotel. When did it start to feel sleazy and cheap? Easy answer. When he offered to pay the weekend in London for the abortion. Brown envelope. Film star role in B-movie over. Comic-strip sex affair. Too old for pure sex he said. She didn't want him to talk about love or did she? The whore feeling distracting from any last bit of pleasure. Without the sex there was nothing. If only Maeve hadn't found out. Using the same hotel was a mistake. Ireland is so fucking small.

Matt was great cover for the assignations although she never told him who it was. He didn't ask. Talked instead about how gay men could give some insight into the pain of splitting sexual relationships from emotional commitment. The unbearable mirror-image of the male tendency to separate taken to the extreme. Trapped in a cycle of sexual compulsion. Consume sexy meat chunk and shit it out again. Flush the consequences down the pan.

She thought of asking Matt to go with her for the abortion but he was really busy. A dilemma solving itself when Mum guessed and made it their female secret. Better for her not to know the father she said. Did she guess? Hold my hand, Mummy. Abortion clinical but feeling sordid. How to shake that off? After the split, Matt told her to go for connection. First connect with yourself. Use freedom to make choices not dance the puppet on a string of projections.

She'd miss Matt even more when she was back in Dublin. He'd be in Venezuela for six months working on some project for school children. She was so mad when he told her that he was going – she refused to take any interest in the details. He still emailed her but the messages had got shorter and shorter. Matthias would be really interested in hearing Brigitte's story. She would wait until he came back to tell him her idea of creating a graphic novel.

Brigitte describing Katharina as 'the unborn' made her curious about Katharina's father. The aunt came back to Berlin in April before the war was over. She vaguely remembered Gran saying something once about Katharina's father being an American soldier. But so far there was no mention of American soldiers. Aisling's parents had never so much as mentioned the fact that the aunt was never married until that day when they were talking about going to the funeral. Her father said then that Aunt Biddy would have had the child adopted if she was in Ireland. Of course everybody would have seen it as a big scandal sixty years ago but even Gran was cool about it now. Maybe the young Biddy was raped. Maybe she had several lovers. Were they Jews or Nazis – soldiers or prisoners or what? Whatever there was, there was something to hide. Aisling was determined to worm the truth out of the aunt. Her graphic novels needed reality not fantasy. Reality had horror enough and the green bomb was a better image than any fictitious monster from another world. .

Kaffee und Kuchen to-day – because Aisling was here. She'd better watch she didn't put on weight. She liked being skinny and usually she could eat whatever she liked. One good thing about not having the baby was keeping her own shape. She wasn't much into sweet stuff but the coffee and cake ritual here was quality. As she went through the routine of bathroom and hand-washing, she tried now to remember a funny rhyme that Matthias had taught her about Kant and cake. She'd learnt it at the time but she should have written it down. Yola stayed to serve the coffee and cake but wouldn't sit to eat it with them. Biddy insisted she take a great wedge of it with her.

'Lovely cake. I must get the recipe for Mum,' Aisling hoped her insincerity didn't show too much. Advise Mum to find a source of good German cakes would be more likely.

'Käsekuchen. Yola made it from a recipe of Anna's. Anna spent hours repeating those recipes with me so that I could remember them. They were like bedtime stories, told again and again. She made me picture the ingredients in my head and reach for them one by one. Käsekuchen. First of all make the pastry case for the base. It's richer than the pastry we make and you can put egg in it if you have it but it is flat. She put dried peas on it to keep it flat when you bake it. I forgot once and got a bowler hat instead of a base. It made Katharina laugh and we ate it anyway. Anna made me memorise the exact quantities of the filling – the mixture of quark, sugar and egg yolks whipped together with egg whites. I see her yet insisting on the lightness of those egg whites. Standing there demonstrating it with her skinny arms. Grating a bit of orange peel and lemon peel when you can get them. She folded her arms to wait patiently until it turned a golden brown colour on top. I waited a long time to cook my first Käsekuchen but I never forgot how to do it. I invited Anna's ghost to share it with Adelheid, Katharina and me. It tasted better than any cake I had ever eaten in Ireland. Those women were great cooks. They even managed to put together something from nothing. There is no cake that tastes as good as the cake Anna and I ate one day together to celebrate her eightieth birthday. The other women made her a 'cake' of crumbs they collected. It was bound together with some butter and sugar that Dorothea had begged from the house where she cleaned and looked after the children and it had even some children's sweets on top. It was tiny –the whole 'cake' not much bigger than a cigarette packet and they all refused to share it with her but she insisted that I have some. She said it tasted better shared. A true Christian.

'Kaffee und Kuchen. That was the dream that kept me going in the Lager and Anna was the perfect companion for it. She must have been a great baker – no it's not baker is it? What do you call someone who bakes cakes – is it the same?'

'Maybe pastry chef or is there a word for someone who does patisserie?'

'Yes or gateau. They still don't bake great cakes in Ireland even with all the wealth now. Our word 'cake' doesn't really cover everything like that here. They make a difference between a 'torte' – lots of eggs and cream and very elaborate usually. The word, 'Kuchen' is often used for something that's got fruit in it but eggs, flour and sugar too. None of this airy faery spongy stuff that we call cake or the fruit cake solid as a rock for special occasions.'

Aisling smothered her yawn. She wasn't interested in cake recipes. She needed more about the horrors of the camp. Real evil to lay her devils to rest. Horrors of war to inspire a graphic montage. Composing a holistic image from fragments of memory. Not too many words.

'So was Anna a Jew?'

'No, I told you, a true Christian.She was what we call a *Jehovah'sWitness.'*

'So why was she there?' Aisling still had not winkled out the reason for Brigitte being in the camp. Choose the moment. Maybe this was a lead in.

'The Jehovah's Witnesses were one of the first groups to stand up to Hitler. Anna was taken to the camp in 1940. They wouldn't work at anything to support war and they wouldn't give the Hitler salute. Everyone says they are fanatics but maybe you needed to be a bit of a fanatic to survive the Lager. Even in the camp they wouldn't work in any factories that made weapons for the war. They worked in Siemens.

'From what Anna said, the camp that she arrived in was a different place from the one I arrived in. First of all it was only sixteen wooden blocks, and a building that housed the kitchen, baths, and offices. The 'bunker', the camp prison, was there from the start and it didn't change much by all accounts. Many of the houses – the villas and apartments on the outside of the camp for the women guards and SS – were already finished. The prisoners worked on building more blocks and more houses. By the time I arrived, the Ferienlager was a memory. All I saw was mud and cold – even the blissful snow when it came seemed to get dirty quickly. All of the blocks overflowed with people.'

'I read in one of Katharina's books that Polish and Germans made up more than half the inmates if you included the German Jews who were the third largest group.'

'Katharina searched always for facts. Anna was German but not German enough for the Third Reich. We were women. Jews. Germans. French. Polish. Italians, Russian, Czechs. There were a few men too but I never saw the men or women in the political block where it was more like a prison than a camp.'

'So where was the camp?

'So near Berlin and yet so far. When we first heard talk about the camps, people called them 'arbeitslager' or 'workcamp'. Maybe that was how it was meant to be at first.

Who knows? I heard tell of other camps worse than ours. I cannot imagine what those places were like and I don't want to. You can't come back from hell easily once you have been there. Our place was a work camp but for slave gangs. Like machines, some of them. I was young and strong enough myself but found it hard to keep pace when they put me on the building work. Bricks passing from hand to hand and we daren't stop. The woman beside me fell one day. I had a choice to reach further for my brick or let it fall on her. I hated the big beast of a woman on the other side of the fallen bundle of bones between us. She kept the bricks coming at the same speed, hand to hand. It was my first lesson in learning to hate everyone there – starting with hating myself for not doing anything to stop her.'

'And the fallen woman?'

'Many ways to fall in that place. The guards picked her up. Punishment block I suppose. I never saw her again. Probably one of the many who died that winter. If it wasn't for Anna. I would never have survived. Anna, Anna, Anna. The first glimmer of dawn has never been so beautiful for me before or since. Anna – so good but thank God not completely perfect. Her faults made her human. No-one could hate Anna. That little bad-tempered bag of bones was closer to an angel than any fat cherub. She taught me to see the light of day as a gift of God. It was up to us whether we opened our eyes and hearts to it. She tried to make me believe our suffering was our ticket to heaven. After one whole night and day standing in temperatures below zero after some trivial 'sin' I can't even remember now, I was ready to drop but they kept us there another two nights. The Bifos looked after each other. When a woman fainted, somehow the others on both sides got their shoulders under her arms, her feet hardly touching the ground and made it look like she was standing until she came round again. How long could we stand it? Longer than we thought we could. I couldn't feel my legs they were so numb and my arms but somehow I could stamp some life back into them. So many rules and regulations, even when the place was falling to bits. They were used to the blokowa making them suffer for nothing.'

Aisling repeated 'Blokowa and Bifos?

'Bifos was one of the nicknames for the Jehovah's Witnesses. They were more Christian than anyone else when it came to the push but the French were Anna's weak point. She was so Christian to most people – even the asocials – but the French! She hated them. All the Bifos were impatient with the French women. They said the French women had Communism and workers on their fancy tongues but they were too refined for hard work. Many of the Bifos were plain country women used to farm work – not that unlike what I had come so far to escape. They didn't fear hard work just as long as it wasn't work for war. Polish women despised the *bibelforszerki* as they called them or Bibelki for short. *Bibelforszerki* was the Polish for *Bibelforscherin,* which was the name the guards used for them – because they knew the Bible so well. Anna said that the Polish women were jealous of the privileges and the principles. Many Bifos worked in the homes of the guards as nannies or housemaids. They had special privileges and a small source of extra food. Never stolen of course because, unlike all the rest of the camp, the Jehovah Zeugen did not steal.

'Many of the Polish women prisoners were *Blockälteste* or 'blokowa' as they all came to be called – so many of the heads of the block who kept the other prisoners in line were Polish and of course a blokowa had privileges. Many Polish blokowa were especially hard on Bifos. Anna laughed at them, "Maybe they are jealous of our principles". It was easy to stir up one lot of women against another. Even the Bifos had very little time for the asocials. I was lucky to wear the red badge. Most foreigners were given political status. Even luckier to be with the lavender Bifos.'

Asocials, prostitutes, petty criminals, French intellectuals. Polish. German country women. Lesbians. What a mix! All at each other's throats. Hard to take in. Itchy fingers on the pencil stub. Banned. Not allowed. Itchy fingers to tell it like it was. Martyrs, heroines, murderers. A graphic novel for Brigitte? Matt would like it.

'So Anna had a lavender badge?' Aisling prompted.

'I've always loved lavender since. Anna told me that she had more wonderful visions of heaven there beyond any dreams before. The lesson for her was that just as evil has no limits, so good has no limits and we would one day find eternity in God's love. She helped me believe there still might be a God but he was not the God I learnt about in Ireland. My own belief in the God that I had been brought up with was not strong enough to survive that place.'

'So did you lose your faith?' Aisling was glad of the chance to ask. She had observed that the aunt sat there with her rosary beads like Granny but she hadn't heard her say anything about a priest or about going to Mass even though it was Sunday.

'No. I believe what I believe. There were good German Catholics too. There's a memorial on Müllerstrasse, not so far from Karstadt, to a Catholic priest who tried to mobilise the Church against Hitler. I learnt that even Jews and Communists didn't have the horns of the devil. I learnt differences on the outside are not as great as extremes we can find inside. I never understood how some of the guards were Catholics too and could go to Mass on Sunday. Günter didn't seem to have any problem with that.'

'Günter?' Aisling intervened to keep him in there, 'Katharina's father?' An inspired guess.

Brigitte gave a sharp look, 'Monika said this?'

'No, I just guessed. He's the only man you mentioned.'

'I kept it from Katharina for a long time. I didn't want her to hate the German side of her. After she found out about him, she would have nothing to do with religion. She didn't want to go back to Ireland either – it is too Catholic for her and she said Nazis were welcome there after the war. I don't know if that's true.'

'Go back? I thought she was never in Ireland.'

'I took her once to Dublin. She was nearly sixteen then. My mother was in St. James Hospital. I would visit the hospital everyday and we would meet later at the bed and breakfast. We ate sandwiches and Katharina would tell me about the Dublin I never knew – the Ha'penny Bridge, the post office where you can still see the marks of the bullets from the Easter Rising, St. Stephen's Green. The memorials to Joyce, to Yeats. Katharina liked Trinity College and the Book of Kells. She found Dublin strange. So many nuns and priests, churches crosses and religious 'kitsch' as she called it everywhere. Even then she was not keen on religion. She said that Ireland exported its creative and talented people like James Joyce or Samuel Beckett and made the lives of those who stayed a misery.'

Aisling did some mental arithmetic. Katharina made her

only visit to Ireland in 1961 – her father was about 10 years old then. Was Dublin really full of nuns and priests in the street at that time? You wouldn't see them now anyway. It was hard to imagine what the Dublin they visited was like. For the first time she wished she had paid more attention to dates in her own history. She'd have to ask her father if Dublin really was that different in those days. It was hard to picture Brigitte and Katharina in Dublin in 1961 and that was the year the Berlin wall went up too.

'So were you in Ireland when they started to put the wall up?

'No, we came back in August just before it started. I was afraid there would be another war just when we were beginning to enjoy some peace.'

'Katharina wasn't born in the camp was she?'

'No, we got out on in April 1945 but the war wasn't over until 8th May.'

'We? Was that you and Günter?'

'Günter – no,' Brigitte looked at her in a way that made her realise that was a really stupid question. 'I'm sure Günter got away all right. All those questions about Ireland that had puzzled me at the time, made sense. He was probably even smart enough to escape prisoner-of-war camps. When he saw the writing on the wall, he managed to get himself transferred to the Army. A good move, I realised afterwards, as there was more chance of escaping as an ordinary soldier. I couldn't help wondering if he made it to Ireland at the end of the war. He left the camp in February.'

'Did the Allies set you free from the camp?'

Brigitte snorted, spraying some cake crumbs into the air, 'Oh yes, it would be good if it was like some of those films where they drove in their tanks and smashed the guard and fed and clothed us like human beings again. No, it wasn't like that. The Russians were getting close to us. The Bibeltiki were more afraid of the Russians than of the Nazis – they were German after all and for them to be captured by Russian communists was a fate worse than death. They co-operated with the guards when the plan came to move us to another camp. By then I had Irma.' Brigitte laughed again but more lightly this time, 'Vertraue mir!'

'Come again,' Aisling prompted,

'I can hear Irma's voice even now – Vertraue mir! – It made no sense to me that we should play with the dogs but she did it and it worked. Vertraue mir!'

'Trust me! Why did she say that?'

'Well it was like a test. I had to trust her, didn't I? She couldn't tell me why we were sharing our precious crusts with those dogs. She just kept saying it and smiling her strange smile. Vertraue mir! She made it like a game.'

'Who was Irma?'

'Irma? She's the only friend from that time who is still alive. It was a lucky day for me the day that she was moved in with the Bibeltiki. No-one else would share a bunk with her because she had a red triangle. Anna was too ill then to care so they put her in our bed. Irma was the only one – other than the Bibeltiki – in that place who managed to keep a little bit of themselves free. They had a way of getting inside your mind and your body so that there was nothing of yourself left. That was worse than anything. Your belly begged them for the vile tepid turnip water they called soup, the muddy chicory mess they called coffee, for the hunk of bread with stones in it that could break your teeth if you had any left. Your head begged them for a moment's peace so you could get some sleep that wasn't cut short by some appell or siren or order that had to be obeyed on the instant. You breathed because you had to obey orders and not for yourself.'

Brigitte spread her right hand on the table cloth – moving everything, then putting it back in exactly the same spot – a movement that Aisling had seen her make a hundred times already.

'So if you weren't there when the camp was liberated did you escape?'

Brigitte's laugh had a cynical echo, ' Escape! I had fantasies every day about escaping from that place. Not that I did much about them. To try to escape was just the easiest way to commit suicide and there were some who did that. When Anna died I thought of it but then there was Irma and I couldn't do it to the others who would be punished for me. Irma wasn't like the Bibeltiki and they were suspicious of her because she was a communist. When they put her in our bed, I laughed.'

'You laughed?'

'Yes, they all thought that I'd lost my mind because we all knew Anna was dying.'

'But you laughed?'

'At home at night when we would kneel by the bed to say our prayers, we would pray that Communists wouldn't get to Ireland. As a child, I used to check under my bed every night for bogeymen or communists. From 'reds under the bed' to 'a red in the bed.' I watched this thin, intelligent woman, marked with the communist red triangle, trying to accommodate herself in the bunk where we slept without disturbing us too much.'

'What! There were three of you in one bed?' Aisling was shocked but pleased with the fresh flow of images.

'Yes, three in a bunk meant for one. It could only work because we were all so thin anyway and so exhausted you would sleep like a stone for the few hours that the place was silent. We didn't sleep at all the night that Anna died beside us in that bunk. Irma prayed with me as I muttered the Rosary in English. She joined in too when the whole block prayed and read aloud from the Bible for Anna. I was glad they did. I couldn't bear to see her thrown on a cart like a carcass of a dead sheep without some sort of funeral. She was only skin and bone by the time she died. Irma helped us carry Anna's stiff body to the trolley where they would come and take her on the cart for the dead before appell. We stripped her ourselves to that they wouldn't do it. We covered her little thin body with two washcloths but we knew they would take them away when they took her off the trolley and leave her naked again. I hoped my hair would stay with her. We weren't strong but she was so light to lift that I wanted to blow her up straight into heaven. Irma helped me get through the next day. She nudged me awake when I was falling asleep at roll call even though she didn't get any sleep either. For a few days we had the luxury of the bunk with just two of us and I inherited Anna's enamel mug to drink from. A legacy I still treasure.'

'Do you mean the enamel can on the shelf in Katharina's room?'

'Yes, I wanted her to have it when I die.' Brigitte sighed, 'but she wasn't interested in Anna.'

'And Irma?' Aisling didn't want her to lose the thread.

'Irma seemed to know a lot more about what was happening inside and outside the camp. German was her mother tongue, of course, and she spoke French too and some English but I found it hard to work out when she had the opportunity to talk to anyone. She told me Germany was losing the war and everybody knew it now even the camp Guards. The Allies were already close and the Russians were getting closer and closer. If we could manage to stay alive a few weeks, we had a chance of life and freedom. I trusted her all right.'

'Did she die too?'

'No she is a grandmother. Katharina has met her many times. 'Irma is not ashamed,' she says, as if my shame hid some great evil. Katharina was so quick to condemn the fascists and to analyse them but she didn't want to know how evil reached into each of us. She wanted me to be the victim or the heroine and I was neither. Kill each other? Kill each other when solidarity was the only thing that could keep us alive. She was disappointed in me.

'Strange – they talk about parents disappointed in their children but I was never disappointed in Katharina. She was a gift from nowhere – even when she took up with that Jules, she was always good to me. All I expected in return was that she would see me out. I wanted to die in peace at home. When she was ill, she tried to persuade me to move into some Altenheim, but an old people's home is a waiting room for death no matter how modern and comfortable. She even said she thought maybe Ireland would be better than living here alone. I had family there who could visit. I will do it my own way.'

Sometimes Brigitte behaved like a spoilt child who had to have her own way especially with Monika. If she was serious about committing suicide, her secret was safe with Aisling as long as it was after the funeral. Time for a break.

'I think I'll go out for a bit. But I'd like to hear a bit more about it sometime, if that's all right.'

'Yes, it helps. Maybe Katharina was right. You're a good child.'

Aisling made a quick getaway after that. She was no child and not good either. But let Biddy dream on.

When she left, Brigitte reached for the rosary beads but dropped them again. It wasn't the rosary that had helped her live with herself then. It was Irma who helped her to clean the thick, dirty mess from down there. It was Irma who held her when she shook in bed that night. The only prayer she said was, 'Thank God, Anna is not here to see this and know this.' It was Irma the Communist who helped her pray in her own words and held her anger at God mixed with her prayer for forgiveness.

What was the word that Irma used that night? Brigitte made her spell it because it sounded as dirty as she felt. S, C, H, Ä, N, D, U, N, G. Schändung. The dung part made her think of summer days, saving shoes as they walked barefoot in the field. The feeling of cow dung between her toes. And then washing them in the brown water of the stream that was always icy cold even in summer, as icy as the sheet in the shower block. Schändung. She locked it all in that word and left it in the dung heap. Later Katharina asked her in English when she worked out the time of her conception, 'Was I the product of a rape?' And then again in German, impatient now.

Brigitte shook her head and in her head she dipped her toes in dung, and then again, and said nothing. Katharina looked disgusted anyway. There was no right answer, consent was worse than rape.

After that she looked up Schändung in Katharina's big dictionary – violation, desecration. Violation, desecration of the tabernacle – of something holy that was something different. Something not of herself. That wasn't the word that Katharina used. She said 'Vergewaltigung' for rape – a word Brigette thought meant murder. No word is right because the act meant life not death. Perfect life with the mess of dirt washed away by Adelheid in the warm water from the big jug. And the clean baby put in my arms. She was right to shake her head to Katharina and speak no more of it.

Irma said other things too, don't let it spoil your pleasure in yourself. Your body will heal. Let it heal your mind. Your body will heal and it will be you who says. Love for the child helped her to see the kindness in Günther, helped her live with the shame that she never resisted. Was that why Katharina was a Jules? Because I turned from men? Now it is too late to torture myself with that question.

Chapter Fifteen

# Torn to Pieces

Something's wrong? Brigitte lifted her eyes. They were back again. Flies on dead meat. The dirty-dishwater-taste rises from a stomach that knows only emptiness or short-lived promises. Closing her eyes and seeing the shadows from the lamplight daring to take the place of the moon and stars, Brigitte willed the moon back to its rightful place over the lake again. Carrying her back to the dung in the byre and far from the dreams leading her to this place. Shadows of light from this little corner of the byre safe from the nightmare where her fingers were raw sausages she chewed for comfort.

A wisp of will whispered its way into the darkness, 'Supper is ready', 'Abendbrot ist fertig.' She wanted to say, I know those words but her throat felt paralysed and no words came.

The word 'supper' that she carried from Ireland had meant something later and shorter – tea from hand to mouth. A bowl for her grandfather, a mug for her father, china cup for her mother and a scramble of other cups for the rest. A slice of soda bread, crumbling in your hand with homemade raspberry or blackberry jam at the right time of year. 'Abendbrot' carried with it the flavour of smoked ham, strong solid bread, a nibble of foreign tastes that challenged her palate –a radish sharp from the garden of Dieter's mother with a host of different fresh green leaves. Dieter wondered at how she had never tasted radish before. In Ireland where most people grew potatoes, onions, carrots and cabbage, surely they could grow radish too. And so many different sorts of cheese. So hard that you had to cut with a sharp knife or so soft that you could taste it with a spoon. Delia had found her one day in the little pantry with a spoon in her mouth and laughed.

The glory of the Sunday table with a white cloth and some flowers in a vase. Clearing away leftover food into the pantry afterwards. Delia kept that rhythm even after the bombs had started to fall on Berlin. In those days the bombs were at night. She feared for this city that she had fallen in love with, where everything was so stylish and tasteful. White tablecloths in the Café Linden – on her first day of sightseeing in Berlin, sitting with Delia watching the buses, the style of the women strolling by. Arm in arm they strolled too – Pariser Platz, the Brandenburg Tor and the Reichstag – the smell of coffee still in her nostrils.

The whispers of 'Abendbrot' carried the taste around the block later, a platter – geisting its way from one bunk to the next, changing what it offered to the memory of each.

'Schinken' someone said, and 'luftgetrocknet' ham came from the dry air like an answer to a prayer. And she could see Delia cut thin, dark slices from the ham left hanging in the larder. She remembered once at home they had something that tasted a bit like it hanging near the fire. Her mother would add bits to the cabbage. They never ate it raw. Only once Michael her oldest brother had come home late and sliced it down on top of fresh scone bread on the table – ready for breakfast. Her mother found a quarter gone in the morning and flipped him with a wet dishcloth. Memories and words to fill desire.

'Roggenbrot mit Butter.' She loved the rye bread smeared with butter. Half with thick butter to taste the foreign taste of the bread and half with fruit gelée from Dieter's mother.

The whispers filled the platter faster and faster – too full for her to take it all in. And to go with it came cans of tea – Kräutertee – Schwarztee… until a mocking voice that she recognised brought the floating platter of small baby sausages: 'Würstchen'… 'Mein kleines Würstchen'… 'Mein Schatz' halted the platter and it wafted away on a giggle. Was it a giggle or a snicker or a snigger – or a giddy bit of repressed laughter? 'Mein Schatz', that was what Dieter said to Delia and then sang in English with an exaggerated Irish accent, 'You are my dear, my darling-o'. Silenced then by, 'Vorsicht, blockowa kommt.'

She hated that word, 'Vorsicht'. First Delia and her 'Vorsicht' – be careful not to be seen talking to the Goldmanns. Be careful not to be out after curfew, Be careful not to speak English outside. Be careful what you say to Herr Schmidt. And then Anna, be careful that the guards and their spies don't catch you looking out the window; don't catch you with your hands in your pockets; don't catch you reading the German newspapers that were used as toilet paper. With the 'forsicht', darkness came in with the draught of the guard to gnaw the bones left over from the guilty-geist-midnight-feast.

Aisling flicked through a magazine. The aunt's eyes were shut and her head was back. She hadn't woken up when Aisling came in and Aisling couldn't see her breathing. Was she dead? There had been a flicker when she said, 'Supper is ready' but then nothing for ages. She'd better not die when Aisling was there. Of course, she must have expected to die first. There's nothing harder than a mother burying someone she gave life to. She heard it said often enough to her mother.

The story of Katharina and the aunt were a bit like Mum and Michael. She hated it when her Mum danced around him – both of them pulling each other's strings and knowing nothing of each other. Michael wore a pullover that his mother bought him not because he liked it himself but because she chose it. She asked him once. Do you really like that silly pattern? He shrugged. It's O.K. She wanted to shake him then. She hated her mum anticipating what he wanted but she hated Michael even more for pleasing her. Everything was OK those days and she knew it wasn't. 'You're such a fucking goody-goody angel,' she said to him the day before he topped himself. He looked at her in the eyes. 'No I'm not. I'm even worse than you think I am,' he paused and gave that weird grin with his mouth to one side, 'Even worse than you.'

'Don't think I don't know why you hang out at Fiona's so much. I know it's not Fiona you're interested in. But I know her big brother's not like you – he likes women.' She said the last bit in her sexiest voice. It wasn't true, he'd never come on to her but she was gratified – Michael looked worried. 'Don't worry – I'm not going to go blabbing any of your secrets. Why should I? They say that it goes with being a Mammy's boy so I'm not surprised.'

And if she had shut her mouth then or if she had told her parents then, would he be still alive? He knew she had the power of a blackmailer. She could smoke a joint openly in front of him without fear of tell-tales. She used to wish she had something wicked enough to hide from their parents to make a secret a burden to him. Stupid wishes can come true sometimes she'd learnt and was more careful with her wishes. Her mother was always on her back looking for signs of 'new boyfriends' – whiffing out signs of sex. Some nice young man to bury the memory of the unborn. Boyfriends! It said it all. Immature gropers without style or substance.

There were too many like Jamie who still acted like he'd done her a favour by screwing her. If anybody had told her the first time would hurt like that and that there would be so much blood she wouldn't have done it with him. Worst of all was him banging away and hurting her she couldn't stop him. She'd put her favourite beach towel on the bed under them – just as well – blood leaking everywhere and semen spewing out of the rubber, like guts spilled out: it made her feel sick. She hurt for days after too. He couldn't look at her straight in the eye after. I didn't know you were a virgin. She said a Hail Mary so fast he had to laugh. At least that bit was over with when she did it with Maeve's dad and he made sure she came.

Losing Maeve meant meant losing transport too. Meant brazening it out to a city-centre gang once too often for comfort. Throw the phone and coin purse and run. Maeve had her own car – a 21st birthday present from her parents. Even if her own parents had the money, they'd never part with it for a car for her. Her dad said so. In his view it was safer to buy your own car when you could afford it. Another reason Aisling moved back home after Michael died. She'd decided she wanted her own car and it was easier to persuade her parents to let her drive their car and to take lessons in it when she was living at home plus the fact that living didn't cost her anything and her dad never thought to reduce her allowance so she had the satisfaction of seeing her savings move into four figures – enough to get her a pair of wheels but not enough to pay the insurance. She would take her test when she got back. That and being over twenty-one should get her into a cheaper bracket. She'd get a letter from her Dad's insurance company too to say that she had been driving since she was seventeen and never had an accident. True because she hardly ever drove.

Brigitte's hinting at unimaginable horrors annoyed her. Aisling wanted the details not hints and fears. It didn't take an expert to work out that Katharina was conceived during the war. She wanted to find out whether Katharina was born from rape. She made a point of asking very deliberately about the dates when Brigitte was in that camp so that Brigitte would know she guessed something so she might as well tell her straight out. Surely Katharina did the same. Her Gran had only once talked of Katharina in front of Aisling and said something about Brigitte's 'lovechild'. Aisling couldn't connect the dead old woman she had seen in the coffin with something that sounded as romantic as lovechild even if everyone knew it was just a euphemism for bastard. Gran didn't know about Katharina's origins. It was enough to know there was no husband for Brigitte. 'I used to wonder why she didn't have the baby adopted. That's what would have happened if she'd had it in Ireland.'

She decided to push the aunt a bit harder if she woke up. The "Erste Frühling" had revived her interest in comic-strip stories. She'd looked up 'graphic novel' on the net and found there was a lot more to comic-book stories in the years after she had tired of fantasy and horror and stopped visiting Forbidden Planet and Sub-City in Dublin. When she went to university she was reluctant to be seen as a dork or a comic-book nerd. She'd tried manga with a promise of a more adult story-line than American superheroes for teens but the Japanese-style graphics annoyed her. She'd given up too soon. There was more on offer. Graphic novels were now being described as 'sequential art', as 'literary storytelling'. She liked the sound of one about James Joyce's daughter written by a daughter about her own father. A mix of past and present. She'd order it when she got home to Dublin. Meantime there were comic-book shops in Berlin. Plenty of them. Good for outings and exploration. Bound to be better than Dublin. But not sequential. More like a montage like a film rather than a story with a straightforward timeline. Not flashbacks either. Montage of memory but with hindsight.

Maybe a private practice with the story of Gerry. The times when it felt like Gerry and Aisling. In another place, the age gap wouldn't be so important. So what if he was Maeve's dad. Grow up she felt like saying. True at the beginning and the end Gerry was Maeve's Dad more than his own man. Mounting in the middle. Grown adults taking pleasure. Nobody's loss. Happier Gerry probably having sex again with Anne. Catholic guilt creeping in again to turn a good fuck into an incident. Maeve's horror at her reaction, "You're not even ashamed." Sorry to be found out. Sorry the pleasure was spoiled by the brown envelope solution. Montage into Maeve's Dad and Anne's husband again. No lover boy left. Not quite true as he came back again in fantasy fucking. No wonder Brigitte was all over the place. She probably saw Günter in Katharina. Nobody else to share the image. Lonely too maybe.

Aisling made a pot of tea and rattled the cups. It worked but neither of them ate much or said much. The aunt insisted on helping clear away. She had her own way of stacking the dishwasher – some method that Aisling hadn't mastered yet and had no inclination to. Let her do it herself. She waited until they were sitting again. The first really warm evening since she arrived. She opened the big windows wide onto the street and sat with half an eye on passers-by.

'I've been thinking about the Lager. It's a bit hard to imagine. Did they torture you?'

'You may think you want to know but you don't really young lady,' her aunt's tone was regretful – not as bossy as usual.

'But I'd like to know. It would do you good to get it off your chest.'

'Katharina has sent you to torture me.'

'Hey come off it. I only asked!'

Brigitte closed her eyes and her head fell forward to her chest. Aisling waited to see if it was one of those two-minute dozes or if her head would go back and the snoring would start – then she might be gone for an hour or so. But this time, it seemed like she wasn't asleep at all. She started speaking even before she lifted her head.

'Maybe it is not so shocking for you young people to-day. You see everything on the TV and in films. You watch images of lots of blood and violence. You think you can rewind the film again and people will come back to life. Even in Ireland, so many people blown to bits in those Troubles – bits of bodies collected in black plastic bags after a bomb in the street with no warning. If they'd known a real war, they wouldn't be so quick to start one. I was glad I was living here then.'

'It was mostly in the North. We didn't see much of it in Dublin – just on the news.' Aisling wasn't going to be side-tracked like that. She wanted a story with face-to-face reality not some story of anonymous plastic bags. Real images in her mind to inspire her. A mix of reality and fiction. Some graphics without words because she would use her skill in creating images to tell the story combined with what was common knowledge.

'So did many people die in that camp?'

'You are more persistent than Katharina. Or is it I am older now or you are younger? I don't know how many – thousands of course but how many thousands I have no idea. The deaths of people I knew were enough for me. Katharina was good with the numbers of people killed by the Nazis but the thousands or millions made no sense to me. Day-to-day death is harder to count. Worst of all were the days when you wished it were yourself. '

'So did you see people die?'

'Too many to count but Anna's death was the one that I mourned most. I only wish the story of "Die Arme" had died with her.

'Who was Diana?'

'There was no Diana there.'

'So what is the story that did not die with Anna?'

Brigitte sighed, 'Some stories are not for telling. Telling can release the devil himself.'

'Your devil?'

'My devil, your devil. Everyone's devil.'

The nightmare devil who came to torture me long after Katharina was born. When Katharina was growing up, I didn't talk of those things. No-one did. Leave Katharina to her facts about millions. How could I tell her those words from Anna's lips gave me worse nightmares than the bundles of rags turning into naked corpses on a trolley? How could I tell Katharina I heard the animal cries and the strange silences with my own ears when maybe I imagined it? How could I tell her I saw the weird procession better than if I had seen it with my own eyes? How could I tell her what I saw in Anna's eyes when she would pray each night for "Die Arme".'?'

The possibility of a true grisly story gave Aisling goose pimples of anticipation. Something she could use which would make fantasy horror images lame by comparison.

'Katharina hated me when I said, the Nazis were bad but we were worse. She wanted stories of heroines or if not heroines, she wanted innocent victims. She should have been Irma's daughter not mine.'

'Matt says we've all got a bit of Nazi in us if we look hard enough. He says it's about abuse of power and creation of scapegoats.'

'Matt?'

'A friend of mine, he's from Hamburg.'

'Sounds like an intelligent young man. They say the phosphorus bombs in Hamburg were much worse than here.'

'Yeah, he says victims can feel guilty either for not resisting or for surviving when others didn't. He can't get over how much guilt there is in Ireland. It creates space for power seekers who use guilt to exploit and manipulate people.

'Is he your boyfriend?

'No. He's too good a friend for that!'

'You met him in Hamburg?'

'No, I've never been to Hamburg. He moved to Dublin with his parents but he stayed when they went back to Germany. Now he's in Venezuela. I wish he was here. You would tell him Anna's story. He can make anybody tell him things they wouldn't tell another soul.'

The blue in Brigitte's eyes flickered, 'You are quite persuasive yourself. I will tell you Anna's story if you are sure you want to hear it. If only I could have seen Anna buried, maybe I could have buried her story with her. Instead I saw her spirit rise up in the smoke from the crematorium that day and heard her laugh. It was Anna's laugh all right and I often wondered what caused such a laugh.'

'So is Anna's story about how she died then?'

Brigitte was silent. Such a story seeks to escape thoughts. Such a story sneaks away from memory. Such a story is in nightmare only. Such a story is not made for thinking or for telling. There are no words to tell it. Some words were spoken then but not many. No words of accusation. Her sins were many. Stealing food. Nobody asked who among us is not capable of stealing food when we are hungry. Dead meat on a platter of bare arms carried past. Later vomiting bile at the thought of it. Push the thought away and it sneaks back inside into the dark where there are no words to release it. She shouldn't have tried to escape. And who didn't dream of escape and envy her for trying? She shouldn't have got caught. They should have caught her sooner.

The others waited, waited and waited. They've caught her – waves of sharp air carried the news. Hunters brought her to those hungrier than hunters. The silence of hungry anger. Anger to energise exhaustion. Beyond the limits of endurance anger. Anger inside and out – pulling and pushing. Anger at them. Anger at me. Anger at you. Anger at her. There was no first movement. No single hand or mouth. Each anger joined the other in bone and blood. We threw you to the wolves in ourselves. We tore you limb from limb. The anger of teeth with no tongue. No flesh to eat. Skin from bone. The eyes of those who carried the remains past the windows of the block that she remembered more than the bits of flesh and bone. Surprising to see blood left to drip. Dripping blood we didn't know in that place. Congealed raw sores and open wounds, blue-black bruises, raw fingers and toes we knew but no blood

177

dripped for long without being licked off. There was no monthly rhythm of blood in the Lager to remind us we were women. Bones we knew with not a scratch of fat remaining rolling on the ground. A joint of meat dripping blood was geist feast food not red reality. We made her an animal, making animals of ourselves.

'Das arme Kaninchen'. But she wasn't really a poor rabbit – not one of those who hopped on crutches from shelter to shelter rekindling some maternal feeling. Not even lucky enough to live through the scientific experiments of doctors. Thrown there, still alive, at those feet at the bottom of legs left too long standing. Those eyes that looked in those eyes that looked on Anna and looked on me – defiant or dead eyes and hands that carried the remnants turned into a skinned rabbit. More skin and bone but flesh too with teeth marks.

Aisling sighed. It was hard to follow the staccato burst from the mumble of blood and gore. No chance for questions. Brigitte had gone back into one of her dozes. Maybe she'd head off to do an Internet search on Ravensbrück. She'd more or less exhausted what she could read from Katharina's collection.

'And how did Anna die?' she asked to see if it would wake the aunt

'Anna was one of the lucky ones. She died peacefully in her bed between Irma and me. She went out on a breath. I was young enough to think that she was a very old woman and eighty years was a long life in those times. Anna's death was a comfort to me not a great pain. Every day that I suffered I would think of her not suffering any more. It was the other death.'

'What death would you mean?' Aisling heard her mock imitation of Gran's accent. Not a good idea. The two of them were radically different characters. Hopefully Brigitte didn't notice.

'Anna said that it was the eyes that were worst of all – wild eyes set in faces of stone with something not of this world. Anna said she saw the devil that day in those faces. The faces kept coming after the parade was over. Some of the bibelki of course saw that whole block as no better than animals anyway and passed their own judgement on them. They accepted the punishment of all for one as their lot. It was true of course. The bibelki often faced the long hours of punishment and they did it together without blame. '

'Anna said, 'in Stücke' – torn into pieces. I could see then skinned and shiny bones sticking out. Hannelore in the next bunk heard her tell me this story and intervened. She said the woman brought it on herself – live like an animal, die like an animal. She knew what would happen when she was caught and worse – she knew what would happen to those she left in her block when she tried to escape. Bringing punishment on everyone was bringing death nearer to everyone. But for Anna nothing made it right to open the door to the devil.'

'I don't understand. What actually happened to this woman?'

'She was in another block – the block for prostitutes, thieves, petty criminals. Many of the Zigeuner were put there.'

'Zigeuner?' Aisling repeated.

'Zigeuner looked foreign. When I heard Anna use that term first, I thought it was another form of Zeugen or witness. She laughed so hard at that, I had to join her although I didn't understand the joke, I asked Anna were they German? She said first yes and then no. "Zigeuner", she said. Maybe another word for Jew I thought.

'Later I overheard one of the British women there say Gypsy and then I realised Zigeuner were similar to the people we call itinerants or Tinkers. When I was growing up there were Tinkers who came round: sometimes people would call them Gypsies. People were afraid of them but they could mend things that no-one else could and they would do small jobs in return for food.'

Brigitte paused again and Aisling prompted.

'Like knackers you mean?'

Aisling was glad Matt wasn't in earshot to hear her using the slang term for Travelling people. Matt had told her off once for calling Travellers, 'knackers' and said the women with long skirts and shawls that begged on the streets in Dublin were linked to Irish Travellers even if they came from Romania .

'Knackers – isn't that where they take horses to die?' Brigitte was puzzled, 'I don't know that word. Katharina said they prefer to be called Rom or Sinti – according to the clan they are part of. An educated young woman like you should know that. I suppose you don't see itinerants on the streets now in Ireland, but you used to have them all sitting on O'Connell Bridge wrapped in shawls and with their long skirts – a baby bundled inside and another one with the hand out. They said at home that they were people pushed from the land during the famine. Other people said that real Gypsies came from Egypt so they were foreigners not Irish at all. The rest of them were just tramps. One woman came to our door every year at the same time with a new baby in her shawl. My mother would always give her a cup of tea and whatever bread was in the house and a few eggs. She used to give her my grandmother's china cup and she would scald it after with the kettle from the range. My mother was a Christian; most of our neighbours would shoot them if they got a chance. I understood a bit better why they were treated as if they were no better than animals even by the other women prisoners.'

Aisling felt insulted when the aunt called her ignorant though it was true she didn't know about the history of Travellers. On the news it said that some of the people who lived in tents on a roundabout with no toilets had a better living that back in Romania where they were persecuted. But not all Romanians were Romanies. She'd have to ask Matt when he came back what the connections were. Anyway there were plenty of people who would call Travellers or Romanies asocials nowadays too. She ignored the insult.

'So Zigeuner are German Gypsies?'

'At least they spoke German and were born in Germany but they didn't look German. Most of them had brown-black eyes and brown skin. Katharina told me many of them were killed in concentration camps.

'Were there Zigeuner in your hut?'

'I thought I told you already that it was mostly Jehovah's Witnesses when I arrived. I had a hard time with Anna at the beginning. She was even more particular than the sztubowa. At night my head would be full of exhaustion. All I wanted was to lie down and die rather than face the nightly rituals of cleaning and tidying that Anna insisted on. I couldn't make any sense of it at first. I couldn't understand who these women were? What fault could be found with them? They were so German and proud of it. Sometimes I was angry at how proud she was her people were allowed to work in the houses of the guards outside the main camp. Later it made some sense. They could be trusted never to try and escape because they were in prison for their principles. They refused to give honour to

Hitler that could only be given to God. There was no escape for them. You could see why the guards respected them. They spoke good German. Their own habits of cleanliness and childcare were close to the camp authorities.'

Was Brigitte dodging out of Anna's story again? It made her impatient, 'But the woman who escaped wasn't a Jehovah's Witness. What happened to the Gypsy woman?'

'She tried to escape but they caught her as they caught anyone who was foolish enough to try. I heard only about one woman who made it. She was on the team who worked in the forest. Somehow she hid clothes there and one day she didn't come back. The pine forest was the place to hide but the dogs always found anyone foolish enough to try. She walked all the way to Berlin on her own. Everyone knew because her friend gave the address of her brother in Berlin and she reached him. There weren't many who even got as far as the forest but anyone who did was usually thrown in the punishment block. Everyone knew that the other women in the block would be left standing until the woman trying to escape was caught. Everyone in the block was punished.'

'So they caught the Gypsy woman?'

'Yes after a few days. Anna saw the guards drag the poor woman, "die Arme" past their block back to the asocial block. She had been beaten so badly by then that she couldn't walk. She looked like a rag doll her arms already out of her sockets. The dogs had been at her too. She must have been half dead already. The guards didn't think it worth their while taking her to the punishment block. They knew what they were doing when they threw her back into her own block. They knew the anger of the women there standing, waiting in hunger, suffering for her for days.'

Aisling looked at her hands. She tried to picture it and couldn't – a group of half-starved women wouldn't have the strength surely? Was it really possible to tear someone limb from limb even someone who was half dead already?

'So the guards stood by and let the other prisoners tear someone to bits? But you told me most of those women were ill and weak. They certainly wouldn't be strong enough.'

Aisling examined Brigitte's face. It was hard to work out what was behind that mask. Why would she invent something like this? Why invent it for her? Maybe Aisling hadn't reacted strong enough to the descriptions of 'that place' so she had to invent something. It's not possible for people to pull apart another human being with their bare hands. Not possible to think of a group of half alive scarecrows using all the strength left to rip the flesh from the bone of another woman.

'Hard to believe, isn't it? And maybe you don't believe me either. And if it's true, who would you say is guilty of that woman's death? The people who created that place, the people who kept that place going? The woman who was the first to demand punishment? The guards who stood by and let them do the work and condemn them all as animals. Then they could treat them as animals and go to Mass on Sunday. We all have her blood on our hands.'

Maybe none of it was true. It was confusing. Brigitte never used the word 'Ravensbrück'. Aisling had guessed it from Katharina's collection. You never heard much about it. People were always going on about Auschwitz, Sachsenhausen, Buchenwald, Bergen – Belsen. Weird. Stuck here with an old woman who was out of her mind. And what if she was sane?

Brigitte looked at her, 'Once you take such a story into your heart, then you also have blood on your hands. Once you really know that other human beings, that other women are capable of such an act, you know that you are capable of it too. It is easier not to know but once you know something, you cannot not know it. You are old enough to know that.'

'Yeah,' Aisling admitted, 'but I think all this business about everyone being capable of it is just a big guilt trip. Not everyone did it. You said yourself that the bibelthingies didn't behave like that even if they were left standing and hungry for longer.'

'That's the point. The Bibelki had the strength and grace of their belief to take them beyond that anger. They had knowledge – or some of them anyway. Once you really know another human being, you know what they are capable of and you can see yourself in her and her in you. But you need to know that to have the strength to refuse or forgive. It is easier not to know.'

Aisling stopped herself from asking, 'What about Monika?' Instead she said, 'Knowing what you are capable of and doing it are poles apart.'

'There is always choice in it,' Anna said. The guards chose that women's fate as another way to make us see ourselves as no better than animals. And if we were no better than animals, then they had the right to control us. To get control of your spirit, your 'Geist' again, you had to know the depths and know how to climb up from there.'

'And if you really know it, then you are as evil as the most evil,' Aisling retorted.

'Yes. So it is. It is knowledge that is hard. It is easier not to know, so it is easier not to believe just as it is easier not to talk about that place. Once I thought sharing something with Mary would help. I could find a way to believe myself without going crazy. I made the mistake of telling some parts of my story to Katharina. She was an inquisitive child. Then she had such nightmares. She spent her time working out how to escape or hide if soldiers came for us, even as a teenager when people died as the wall was being built. I learnt it was better not to bring back those memories.'

Her face softened. 'Sometimes I told myself I had imagined the worst, that it was a story told to frighten me. Blamed my poor understanding of German. That it was a nightmare on one of those days and nights when every day was a waking nightmare. Then I would see Anna's face and hear her prayers and I knew she does not lie.'

Aisling found herself torn between wanting to be drawn into belief and wanting her own scepticism to win. She was silent now. She had got what she was looking for– something so evil that it gave her goose bumps. How could she use it? She liked the Aunt's angle; making everyone responsible. You could make a great horror-comic out of the images but one without baddies and goodies – horror lurking everywhere under the surface. Too many comic books were just like novels with the good triumphing over evil. Not true to life. A good story with a bit more depth was needed for a graphic novel.

Chapter Sixteen

# Rituals

'Das Badezimmer ist frei.'

Aisling was tired and ignored Brigitte calling out to tell her the bathroom was free. There were some things Brigitte seemed incapable of saying in English. Usually, Aisling took it as an alarm call to get up, washed and out for 'Brötchen'. The trip out for fresh bread and rolls was a part of the breakfast ritual that she really enjoyed. Queuing was even fun because she had to decide which to buy for herself – plain white crusty rolls; or triangles with crunchy pumpkin seeds; or a round one with sunflower seeds; or a rectangle of rye; or a 'Splitterbrötchen', which she liked better than croissants. They knew her now and would repeat what she said in German smiling at her. Brigitte had one white roll but she always told Aisling to buy five. Every other day there was the big decision on which half-loaf of bread they should have for 'Abendbrot'. Aisling preferred the rolls and would eat what was left over from breakfast for snacks in the day.

But this morning she stayed in bed. She couldn't sleep. She wished she could rewind the evening back. Wished she had gone out after Abendbrot. The old woman was right. Secrets are better left buried. Once they are out they change things.

Something was finished but what? Graphics and more

graphics needed for the graphic description. She should have binned the vicious cartoon she drew of Maeve instead of showing it to Cathy, who loved it of course. Queen Maeve. The hurt in her eyes worse than the cold, silent mouth. 'Maybe the cartoon was worse than having sex with her dad. Thankfully Michael tore up the cartoon strips she did of him. No more. The price was too high. This would have to be different.

Brigitte was dismissive when Aisling had asked about Katharina's books. Books and more books about the times Brigitte wanted to forget. Memorials, lectures, exhibitions to drag back times and deeds better forgotten. She sat up in bed and reached for her drawing pad. Skinny, striped people walked from the tip of the pencil stub in her hand as she leafed through. "Everyday life in a Women's Concentration Camp 1939-1945". Graphic artists there too. Drawings and portraits. Compare the French "Living Room" – black lines of half-starved people – with the plumper Czech quarters. Different times? Different treatment? Different backgrounds?

She waited until long past the usual breakfast-ritual time. When she did get up about 11.30, the breakfast things were still on the table. Brigitte had moved to her favourite chair and was dozing. She roused herself then and muttered an attempt at a polite, 'Did you sleep well?'

Aisling said, 'Fine thanks.' No apologies. She'd done nothing wrong, had she? Aisling prepared a breakfast like she did at home – toast and some juice – usually eaten at the breakfast bar on her own. She took a tray into the dining room. Brigitte said 'Guten Appetit' and then nothing more. She said 'Good appetite' in German before every meal. It was a Sunday. Yola didn't come on Sundays. Aisling cleared the things away on her own while Brigitte dozed. She hated this feeling of being out of place – not knowing where to put things. She swore she would keep the ritual for the next few days – it was easier.

As an attempt at a peace offering Aisling showed her the graphic novel she had been reading, "Der Erste Frühling": a retelling of a family story in 1945. Easy to read German especially with the graphics.

'A comic-book – do you think I'm a child? I can read German! I don't chose to read about those times.' So this "comic-book" was one more attempt to get the aunt to recall. The present tense touched a gutstring. Strumming sounds for graphics stripping across her brain.

'Graphics are not just for children! Graphic novels are for adults too.' The best novel I have ever read and the best film is all graphics – a Persian woman Persepolis. Protective of my secret heroine. The one I wish to be.

Brigitte spotted it. Her turn to put the needle under the skin. No pathetic old dear but a sparring partner without gloves. Never heard of comic –strip novels. Why did Aisling care about comic books when she cared so little about anything else. Rhetorical.

Defensive then. 'I do cartoons'

'I suppose you draw me too? An old biddy waking her daughter alone and waiting for her own death.' Brigitte laughed at her when she blushed then.

'Alone? I'm here.'

'So you are.' Shrewd eyes to see through her. 'You're not as bad as you think you are.'

What did she mean by that?

Brigitte blinked out the sunshine. She would ask Aisling to draw the curtain when she came in from the kitchen. So many moments of sunshine flashing back. The still blue heat of that beach in Greece. Once upon a time they lived happier ever after in those moments of sunshine. Now it washed over her and ebbed out on a draught of air swept in by the voile curtain. It took with it that glimmer of the first Spring when sunshine could tempt her out of the cellar. When she moved from the cellar, she wrote her name on the frame of the main door as she had seen others do. If Dieter or Delia came to look they would know she was alive. She cried as she left the half-ruined building – tears that didn't flow for Anna.

Sunshine carried her belly in search of work and food for new life, when she wanted only to die. Brick by brick she scraped and piled. Happy to help the city stagger to its feet and dare to put its full face to the sun again. Kaffee with Adelheid on the pavement at the Café on Kurfürstendamm, wishing she had taken off her headscarf and rolled her hair. Some of the women were even wearing hats. 'Did they live through our war?' Adelheid muttered in her ear.

The rhythm of years when autumn followed summer year after year merging now. Brigitte closed her eyes to catch the roast glow of autumn sunshine chasing the heels of her Katharina – catch a leaf and make a wish she called out. Rehberge Park – collecting leaves together for a school project. The feeling of pride swelling up inside me – she was only five years old and already she could tell the names of trees, and her Mama had to buy a dictionary to find the name in English. The only leaf that Mama could be sure of was the oak.

'But Mama' – her forehead wrinkled with that old woman look she had sometimes– 'you lived in the country. Have they no trees in Ireland?'

The pain that shot up her leg opened her eyes again and she saw only Peggy's granddaughter – to-day the sharp face paler than Katharina's in the coffin. No make-up. Probably they put make-up on dead people these days. Katharina would hate that: she never wore make-up. Maybe this child will help me kill those moments of joy so that I can let go. The pain of remembered joy – maybe greater because it was so unexpected – is the worst. But who can ever say they know the worst?

Things could be worse. Irma laughed at that even on the long march towards what we thought was likely death. Luckily her laugh was the laugh of a happy camper, low and throaty, and ready to change to a cough at any moment. My mother hated the saying because the pessimist used it to escape the moments of joy in life – always imagining something more hurtful or heart-breaking than what had happened already, which was bad enough. The optimist used it to say what had happened, which was bad enough, was not as bad as some other imaginary event. The explanation took several kilometres because so much of her energy was taken up with putting one foot in front of the other. The longer the better. She even tried to tell some Irish stories in German. The mental effort raised the pain from her feet. Telling stories to 'shorten the road' was always the way especially coming home from the bog on a summer evening after making the most of a dry, sunny day. Thoughts of the bog, back-breaking work and being bitten by midges had kept her in Berlin. Now even that was a glimpse of heaven.

'The Irish should be philosophers of death,' Irma said one day but she did not understand what she meant. She still didn't understand it. Irma could imitate my words and accent in English, 'You have helped shorten the road for me.' They didn't know yet how long or short the road would be.

Aisling shifted uncomfortably in the silence. Brigitte was stranger than usual to-day and she couldn't help worrying that she'd pushed her too far last night. It wasn't going to be easy stuck here until the funeral. Monika had rung yesterday. The funeral would be on Thursday. Maybe they could enter the Guinness Book of records for the longest wake ever. At Michael's wake, she had hated the people who tried to cheer them up by remembering the good times. But maybe it was different when you died as an old person. When one of Gran's friends died, she would talk and laugh about the times they had together more often than she would cry about them.

If only this was a proper wake, at least with people calling around, you didn't have time to sit being morbid. It made it easier to talk of normal things – the weather, the TV or holidays without feeling that it was some sort of sacrilege. Here with Brigitte, there was so little for them to talk about. It seemed safer to stick to the only subject that she cared about.

'Do you have any other photos of Katharina?' Aisling's eyes indicated the one that always sat by Brigitte within touching distance.

Brigitte looked down at Aisling's feet wound round the legs of the chair. The girl rarely relaxed. Words came to her lips but she bit them back, letting them loose only in her head, 'Don't be polite with me, young lady. I know your weakness. I can smell it. If you are going to survive you have to know it too.' She permitted herself just a small twist of the knife that Aisling had given her. The girl had her own reasons for getting away from Dublin – that suited Brigitte fine. She had no need to feel any sense of obligation.

'Do you use photos to bring back memories of your brother?'

Aisling hated Brigitte then – hated her for the casual swinge of the blade that sought out her weak spot but hated her even more because she saw through Aisling's veneer of visiting relative. Revenge for the break in their ritual. 'That's different... I didn't... I'm not a mother.' Her childhood stammer came through her anger.

'You didn't what? Maybe you didn't love him enough? Maybe you wished him dead sometimes. Maybe you would have behaved differently if you knew he was going to die. Maybe you know what it is to feel guilty.'

The cruel bitch, did she know something more or was she guessing? Surely Gran never guessed any of it and what would she know anyway and what would she tell – sister or no sister? It was her own evil mind. Aisling turned it back to her, 'So what if I teased him sometimes. Why not? He did worse to me and to my cat. Should I feel guilty for that now – just because he topped himself?'

There – it was out. What she wasn't allowed to say. It was no accident. Everybody thought it, even Mum but no-one was allowed to admit it. Brigitte didn't seem to register it so say no more and hope for the best. She's hardly going to big mouth it to Gran. 'There's something about Brigitte, Bridget, Biddy that is different from other people, I've met,' Aisling thought then, 'Could it be just that she's a mix of Irish and German? Not that: in some ways she's more Irish than Gran. It's something about not play-acting a role. She's not the 'poor mother', the 'grand aunt'. It leaves space for me to think about who I am. 'Very profound, I'm sure, Aisling. Maybe you should switch to philosophy at uni next year,' she told herself. Time out would be best but how to keep her allowance. Maybe even time out in Berlin?

'Are you sure everything is OK? It's taking long enough?' Text exchange with her father again. 'Everything is fine.' She wanted to do this herself. To be treated like a whole person for a change. She wanted to be away from Michael's ghost long enough to work out what her next step would be. Bad and all as Biddy was, she treated Aisling like an equal.

Brigitte sat with half-closed eyes.

'Are you O.K.?'

'O.K.? I will never be O.K. now. Katharina's agony was worse than anything else I have ever suffered. I thought I had accepted all the suffering in the past – even the time she left me to live with her Jules. But watching her die made me question everything again. I asked myself, what if I had been prepared to die like one of those martyrs from my mother's prayer book, then this suffering would never have come into the world. Maybe I could have chosen death not violation and gone straight to heaven.' She paused. 'Even that is not true,' she added quietly, 'There was no real threat of death. And what was violation? Surely more resistance than I felt or showed after the first time. How to tell her I was more afraid of the blockowa than of him? Which would be better? The child of a rape or the child of consent with a Nazi? I couldn't work out which would hurt her least.'

Aisling found herself touched by a novel sense of gentleness and forgiveness. Where did it come from? She watched as Brigitte searched around for a cigarette.

'You shouldn't smoke; it's bad for you.'

Brigitte laughed her odd, crackling laugh making Aisling's mouth water for the taste of her bitter chocolate.

'You mean it might kill me. Hardly before the funeral and afterwards it would suit me very well. If I had the courage back then, I would have killed both of us. I wished myself dead so often it was a surprise to me that I lived and a shock to find the child I didn't want to bring into the world could bring me such happiness.' Brigitte drew on the cigarette and blew the smoke into the air. Aisling watched it rise.

'Oh, we had happy times – happiness that I never expected to find. A pure gift. But once you have that happiness, you want to hold onto it and that is where you make the mistake. If you live to be as old as me, you might learn how wrong you can be about everything.'

For a moment Aisling felt the power in her own hands. Maybe I can turn on the happy times; or go for the secrets; the guilt; the story that silence couldn't hide? It was a good feeling. Like something had happened inside her. She surprised herself when she went for the kinder option without the kicks.

'That's one way you're different from Gran. She thinks she's right about everything,' she said.

'So Peggy hasn't changed then?' Brigitte replied and they laughed together.

'I think wakes are a good idea. People can talk about happy or sad memories. Gran had a good laugh at Michael's wake. A good wake is better than a Mass where more than half the people who turn up don't believe in it anymore. You can laugh or cry. You're aware of the person – the good times and the bad times. Other people there mean you are not so caught up in yourself.' The compassion she felt as she spoke surprised her.

Brigitte felt it slide along the smoke line from her cigarette. She could feel them burning Katharina now, just as she felt them burn Anna. 'Not being caught up in yourself. Yes. Not necessarily from a wake or even a death. That's a gift at any time. Maybe Michael's gift to you? I would've liked a wake for Katharina – or maybe I mean for me.' Her tone was so soft it was hard to hear her.

Aisling pushed a bit more, 'So we can have a wake while we're waiting. What makes a good wake?' She dredged her own memory for some story about Katharina and found only a conversation over Christmas dinner once as the time for Gran to ring her sister approached. It was Michael who asked, 'Who is Aunt Bridget anyway?'

'You've never met her – she's your Great Aunt, your Gran's sister. She lives in Berlin with her daughter, Katharina.' Mum popping into the conversation with that cheerful and super normal tone as she dished out an extra helping of turkey, making Aisling smell a sensitive point.

'Grand-Aunt,' her father said to Michael, 'She's my aunt and your Grand-Aunt.'

'Oh Brendan… stop being so pedantic – who cares Great Aunt or grand aunt. He's only seven.'

'So what is she to us, this Katharina?' Aisling remembered the conversation because she liked the idea of Berlin and the idea of a cousin in Germany.

'Oh she'd be your second cousin. Isn't that right, Diarmuid? I'm not much good at all this first cousin or second cousin once removed, twice removed – aunts and cousins are far enough for me.'

'And how old is she?'

'She's a bit older than Daddy.'

Aisling lost interest then but remembered it as the time she first really registered what an umbilical cord was. As a child it was all willies, tits, bums and trying to work out how her mother's vagina could ever stretch enough to bring out a baby – like a turd from the wrong hole. Her father said something to her mother about Bridget and Katharina had never cut the umbilical cord and that was why she had never married. Her mother had said, 'You're one to talk.' She didn't say any more as Gran was only in the other room on the phone but Aisling heard her mutter as they cleared the table, 'Try shaking your mother off at Christmas or any other family occasion.'

'What's an umbilical cord?' Michael asked and both her parents jumped back from their whispered scraping of the plates to answer him.

'Katharina didn't live here when she died, did she?' she said now to Bridget to keep both of them from drifting off to another space.

'Forty-five years we lived here together before she went to live with Monika. We came here when she was a baby. I found this apartment myself –repaired it with my bare hands before she was born. Somebody else had broken in and made a mess of it – the door was left hanging open. Adelheid made me move in before someone else could get it. Forty-five years.'

'What? You squatted this apartment?' Aisling laughed. The idea of someone Gran's age being a squatter was just too funny. She'd heard of people squatting in London and Copenhagen – people her own age or even her parents' generation – but not grannies.

'Squatted, you call it. That's an ugly word. I call it doing something for my child. What could we do – wait for someone else to help us? The war was over and everything was in chaos. Adelheid knew the old woman who lived and died here alone – she used to look after her. Sometimes later people came back looking for their home back. We were lucky. No-body ever came back. She had a son but maybe he was killed in the war. When the landlords came to collect the rent I told them that I had lived here with her before she died. They put my name on it so we were legal tenants then.'

'Maybe the old woman was a Jew?'

Brigitte looked at her suspiciously, 'You are like Katharina – always questions, questions, questions. How would I know? I didn't want to talk about those times. I had worked hard to put them behind me and she wanted to throw them back in my face. So many others had their stories buried with them. Why should mine not be buried too? But Katharina was so strong – so determined. She made me angry with all her questions. Why did she need to know so much? We did what we had to do in those dark days. Why dig up the past? You can't change it. What's done is done. What's gone is gone. People think – if I were you I would do this or that. No-one knows what you would do in another person's shoes.'

'She told me that she had a right to know who she was and who her father was. She accused me of secrets, lies and silence and even of spinning her so many other stories she didn't know who she was anymore.'

'So why not tell her the truth?'

'The truth. What is the truth? To survive, you have to make up your own truth.'

Aisling laughed, 'You can't make up the truth. The truth is the truth.'

'What is truth to me may be lies to you.'

'Gran said Katharina's father was an American soldier.'

'Maybe they wanted to believe that and maybe I let them. There were so many fatherless children when Katharina was a child, it didn't bother her much at first. Only later when she became interested in the war and started to read books in English. But she got too clever for me with her dates and her history. She wanted to know how I could be with an American soldier before the war was over. I told her that I didn't want

197

to dredge up the past with its memories of hunger and want, but she persisted – questions, questions, questions.

'When the heart of Berlin was torn apart by the wall, she started to tear me apart too. She used the excuse of studying history to question me about dates of this and dates of that. Why should I remember dates? She told me once her friend's mother was raped by a Russian 'liberator'. Who told the child such stories? I was afraid dirty talk with coarse words would get there before I told her about her father but I could never find the words. When I was young these were things that no-one talked about. Once she asked out of the blue – was she born premature or full term? It was time to tell her then of her birth.'

'So she asked if she was conceived in the camp,' Aisling put her hand over her mouth to hide the grin. It was a bit obvious wasn't it? She had sussed Katharina was conceived while the Nazis were still in charge before she heard Günter's name as the father. Katharina must have worked it out for herself long before Brigitte told her the truth.

Brigitte looked at her, 'So, like you, I understood what she was asking. She didn't question it when she was younger. She knew many Americans and knew only kindness from the Americans I worked for. Many of them went back to America. Some came back and brought her American dresses with petticoats and frills. It was only later, when she was a teenager, that she started counting and adding up the answers to questions. So where were you in January 1945? I told her I was in Berlin. I didn't want her to know the story of that place. Better to bury it where it belonged.'

'So where was the camp?'

'A place called Fürstenberg. One good thing about the wall

was it cut me off from that place. Katharina went there anyway to the Memorial the GDR built. Much good a memorial would do the people who died there but every year she tried to persuade me to go with her. When the wall came down she wanted to help with the new museum and the questions started again. She told me the Russians used the houses where the SS had lived and they didn't even realise it. She wanted more and more detail of what happened there. It's history, she said. Help me be a better teacher. She said that Irma told her more than I ever had.'

'I didn't know it then but the best days were the hard days of hope before the questions – watching Katharina go to school, grow up, speak German like a native and English better than me. There were shops with food and clothes and work to be done to earn the money to spend. We had our own home. We had put the bad times behind us. The wall brought fear and death back.'

'But you must have known they were building the wall. It wasn't something they could hide, was it?' Aisling didn't try to hide her amusement.

'There was always the Russian Sector and some guard and it became harder and harder for people to move freely between the Russian Sector and the other sectors but we didn't really see it coming. You'll learn soon enough it is easier for things to seem obvious after the event. At the time, it didn't happen at once and yet it happened all of a sudden. I remember 13th August 1961 better than my mother's birthday. Of course we noticed that there were more and more patrols of the Russian sector marking the line between us and them but it was only more of the same. We saw it coming but didn't recognise what we saw until they put the fence in front of the patrols. And even then we weren't ready for the declaration of the border and wall being built and the way they split streets and started to clear houses.

'We went to watch as people came under the fence in the first days with suitcases and bundles. Then there were more and more soldiers: later great machines making concrete barriers and the shooting started. We were so afraid of another war. I tried to stop Katharina going near there. I told her about the tunnels and secret ways that people found to get to our side of the fence so that she would look in other places in our streets. I told her she saw more by looking at the television and persuaded her to come with me to Adelheid's. She already had a television and used it to get a bit of extra cash from neighbours. She would never take money from me but I always brought something.'

'The museum that I went to in Bernauer Strasse has lots of photos and some films. It's worth a visit,' Aisling suggested.

'I've never been,' Brigitte replied.

'Well you should: it's free too.'

'I hated that wall. With that wall came more and more questions. I should have known that those questions were leading somewhere. 'Did the Americans liberate you?' Katharina asked on the way home from watching the T.V. at Adelheid's. I told her how we left the camp in March.'

'So where were you when the Russians reached Ravensbrück?' Aisling was beginning to realise how frustrated Katharina must have been. Her own mother's insistence on telling and explaining was intrusive but it had advantages.

'You are just like her, questions and more questions. We had already left on the long march to the north east. It was hard to remember dates. Was it winter or was it already Spring?' Brigitte mimicked Katharina's curiosity.

'I told her about the time that Irma filled her mouth with snow. She talked about the best sorbet she had ever eaten in a restaurant in Vienna. Zitrone und Limone. I knew Zitrone was the word for lemon and I could taste the sharp sourness. 'Was ist "Limone"?' I wanted to know – it sounded like it should be lemon too. She told me like a lemon only green. I'd never seen such a thing. Then she suddenly said, 'It's Lime, Lime! I almost spat out my bread. You eat lime? I told her we put lime on houses to make them white. It was her turn then to be astonished.

'Ahh... You mean Kalk – Chalk white. I told her how we laughed at that – the small white house in Leitrim was as far from limes in Vienna as that snowy place was from reality.'

'But you lied to Katharina, didn't you?'

'That was no lie. Irma and I did eat snow together.'

'Yes but about the camp,' Aisling knew well this technique to tell a part truth as a good way to distract from what actually happened.

'We left in April after Anna died. Katharina went to the camp after the wall came down and the Russians had left,' Brigitte looked defeated, 'but there was a wall between us that never came down.'

'I'm sorry,' Aisling said, surprised at the tears in her own eyes.

'I'll rest now,' Brigitte put her head down.

'I'm off out.' Aisling left quietly, ambivalent about her escape. Questions about why Brigitte ended up in Ravensbrück and how she got out again would have to wait. She wanted to know more but it felt like picking at someone else's scab. Intrusive but compelling.

Chapter Seventeen

# Escape

Lunch was ready-prepared by Yola on Saturday– Gulasch. They would eat it with noodles prepared by Brigitte. Aisling dipped a spoon into the thick sauce. She was glad she had come back. Brigitte asked her to open a bottle of wine and lay a white cloth. They would make an occasion of it. As she laid the table, Aisling made Brigitte laugh with stories of her waitressing. She promised herself she would get another bit of the story this evening. Brigitte needed distraction anyway. When she got into one of those long, dozy pauses, she seemed like she had one foot in the grave. When she spoke of being young in Berlin, she looked younger too, even when she told horror stories.

'You know when you said you left the camp in March. How did it happen? Did you escape?' Aisling could hear that the question, which drifted in the direction of Brigitte on the billow of the curtain, sounded too light to face Brigitte's solid silence. Brigitte had withdrawn into herself while Aisling cleared away the dishes. For no apparent reason her mood had turned foul. But the question achieved its purpose of provocation.

'Escape?' Brigitte's saliva gathered at the corner of her mouth. 'Even you would like pretty words to end the horror story. But there was no place for pretty words even in dreams.'

Brigitte spoke then as if to herself, 'Flucht, Flucht, Flucht, Flucht,' For a moment Aisling thought she was swearing at her before she heard the German word for flight come through into her own consciousness.

'I learnt that little word, 'Flucht' had a big meaning in that place. A word that carried as much fear as hope on its wings. I learnt the reality of 'Flucht' was to see the pieces of what was once a person spread out on the electric wire above our heads. Like a crucifixion. 'Flucht' from that place was death or worse. I told you already what they did to the woman who tried to escape. I was more afraid of escape than I was of dying in that place. Are you too young to know that you can never escape from hell once you have been there?'

Aisling bridled, 'I'm not too young to imagine a bit of hell.' 'Don't let her wind you up,' she told herself: it was Brigitte's way of keeping the story inside herself – not sharing it. Aisling was keyed up with the hope of more graphic detail of the horrors fluttering somewhere between her abdomen and her fingers.

The last story had given her replacement nightmares. Better nightmares for graphics, and no more Michael and his eyes popping out. But Brigitte was somewhere else now – her head sunk onto her chin. Aisling thought she was asleep until she spoke again in a lower tone.

'When I saw what could happen… even though I was only a short time in that place, I tried to dismiss 'Flucht' even from my dreams. I think if I had found the gates open and unguarded, I wouldn't have walked through when I knew what could happen. Oh yes, it's very easy for you, so young, to plan cutting wires, digging tunnels, outwitting guards, using disguises. I thought about those things too in my days of waiting before they came for me. There were even some in there too who were foolish enough to dream but not many were foolish enough or desperate enough to take the consequences when they saw what failure brought.'

Were those tears or did Brigitte rub the light from the street lamp from her eyes? She seemed to hear the unspoken question.

'I haven't shed many tears in my life about that. The tears are only for myself and for us because what we could do was worse than anything they could do. Katharina was angry because I wouldn't talk about what happened there. 'You can't bottle it up, Mama; one day the cork will blow off.' She was wrong. She was the one who brooded over it and let it eat its way through her insides. If only I could have told her the worst, she would have understood but it was too late then, it was already eating her.'

Aisling felt again the flutter of hope that she would get to hear some more of the gory detail Katharina had missed. Reality horror. The way Brigitte looked at her when she spoke gave her the shivers.

'Who knows who can live with knowing how far you could be pushed away from ordinary human feelings? Brave stories of the good and the bad didn't belong in that place. I learnt that there – there are no good and bad – there are only those who are brave enough or foolish enough to stand up for something and those who aren't. Either way you can be an angel or a devil. And the angels and devils are here on earth. There's no heaven but what you make yourself.'

'So you don't believe in life after death?' – 'What would Gran make of this?' Aisling wondered.

'Life before death is good enough and bad enough for me.

Why would I want to live through hell again? And the bits of heaven with Katharina are inside me forever.'

'So you don't believe in God?' Aisling persisted.

Brigitte looked at her strangely. 'If there was such a God with the power to allow things to happen or the power to stop them and he could stand by and do nothing, I wouldn't want to have anything to do with him anyway.'

Aisling took a few moments to get her head around this one, 'So basically you're saying God, if he does exist, doesn't deserve our belief in him.'

'Whether God exists or not, it's not my problem. I long ago stopped caring about God. I am sure the devil exists because I have seen him operate through evil done by desperate people.' Brigitte sighed, 'I suppose I have seen God too through the good done by people who were just as desperate. So I cannot say. It's irrelevant to me. What do I care about the afterlife? Sometimes I hope there is something there for Anna, for my mother and father. Maybe there is and maybe there isn't'

'And Katharina?'

'Yes and Katharina too. Somewhere we could live again our moments of joy.' Brigitte stopped to breathe in the smell of growing herbs on a hillside in Greece when she was already a grown woman: stopped to feel the chestnut glowing in her hand, matching the bright questions from Katharina's mouth and the light that shone from her hair when she was a school girl. 'Yes, if there was heaven, it would be a place to undo my cruelty to her when I sent her off to her Jules with my coarse curses and with tears in her eyes.'

Aisling was surprised to find tears in her own eyes now. What a life! She resolved then she wouldn't tell Gran everything after all. Gran would gloat a bit and lift her rosary beads down to pray for her wayward sister with the bastard child. At least this horror movie of real life had more meaning than fantasies about heaven and hell.

Suddenly Aisling thought rape – why not rape? That could account for a lot – Katharina was probably the product of a rape and Brigitte just didn't want to admit it. In Gran's view of the world, rape was something that women brought on themselves. So Brigitte would feel guilty about it. Aisling stored that thread of the story for another time when the aunt had a few Schnaps in her. It was no wonder Katharina found her mother frustrating. The aunt couldn't answer anything straight – you needed to time everything. She was worse than Gran on that score.

But if you could get her started on a story and keep her going, she was almost back there and it was like watching someone on T.V. She searched now for something that would get the aunt going again: 'So how did you get out of the camp?' She put emphasis on the how to distract from whatever.

'I was only there seven months but it was the longest seven months of my life. There were so many people who died or were gassed or killed in some other way I didn't expect to live through it. Waiting, waiting, waiting. Worse than waiting for Katharina to move out. Worse than waiting for Katharina to die. Worse than waiting now for Katharina to be buried. Waiting for Anna to die in the camp – hours that were as long as days. What would come first – the end of the war or some new torture of desperation? Waiting without knowing is worse than living without hope. People talk of the numbers who died. I marvel yet that there were some who lived all those long years there. I wouldn't have survived so long.'

'So how did you get out?' Aisling put the emphasis on 'did' this time.

'Irma saved me. She came to our block when the whole place was falling apart. We talked of looking forward to spring. We meant surviving that place. We could smell the fear of the guards rising as the Allies advanced on the East Front or the West Front. Irma wanted me because I could help her communicate with the British or Americans if she needed that. It was her who told me that I had been arrested after the Allies had entered Germany in September 1944. I didn't even know that the Allies had made it that far. She was a red star but wasn't cliquish like some.'

'The end of the war must have been hard,' Aisling prompted.

'In those last days, the place became chaotic. That caused problems too. The more the fear rose up in the guards, the more unpredictable they were. The women were worse than the men. Only once, while Anna was alive, did I ever see signs of feeling. There were some good singers in our block although it was mostly hymns that they sang. They weren't supposed to sing but sometimes, like around Christmas, even the guards couldn't stop it.

'The worst of the guards was a women built like a tank. I heard someone once murmur her nickname. I thought they said Tänzer – Dancer not Panzer. Anna loved that new nickname. It was hard to imagine her dancing so that made it even funnier. We giggled like schoolgirls about 'tanzen' when she was near and the best was that she never knew why talking about dancing made us laugh.

'One night around Christmas she asked one of the women in our block to sing a song about a pony. It was some well-known

German folk song they told me. I couldn't really follow what happened this pony but it must have been a sad story because she cried. Anna and I hugged each other with laughter later. The Panzer had an underbelly. There was delight near happiness to see some sign of weakness in the monster. I hated her and I hated her dog, which was like an extension of her. They all thought more of their dogs than they did of fellow human beings.' Brigitte paused again and Aisling filled her glass with water. They sat in silence for a few minutes. Brigitte's tone was so low when she started the story again, the street sounds seemed louder, 'After Anna died in January, life there became more and more unbearable. It was harder and harder to keep clean – the showers and toilets hardly worked any more. The guards did nothing except talk amongst themselves and beat anyone who stepped an inch out of line. Irma taught me how to be like a shadow. Taught me how to show respect even to the guards without fear and without accepting the ugliness and cruelty. She is my best friend even now. She is so clever too. '

Pause. A dog barked into their silence from the street. Brigitte's voice became stronger and louder. 'One day I couldn't believe my eyes when I saw Irma lying down on the floor and playing with Panzer's dog. She would let it lick her face. She even gave it a bit of precious bread. She dared me to do it too. The only reason I did it is that I had been practising how to keep on the right side of that dog. My brother Liam taught me how to not be afraid of dogs. He said they could smell your fear but if you could control your fear they would pass you by and bite someone else. I wanted to impress Irma. I needed her respect.'

'Does she live here?'

'No, she lives in Austria. She always sent me a card at

Christmas with photos of her children and grandchildren. Now she goes nearly every year to the commemoration and she visits me when she comes. She says it helps to visit and to remember and that I should do it too. Katharina and Irma talked and talked about those times and what they have done to make it a museum. How could they make a museum of that place? They should have put bulldozers through it long ago.'

'So if it's a museum, I could go and look?' Aisling perked up —might make an interesting day trip. She could check out for herself what was true and what wasn't.

'Nowadays it is easy, you can go there by train from Berlin to Fürstenberg and you can walk to the camp. She always asked me to go but I never want to see that place again. I'm glad that the Russian soldiers used it all the time Katharina was growing up. The only regret I have now is that the Russians didn't destroy that place before they left. Now it is a place for students and tourists, Katharina told me. She went with Irma when Irma visited us for the first time in 1992. She went back again with her Jules. Now they have talking films and photos. She was cross with me for not telling her more. She wanted me to do one of those videos she found there.' Brigitte mimicked Katharina, 'Mama, why didn't you tell me it was as bad as any concentration camp. You talked always about the Lager you spent months in as if it was more of a workcamp. I didn't know it was like Belsen or Auschwitz. It's typical that because it was mostly women, no-one hears about it – not even in Germany.' She made it sound like a conspiracy. I didn't tell her most of the people who survived that place don't want anyone to know about it. What good is talking about it now? To bring the misery back? Every time Katharina went there, she came back from there with questions, questions and more questions.'

She mimicked Katharina again: "How did you get out? Were you still there when the Allies liberated it? Were you on the death march?" I laughed in her face and told her that we ran away into the woods and then took a train back to Berlin. Katharina was angry then and told me she found out more from Irma in a few hours than she did from me in a lifetime. I reminded her then of her favourite bedtime story when she was a child – the story of Mitza and Biddy, the two cats who escaped into the forest and hid with all the other animals from the hunter and his dog. If they were captured they would be taken back to the place of cruelty they had escaped from. If they fell down and couldn't walk any further, the hunter would shoot them. "Mama, you and your riddles," she said and looked at me as if she despised me.'

'So how did you get out – was the War over then? Did you really run away into the woods and then get a train back to Berlin?'

Brigitte laughed her throaty laugh, 'Almost true. So what's wrong with that?'

'Not a thing,' Aisling replied, knowing now that she would hear more.

'Katharina says Irma told her we were freed by the Soviet army. But Irma would say that. Even now she is still some sort of Communist. I don't talk to her about politics. We weren't freed by anyone. It was more being ready to take the... the what?' Brigitte stopped, 'So many words in German and in English and sometimes I can find neither of them – die Gelegenheit.'

'Chance, opportunity,' Aisling prompted.

'You know more German than you let on, young lady, you should practise it more. You never know when it will come in useful. Das blinde Huhn findet auch einmal ein Korn.'

'Die hund? What has the dog finding its corner got to do with anything?' Aisling asked.

Brigitta laughed so much she nearly choked. 'I said the blind hen can always find some corn. Huhn for hen, hund for dog, Korn for corn not Corner for corner.'

Aisling blushed. She hated being made to feel a fool. 'So what actually happened? What did you do?'

Brigitte coughed new wind into her sails from the laughter and took a breath, 'There was no point trying to get past guards in the camp – getting caught and then everyone in the block would be punished. I wouldn't have risked that – not even for Irma. The guards were more and more jumpy so we knew something was happening. Irma found out that they planned to move us to another place. There were so many movements of people in and out; none of us knew what would happen from one day to the next. Every day there were whispers that the Russians were getting closer on the Eastern Front. Irma pieced together every snippet of news. Even the Zeugen Jehovahs would listen to her. They were more afraid of the Russians than the German guards and many planned to flee with the families of the German guards if they got a chance. Irma told me always to be ready and to stay close to her. She didn't need to tell me. I clung to her like a baby – night and day. She told me I should try to keep some bread if I could. Hard as it was, I managed a bit,' Brigitte paused and lit a cigarette.

Aisling watched the smoke rise and breathed in, telling herself it was a joint. An imaginary joint was good enough in this strange new space of listening and watching herself and this old woman, who was becoming more and more of a person as the days went by. The young Brigitte from the War didn't fit so easily into 'the aunt' box.

Chapter Eighteen

# Liberation

'Waiting is the worst,' Brigitte breathed out another column of smoke into the streak of sunlight that crossed the room, bringing with it the sticky heat of the street. Aisling sat in cut-offs and a sleeveless t-shirt with her legs slung over the arm of the sofa.

'You are a persuasive young lady. You make me want to talk. But you must first show me your drawings.'

'What drawings?'

'The drawings in the book beside you. You told me you wanted to tell Anna's story with drawings like a comic-strip with only a few words?'

'I haven't done any drawings of the camp yet,' Aisling lied.

'Take care not to make lying a bad habit, young lady.'

'O.K. so I've made a few sketches but nothing I could show anyone yet.'

'You have no need to be shy with me.'

'I'm not shy. I'll show you later. You didn't finish the story of your escape and you haven't told me why they put you in there in the first place.'

'When we knew the war was nearly over, it fed hope. We watched the guards make a big circus tent to house women who came from other camps. You could hear it flap in the wind.

Those creatures barely had latrines and no tap for water. No beds. If they were lucky they had something to lie on. I could see them sometimes with their spoons held up to catch the rain or their faces and mouths open. Irma risked her life many times in those last days of chaos to take a bucket of water to them. To me, she whispered words – not long now. We knew something was brewing when the Red Cross came and Suhren let them take several thousand of women with them.'

'Suhren?'

'The camp chief, a name without a face for ordinary inmates like me. Irma found out he allowed the Red Cross to take prisoners of war from England, France, Denmark and Belgium. It was rumoured there were well-known women among them and Suhren was hoping that they would speak up for him later. Irma tried to persuade me to put myself forward with the other Irish.'

'There were more Irish in the camp?' Aisling found that unexpected.

'Only two. They were Irish but they were in the British army. Probably undercover agents. We managed whispers across the brick line on the building work. I was glad it wasn't easy for us to meet. I didn't want any part in the war. All through the war Ireland stayed neutral. I was afraid the Red Cross would send me to England or back to Ireland. If the war was really over, I wanted to go back to Berlin. My love affair with Germany wasn't over in spite of Hitler. I trusted Irma more than any of them, so I stayed with her. She knew they would move us all in a few days.'

'So you didn't escape?'

'Not so quick, young lady. It took time. They moved the end blocks first on 27th April. From the size of the first column,

Irma worked out that there would be at least three lots of us and we would be in the second or last. The guards were even more jumpy than usual. We hardly slept that night – more waiting and waiting, then it happened so fast. Appell was even earlier than usual. They called out the numbers of those they were moving. I listened so hard that I didn't even hear my number but Irma nodded to me. I followed her every step. We breathed the sharp air of dawn. I said goodbye to Anna when the sky turned pink over the tall pine trees. Everything was confused and disorderly leaving the camp. If you were lucky you could find some of your belongings on the tables made ready for those of us in the column. I got my bundle tied up in Delia's Sunday tablecloth – just as I had left it. The most amazing thing was the Red Cross parcel we were given as we left. We didn't even have time to open it as they marched us out. It was cumbersome to carry but the whispers of bread and sugar kept the string tied to our numb fingers.'

Aisling poured them both some water then sketched a few outlines in her book, ready to work on later. The aunt watched her but continued with her story without commenting on her drawings.

'There were about five hundred of us in our group. Even Irma had no idea where we were headed but I could see her take bearings. As the sun rose, it made the steam rise on the cool earth like a low mist. I thanked Anna's God she was dead already; she would never make it through this. The first day we walked non-stop. We were marched so fast we almost had to run, those wooden clogs flaying the skin on my feet. First we were on the main road in the direction of Neustrelitz but not for long. There was a sign KZ, which led us into the forest. Irma was happy when we crossed the train tracks. She was obsessed with trains. She needed trains to be there to reassure her she would make it back to Vienna. All day we could hear the sound of cannon from the east – the Russians. Irma liked that too. Well she would, she was a communist and saw the Russians as her allies but the Zeugen Jehovahs were more terrified than ever. At that point I didn't care about anything except putting one clog in front of the other. At times I was sorry I didn't ask to be among the Red Cross group. We had little energy or little breath to talk,' Brigitte stopped to take breath.

Aisling was afraid she would fall back into a doze and stop the story, 'and the escape..,' she prompted.

'The escape... ' Brigitte paused again, 'Well, I knew Irma was planning to use this march as a chance to escape. It was a matter of time and luck. Moving too soon meant death. Too late could mean being caught up in the last struggle with the Russians coming from the East. Even the Zeugen Jehovahs were thinking escape at this point. Irma watched and waited. One woman in our column who tried to disappear into the trees was spotted and the guard went after her and shot her on the spot. Better to wait – something would have to happen soon. Later we came close to the main road again and now we walked alongside the railway and sometimes we could see the main road full of people – German soldiers, trucks, civilians.'

Brigitte stopped to take some water and Aisling poured some more.

'I don't know to this day how Irma picked up the rumours that the Germans were planning to blow up the munitions factory at Fürstensee in the afternoon. Irma had antennae and could pick a whisper from thin air. She must have overheard the guards and understood why they marched us at such speed. We found out later the local people were told in the middle of the afternoon what would happen so they had to leave their homes. Irma's eyes were bright with warning when the time came to pass on the news. Sure enough at some time in the afternoon of 28th April, there was a sudden almighty explosion – so close everyone in our column including the guards ran for more cover among the trees. We intermingled with some local Germans who were taking refuge in the forest.'

Aisling fiddled with her pencil. Making more notes now. This part would be better told without any words. And the faces full of terror?

'Were you more afraid of the explosion or the guards?'

'There wasn't time to be afraid. Everything was so confused. We didn't know whether the guards were still with us or not, or whether they would come and shoot us on the spot for running. From the Bifos in our group, we heard some of the women guards were waiting for the chance to run away and some of the Bifos from our block had joined with them, but there were other guards ready to shoot any prisoner. Irma pushed us through exhaustion deeper and deeper into the wet marshy land. They couldn't reach us with jeeps there and it was hard for the dogs to keep track. Later in the evening a group of us collapsed on the damp ground. Irma found a spot for us to sleep on the damp earth under the trees near a lake. At first it was so welcome just to lie there and breathe in the smell of clean earth and trees but after a couple of hours, the cold woke us. We all knew by then that blowing up the munitions dump was a sure sign the war was over. We celebrated by washing our feet and our faces in the lake by moonlight. Irma pushed us to walk through the rest of the night. Sometimes a stumble on a tree root would wake me as I dozed.'

'What, you slept while you were walking along?' Aisling cocked her head to one side.

'When you are tired enough, you can sleep anywhere, even on your feet.'

Aisling wanted to tell Brigitte to wipe the trace of chocolate from the corner of her mouth. It took the edge off the drama. The march of prisoners with their German guards – right in the middle of the war with the advance of the Russians on the one side – was something to live through. A good antidote for boredom. Enough terror and heroism to match any comic but rooted too. How to get over the confusion and keep the sequence easy to follow?

'So if the Russians were coming close to you, where were the Americans and the British?'

'I don't know about the British but the next day we saw American planes in the sky. It was on the third morning when the sound of birds singing woke me, I knew something had happened. Irma was awake already. Later we learnt that by then the Russians were already at Fürstensee. So we knew either the Russians or the Americans would round up the rest of the soldiers and guards. So we were free. Free to be hungry in the middle of no-where. Free to wait for crazy guards to shoot us for fear we would incriminate them. Irma and I still had something of our Red Cross parcel and we breakfasted from that – bread sprinkled with a bit of sugar. We drank the water from the lake. We hid during the day in a hollow. Irma made us collect twigs and branches to conceal us from guards fleeing the same way. We shared the last of our Red Cross parcel. Irma was elated – the Communists were going to rebuild a better world and she would be alive to see it. She knew better than to say as much to the Bifos though, and even joined with them when they prayed in thanksgiving.'

Aisling struggled to picture this group in the woods, 'So how many of you escaped?'

'Well there were lots of groups who had done the same as us. At first, there were about thirty of us still together. Irma's clogs cut her feet and mine were in shreds but now we could stop and pad them with moss or leaves from time to time and wash our feet in the lake. When it came towards night on the third day more and more small groups split off, looking for somewhere to shelter. It was hard to sleep on the cold earth even though we were exhausted. We were left in a group of seven. Five of the Jehovah Zeugen, Irma and myself.'

Aisling twisted her hair around her fingers. She was listening but it was hypnotic, this slow unfolding of the action. Her mind wandered a little. Was it time to have her hair cut off short when she went back? Some way of marking the change of plan for her life.

Brigitte shivered, 'I can feel the special chill air of those nights in my bones even now. It was April but cold in the open air when we were wet through. Without Irma even then I could have lain down and died. I would have been happy with the freedom to die there under the open sky with no guards to kick us to death. But it took the Bratkartoffeln to make us cry.'

'Fried potatoes made you cry?'

'One evening we came to the edge of a small village. There was a small house with barns attached. Irma suggested Hannelore, one of the Bifos knock the door and ask for shelter. Irma was clever; Hannelore was a country woman and German too. The rest of us waited in the trees. Hannelore came back to tell us that an old woman came to the door who was even more terrified than we were. She could hear children whispering somewhere inside. The old woman said we could sleep the night in the barn. Later we learnt that there was an old man there too. Their son was killed on the Eastern Front and their daughter worked on the railway. They were openly relieved most of the group were not foreigners and seemed surprised to meet people not unlike themselves who spoke German. In the evening we smelt the potatoes and onions frying. Our mouths were watering as we talked about whether we dared ask them for something to eat. Then the old woman came with two large pans of fried potato and onions and put them down for us on a bale of straw. They even gave us a jug of milk. We all cried then. At first the old woman couldn't understand. 'Tut mir leid, tut mir leid,' she kept saying but whatever she was sorry for, we never really knew. She smiled when Hannelore kissed her hand and said prayers of thanks. Laughing it off with, 'Tears are good because we are short of salt.' She brought the old man – her husband – out to sit on the bale of straw. They wanted to know if Drewin had been bombed in the great explosion. They had some relations there.

'Irma was able to tell them about the munitions dump and as far as we knew there were no civilians killed. The old couple were more afraid of the Russians than prisoners or German guards and were keen for us to stay although it meant they had to share their store of potatoes. When their daughter, Dorothea, came home, she took us into the house and allowed us to sleep in their loft. I could have stayed longer but Irma was keen to move on. Dorothea was able to tell us about the railway. Many trains had stopped running but the connection to Neustrelitz had been working fine all through the war.'

Aisling flicked her hair back. She enjoyed the new sensation in her stomach. The need to get this story out, to get it to work as it was unfolding in her head. She would experiment with a long strip – mixing styles with and the sharper German graphic of "Der Erste Frühling" blended all into her the unique montage of memory. She wanted to pin down this reality.

'Can you show me on a map where you were?' she asked.

'Maps! Maps indeed,' Brigitte sent out a snort of smoke. 'Katharina has maps. She wanted to go there to walk in the woods. She wanted me show her on the map where we walked but what do I know of maps? She went anyway. She got her pass to cross the border even before the wall came down. I followed her to the crossing point at Friedrichstraße to watch her queue there. It was the first time I spotted the Jules. I wanted to watch her leave me because I thought she might never come back. When she came back she made it sound so easy. 'We took a train to Fürstenberg,' she told me. 'We?' I asked – 'who's we?' 'My friend, Monika,' she said it as if she had told me but she hadn't. 'We had a beautiful Spring day in the woods,' she said. 'But it was eerie too. Like a graveyard.' I told her I had seen enough of those woods when we were marched out of that place. They didn't make it to Wesenberg – it took longer than they planned and they had to get back across the border.'

'So what was at Wesenberg?'

'Wesenberg is where Irma led us after our stay with the old people. We couldn't impose on them anymore and Irma was impatient for news. Seven more mouths to feed were too many. Before we left we helped them plant a field of potatoes and laughed with them about the day we would come back again for the best Bratkartoffeln ever when the crop would be ready. The village where they lived had only a few houses.

Below something it was called. Katharina could tell you. Neustrelitz was north from it and Wesenberg west. Dorothea told us Hitler had committed suicide on the last day of April but the Nazis were still in control of Wesenberg even then. Many of the people of Wesenberg had left their homes and fled in those days because they knew that the Red Army was very close.'

Aisling sketched more images in her head – the Red Army was a good ambiguous image, 'So how long did the Germans let you stay with them?'

'Irma was our scout and went out alone every day to find out what she could. She kept her prisoner dress on but with a coat over it – just in case there were some SS guards also hiding in the woods. One day she spotted some Red Army soldiers with a horse and wagon searching the woods. It was proof that the Red Army had reached Wesenberg. Irma convinced us that it was safe to go there – even for the Bifos. So we walked there – it was already 2nd May and summer was in the air. We had dry clothes and nights were getting warm. We were in high spirits and joined with the Bifos singing hymns while we were still in the woods.'

Aisling grinned as she made more sketches. How to get the image of these half-starved women – a Catholic, a communist and some Jehovah's Witnesses singing in the woods?

'So you made it to Wesenberg?'

'At first Wesenberg looked a bit like a ghost town except for the Red Army of course. A group of soldiers in a jeep challenged us but we explained we were prisoners and Irma showed them her red triangle. They directed us to an empty house where we could stay. We waited there while Irma went with them to the Commandant. On her way to speak to the

Commandant Irma found out many houses were taken over by women from the first column. Some women whispered of how the soldiers were crazy for women. Irma advised us to wear our prison dresses and hide our hair for protection. We were pitiful enough looking but that alone might not be enough. We heard stories telling us nothing was a protection in the first days, so we were lucky we had stayed in the woods. Maybe Irma being a Communist protected us. Who knows?

They gave her a small haversack filled with bread, sausage, potatoes and even a bottle of wine. We made our own feast and exchanged stories with some of our neighbours from the Lager. A strange reunion. Were we prisoners again or free? We didn't really know. I thought we would be trapped again. The Red Army Commandant had been impressed by Irma's knowledge of Russian and insisted that she work with them as interpreter. She couldn't say no. So much for freedom I thought. But they rewarded her well with food for all of us in return and Irma said it was too soon yet to go to Berlin. There was still fighting there. We stayed two weeks in Wesenberg.'

'And have you ever been back in Wesenberg since then?' Aisling asked.

'Never,' Brigitte was emphatic, 'and I have no desire to go there. One of the best things about the GDR was the wall they put between me and those memories. After 1989, Katharina would ask me every summer if I would go there with her: "Monika can take us in her car, Mama, you don't have to go hiking." Monika and her car indeed! I never understood why she wanted to take me with her.'

Aisling shrugged in sympathy to the dead Katharina, 'It's part of your history and hers too. She probably wanted to understand you better.'

Brigitte looked at her, 'I'm her mother: what more does she need to know than that? She wasn't even born then.'

'There you are. She wasn't born but she was there..' Aisling searched for an old-fashioned way to finish saying what she meant, 'She was on her way, wasn't she?' No wonder Katharina got frustrated. Brigitte could be so stubborn and secretive.

'I didn't know. No-one in the Lager had their monthly bleeding.'

'You didn't know then so now you try to hang on to secrets that are no secret any more. Makes a lot of sense that does.'

'Irma wouldn't say if we were free or not when I pestered her. I knew that Irma didn't tell her Red Army boss we were leaving but I said nothing. Now it was just the two of us. No need for anyone else to know. It was too difficult anyway to say goodbye. We left by bicycle very early in the morning for Neustrelitz. Irma had claimed the bicycles from behind the hotel used as Red Army headquarters. She still insisted we wear our prison dresses – now clean and crisp and headscarves too. They might still offer protection and we would save the civilian clothes that we had 'borrowed' from our absent hosts in Wesenburg. We went straight to Neustrelitz station. There was no timetable and we had no idea how many trains there were so we sat in the sun and had some bread from our Red Army rations and waited. It took a lot of waiting and two changes to reach Berlin but we made it.'

Brigitte paused and within minutes her head sank onto her chest. Aisling left her to it – the last thing she wanted was to help to put her to bed.

Chapter Nineteen

# Post War Letters

Berlin 18<sup>th</sup> September 1945

Dear Mary,

*My mother wrote and told me you had your first child, a boy. I'm sorry not to have celebrated your wedding or the birth. The last few months I have been too tired to write. My congratulations and good wishes. I am a mother now too, the mother of a baby girl. I hope you had an easier time in childbirth.*

*Katharina was born on 8<sup>th</sup> September at 9 o'clock. When the child was coming I felt it like the flesh was being torn from my bones for hour after hour. Then it was past – the sweet relief when you knew you could do nothing more and nothing else. I could cradle her so small, so healthy, and so beautiful. The memory makes me cry still. I wasn't ready for the head of black hair and the old woman's face with the dark eyes. Mine and only mine from my own flesh. A tiny bloody bundle. Her little face screams past the images of war. She has marched through my flesh and replaced the procession of death.*

*Down there hurts badly too but it is strange to feel a pain which doesn't make me miserable. I feel happy sitting here in a clean bed with the child lying sleeping beside me. I have a good neighbour, Adelheid, who found a big old drawer for the* baby to sleep in. I met her when we stacked bricks together. I already slept to-day so I am not tired. Another day of rest and then I go to work for the Americans but I want to write to you first.

I baptised Katharina myself while Adelheid was seeing the old woman off with her bottle of brandy – the last remnant of the booty from the apartment that cost us so much energy to drag through the ruins of Berlin. The apartment was a safer hiding place than the cellar after all. No-one dared climb what was left of the stairs – not even the Russians. People say that the Russians didn't like going into apartments that were too high up anyway. It was the women in cellars or in the first floor apartments who suffered most in those first days of the Russians. Thank God to have been saved that fate.

We learnt in school baptism can be carried out in emergencies, didn't we? During the war, it was hard at times to keep any faith. Katharina is a name I heard and liked the sound of. I should call her Adelheid because of the kindness my friend has shown me. She was there the whole time better than any family. She found an old woman from somewhere to help her. A mid-wife? I didn't ask. I didn't want a doctor and they were too hard to find anyway. I focussed on the meaning behind Adelheid's German words to distract me from that pain. 'I've done it three times and it doesn't get easier I tell you but you forget the pain after, I promise you – until the next time!' I welcomed the pain. It fuelled my defiance of all and everyone who would deny me Katharina. I don't give a fig for what the family or neighbours in Ireland would think because she had no father. Katharina's father is already married so I will not tell him.

While in labour, I cursed all the armies that marched

*through Berlin in foul language I didn't even know I knew. Adelheid and the old woman cheered me on. They knew that I was cursing even if they didn't understand the words. I haven't told my mother about Katharina yet. I will keep this letter until I write to her.*

*Many will think the worst of me, but Katharina is my joy. Please tell no-one else, it would hurt my parents. I will never bring Katharina to Ireland to shame them. The shame is only mine. Katharina will never miss her father. I will be father and mother to her.*

*I have a new job working for the Americans. Speaking English is a big advantage. God forgive me for telling them I speak German. I know only a little but more than they do.*

*Your friend, Biddy*

*1ˢᵗ November 1945*
*Dear Mary,*
*The feast of all Saints or is it all Souls, I've forgotten which is which but the memory of winter nights at the chapel clings to me like damp autumn mist — going outside to pray, then inside the chapel, going out again. Each visit earning grace for the souls in purgatory — naming the names of my grandparents, aunts, uncles, my little cousin who died of pneumonia. It's a far cry from my life here, where I rarely see the inside of any church.*

*I haven't had the heart to post my letters to you yet. It is not fair to burden you with my secrets. I will write until the paper runs out. When I have time. Caring for my Katharina and working for the Americans leaves me little time for writing letters or for thinking of the past. I wasn't ready for the rush of love that lifts my step every day when I pick her up from*

Adelheid's. I am sure no mother ever had such love as I have. It feels sinful to take such pleasure in her. My love is stronger than any feeling that I ever had before. I could have my pick of the American soldiers but I run from them — home to Katharina.

I rarely leave her in my free time but to-day I made an exception. I went back to visit the bookseller. I haven't been there since Katharina was born but I asked Adelheid to keep her this afternoon. Katharina cried all night last night as if she was testing my love for her. Even so I left her with Adelheid. To-day I have a free afternoon. I will go alone to a bookshop I know. I tell myself it is for a book on German grammar but I know I will look at the photographs of Hamburg the bookseller keeps hidden in a drawer. He takes them out only for those who question him in such a way that he can recognise that you too have a part of your memory that is like a bit of charred wood. Each time I go I swear I will never go back but my feet lead me back in spite of myself. Like a drunk going back to his hidden bottle of whiskey. Maybe it is a way of burying my secrets and my memories — putting them back in the drawer with those photographs.

It helps to look at German people who suffered much more than I did. Even though it was a couple of months since I was last there, the bookseller didn't ask what I wanted. After he has passed the time of day and said something about the weather, he passes me the envelope. I feel somehow dirty in spite of the compassion in his eyes. It takes one to know one. We both know that his mind is burnt by the firebombs that took his home, his wife and his two boys. Such a mind cannot make the connection between memories of life before and life after. You have to split your mind and start again as if such

227

*memories come only from fantasy — some crazy story that is too impossible to be true. If you don't do that, you can go crazy yourself. I am thankful for the bombs and fires in Berlin which burnt many holes in my memory. Such images do not belong in the light of day in the time before or after.*

*I say 'their' and 'they' for those days. I cannot say 'our' homes and neighbours. Memories and questions that stayed in some dark hole while I was in the camp creep back now in the shadows of the evening light in our apartment. Sweetmeats that were offered sometimes in that place. From where did they come? Anna refused them always even as a gift. The old man who came one day to whisper to the butcher — and then came no more. Before he left to look for work or food in Brandenburg, he told his wife that he had left enough bear meat with the butcher to last until he came back. But he never came back and some said it was not bear meat that he left — it was too tough. I am not sorry we can afford very little meat. Even the sausage that I put in the lentil soup brings the smell of darkness and the wet wool of an overcoat. Sometimes I see another face on Katharina's.*

*It is a comfort to write to you. I doubt I will ever tell another living soul. Perhaps one day.*

*Your good friend, Biddy*

Aisling fingered the rest of the pages — all left blank. So what happened to the friend Mary in Ireland? Did they ever meet again? Were there other letters posted? She felt let down now. Questions with no answers. Now Aisling would have to burn it for her — or bury it. She felt a rush of pity for the old woman. The baby that she had suffered for and probably sacrificed a lot for was dead. No wonder she wanted to put the pages in the

228

coffin with her. Sixty years' worth of Katharina gone as if she never existed. Left only with memories and ghosts.

Brigitte didn't even have religion. Without an afterlife then all the bits of Katharina that made up her life just fell apart now. Her computer with its empty files – wiped clean for Brigitte. The books on the shelf – some of them with an article by Katharina – they looked pretty boring. She would never be famous and live on in people's memories. It was the little things that Aisling found spooky – like the hairbrush in the bathroom – she knew without anyone telling her that the hairs in it belonged to Katharina. How long would it sit there until someone binned it? Would it have to wait until Brigitte died or was dragged off to a nursing home? Brigitte would kill herself rather than let that happen. Aisling agreed with her there. She would rather commit suicide than go to one of those nursing homes full of old, sick and half-dead people.

And why wait? Now she had a glimpse of why Michael did it. Memories of some of those weird conversations they had sometimes pushed their way back. What was the point of stuffing your life full of things you wanted to see, to do, to eat, to wear, to hear – only to see it all disintegrate back to meaningless crap when you weren't there to hold it together. Gawd, she was getting so morbid stuck in this apartment with Brigitte! She'd be working out a suicide pact with her soon. She was glad of the drawing. She needed something to keep her from losing it.

She would show some of them to Brigitte. It had felt good to be working on the rough ideas while the old woman talked. How to work the layers of the story together? She needed to study sequences to help her develop her own style based on montage. There could be nothing casual about it. Sometimes maybe like layers of a hologram. She wanted to do more graphics. Give up the course in Dublin. Why not look around for a graphic art course in Berlin? She could stay with the aunt until she got a place of her own. Somewhere Matt could come to stay when he came back to Germany.

She fell asleep but woke again out of a dream where someone was holding her head under water. No sound from Brigitte's room, probably in the bathroom. Aisling waited to hear her call out, 'Das Badezimmer ist frei.'

## Chapter Twenty

# Arrest

Aisling laughed aloud. It was the look on Brigitte's face that killed her. Evil – the killer instinct. The poor fly didn't stand a chance. Brigitte was up and out of her chair without the usual palaver of support from her stick, aiming her weapon of destruction. Where did that come from? Reminding her of parts of Brigitte's story still missing. She had a way of deflecting attention until and if she was ready to share something. How did she end up in Ravensbrück? Was she really as naïve as she made out? She was so secretive all these years; surely she must be guilty of something? Speculation. Did she kill someone? She didn't kill the unborn child she carried as Aisling had. Avoid the pit that opens there. So many stories of women who had good reasons for termination. Terminator not murderer. Mum said those holy gracies who claimed abortion as murder were total hypocrites. A fertilised sperm is not a person. Whose right to life? The church with all its abusing clerics ruining lives and hiding it. How did they dare come out against a woman's right to choose?

'You're not very keen on flies, are you?' Aisling said for something to say Brigitte turned on her, 'You are just like Katharina. "What harm in a fly or two?" she would say. "They die in a day or two anyway, so why cut their short lives shorter?

Those sprays you buy to kill them are likely to do you more harm than one or two flies." I keep my own counsel on that. Who knows what they have been feeding on last?'

Aisling was distracted by dodging the fly spray, otherwise she would have considered a mild correction of the tense. Time to face the end. Time to use the past tense when talking about the daughter but she turned it into, 'So why do you?'

'Why what?'

'So why do you hate flies so much?' Aisling was a dab hand now, as her father would say, at Brigitte-style conversation. She could keep the thread of Brigitte's thoughts even when she lost it herself. Just repeat something in the right way and she would pick up the tune again. Generating more images in Aisling's head than she had time to sketch out. Brigitte did not answer right away and Aisling wondered if she had dozed off again in the silence – still holding the can loosely in her hand.

Aisling wriggled on the sofa. It was the original 70s style – low and well-padded in imitation leather. Did she dare put her feet up or nick the footrest from its place near Brigitte's chair. It wasn't as if it was in use at the moment but the movement might wake her again. Then Brigitte's head lifted and her voice came clear and flat as if from a distance like an old-fashioned radio.

'You would hate them too if you had lived through those days of death. Even when the war was over, there were flies, flies and more flies. We scrubbed and scrubbed in every spare moment and still they would come from nowhere – mocking our efforts to be clean. They treated the dirt and destruction of our lovely Berlin as their special feast. I couldn't stand it.'

They had this day to kill before the fuss of the funeral took over. Both were tired. Aisling had woken several times in the night – lights on in the hallway – loo flushing. Brigitte hadn't slept much at all. Aisling dozed again after she heard the bustle of Yola arriving, helping with washing, dressing. They had both spun breakfast out as long as possible – the ritual for getting Brötchen was well established and Brigitte still had a good appetite for an old woman, even on the eve of her daughter's funeral. Now even that distraction was gone and Yola with it. Aisling's unasked question burned a hole in the paper: what had Brigitte done to warrant ending up in Ravensbrück?'

She fiddled about with another Gran-type foot-rest thing she had spotted in the corner – manoeuvring it with as little movement as possible to get her feet on it. If this was Ireland there would be action: somebody would be fetching people from the airport; somebody would be at least talking about how to make sure everybody got a bite to eat. She could remember her shock that her mother could think thoughts like that with Michael lying in the coffin beside her. Her mother didn't leave the coffin except to go to the loo or wash herself. She moved to the armchair at night and slept there – ignoring her dad's entreaties to come to bed. She even gave up on her make-up because her tears kept washing it all off. If this was Ireland, Auntie Betty would be off to get her some waterproof mascara for the funeral.

Death didn't stop people in the way you would expect. You'd think that things should be different when someone dies. Everything. At first it's like that. You hear a clock ticking you never noticed before – like that damn brass monstrosity on top of Brigitte's sideboard. When Michael died, she felt strange just brushing her teeth. It felt like an insult to the dead person to do normal things. But it didn't last. Now she didn't think of him first thing when she woke up. Even so, she was sure she

missed Michael more than any of them even if it was her fault..
He was the only one she could say something like that to. The
only one who would notice the same things. And she didn't
even know it until he wasn't there. His photo on the wall –
with the naff thing under it for flowers would mock her too –
Mum and her bloody altars. Saint Bloody Michael was no saint.
Would it make a difference to Mum if she knew everything?

Here there was no last minute shopping to do. She'd hung
her funeral rig up on the day that she arrived. All she had to do
was step into it. Now they had time to kill and why not kill a
few flies to pass the time and cut the mockery. No-one to feed
or meet or drag out of the pub and sober up. It was a pity really
that her Dad had discouraged his Uncle Mick from making the
trip. He would have provided a bit of distraction and Aisling
would have the job of finding him and sobering him up.

'Uncle Mick would have come if Dad had helped him, you
know,' she said aloud. 'He came for Michael's funeral.'

'Your Dad's right. Mick's not fit and he would have been
more of a worry than a comfort. He's never been further than
England anyway. Even the trip back home is too much for him
these days. Can you imagine him surviving in a Kneipe here?'

'Well I can actually, I think he'd have little bother with that
end of things,' Aisling retorted.

Brigitte rattled an attempted laugh in her throat, 'You're
right, it would be getting him out that would be the trouble.
Besides Mick would cry and Katharina would have hated that.'

Brigitte did not want Mick's tears either. He sobbed like a
baby with tears bumping down his spread-eagled pink nose when
they were putting their mother in the ground. John-Joe
muttered to Marion, 'The beer has to come out somewhere' and
she muttered back, 'Maybe he would cry less if he had visited

more.' John-Joe now sitting in his own chimney corner – by an oil-fired Aga in the big house on the hill – passing judgement and waited on hand and foot by Marion. They weren't the sort to put themselves out even if they were fit enough. Their four children were all in the States. They flew in together for their granny's funeral, stayed in a hotel at Dublin airport, hired a car and drove up and flew back again the day after. Brigitte had the feeling that they were glad to be out of reach.

'What about your brother James?' Aisling asked. She remembered that he lived in Boston. Granny had a card from him every Christmas – with one of those letters about what his children, his grandchildren and his great-grandchildren were doing. Granny would read bits to her father. She would sniff then, 'Fancy photos and letters are all very well but you never heard what happened to his American wife and none of them came back even once with him to visit.'

Brigitte's tone in response to Aisling's question was matter-of-fact: 'Don't forget he is two years older than me. I won't be going to the States for his funeral, never mind the funeral of one of his children.' Brigitte could see him in the doorway – James, stiff and upright, carrying a cane to hide the weakness of his bad knee. He was probably still fit enough but he wouldn't travel to a funeral of someone he didn't know at all. She respected that and wouldn't ask him. 'The only one that I miss here is Liam,' she added.

'Which one is he?' Aisling asked, 'I don't remember him at Michael's funeral.

'Peggy said he didn't go. He doesn't have much time for her or for your father either. There was a bit of a falling out after our mother died.'

'Is he the one that lives near Gran's old cottage?'

'Yes. That's what the fall-out was about. At some point Peggy persuaded our father to leave the cottage to her and it only came out after our mother died. Liam was mortified. He was the one who farmed the land and was the one who looked after our mother and father more than any of us. The cottage should have been his by rights. The rest of us thought that Peggy would give it up but your father then got involved with solicitors and what not. Liam never spoke to him after.'

'Well he's right, if Gran did nothing all those years. But my father said Liam would just let the old house fall into the ground if it was up to him and it was Gran who put a bit of money into maintaining it over the years.'

'Your father has a point there, but I think it was Liam's feelings that were hurt more than anything. I told him that it was so long ago that the old folks had probably forgotten but he felt otherwise.'

Aisling wondered why her parents had never revealed this bit of drama. When they'd talked about Liam, they just said he was as odd as two left shoes and should be ignored. Aisling decided to speak to him the next time she was up there – even if he did ignore her. She liked the idea of getting the story of the family feud from his point of view. She wished he were here now. Anything to relieve the boredom of a wake that was no wake. Worth a try – ask her the burning question.

'You never did tell me how you ended up in the camp. What did you do? Did you fight against Hitler?'

Laughing to choke at the question. 'Me fight Hitler! Maybe Katharina would have been proud of me if I had. Not me. A simple no-body in the wrong place at the wrong time Sure wasn't I a foreigner? I was lucky enough that it took as long as it did to arrest me. They wanted to question Delia.'

'Delia?'

'The woman I worked for. I loved my job. I was part of the family. I stayed in Berlin because I wanted my job back when the family came back to Berlin. I was afraid if I went back to Ireland, I'd lose the chance and be forced to stay on the farm.'

'But the war?'

'I was sure Hitler would win the war. Nobody expected the Americans to come in on the side of Britain. I didn't expect it to last very long.'

'So what did Delia do?'

'Nothing, none of us did anything. I stayed in Berlin when Delia took the children to Bavaria. They must've known. When the Gestapo came, I showed them my papers. I was naïve enough to think they would do nothing to me because I was an Irish citizen and Ireland wasn't in the war. Maybe if I had been able to speak better German they wouldn't have taken me for interrogation. I told them everything I knew. I gave them Delia's address in Bavaria. I told them Delia's husband was a doctor in the army. They asked the same questions again and again and I told them everything again and again. They showed me photographs. I recognised one man who was friendly with Dieter. It was a long time later when I found out Herr von Trott, the dinner party guest, was involved in a plot to assassinate Hitler. At the time I heard only about the attempted assassination when Herr Schmidt, the blockwart, celebrated the survival of our great leader. I don't know how they found out Herr von Trott was a dinner guest in the years before the war. Maybe Herr Schmidt. They must have believed whatever Dieter told them because he was never even interrogated – Delia neither. They couldn't place me. So it was safer to put me away. Once there, you couldn't expect it to make sense. There was neither rhyme nor reason to the camp. Towards the end of the war, everything was more chaotic. Anybody that looked for some meaning in it wouldn't last long, I can tell you. You had to make your own way through it – one day at a time. What am I saying? More like one hour at a time.'

Brigitte took a tissue out of the packet that sat on the table beside her chair and carefully sealed the packet again. Aisling watched now as Brigitte put the tissues back in their place – beside the bar of chocolate.

## Chapter Twenty-One

# Alter St.-Matthäus –Kirchhof

'I want to go there before Katharina.'

The aunt made this announcement as if Aisling knew what she was talking about. Aisling was tired of playing mind-reader. Had she totally lost the plot? Go where? A suicide attempt? Or was it gaga speaking? Go to Ireland? Go to Karstadt? Go to deepest Peru? She stopped her own little thought merry-go-round. When she spoke she heard herself sound like her father humouring Gran, 'Where was it you wanted to go? I missed it.'

Lunch was cleared away and Aisling had decided that now was the time to make her escape for the rest of the day before the big event so she warned herself to tread carefully.

'I want to go there to see for myself what Monika has arranged for Katharina.'

Aisling covered her mouth to hide the smile. So it was Monika now. That was progress. No longer was Brigitte calling Monika 'that Jules.' She must mean go to the church or the graveyard.

'So what has Monika arranged?' Aisling was glad of the chance to ask. Brigitte hadn't relayed the content of Monika's visit the previous day and she wasn't sure what to expect at the funeral.

'The remains will be delivered to the chapel and there will be a service there before Katharina is buried in *their* grave.' Aisling noted that the emphasis on *their* was hardly noticeable now – another sign that there might be a move to a bit more reconciliation with Monika.

'So where's the chapel?' she asked. She'd been wondering what sort of service but Monika and Brigitte were so prickly about everything it seemed safer not to ask.

'There's a chapel in the graveyard. That's where I want to go. A pastor will lead the service – a woman who is some friend of Katharina's. I didn't know she had any friends like that.' Brigitte's tone was quite flat and resigned. No sign of any spitting anger this afternoon. She looked older too – and defeated.

Aisling felt quite perky but hid it as best she could. Brigitte clearly didn't think it odd to have a woman pastor. There was no drama in her tone about that. This was clearly no funeral in the grand Irish style. Coffins, queues and a funeral Mass that was so long, you were jumping for joy with relief by the time it came to bury someone. A very different funeral experience would be interesting to take home.

'Tomorrow Monika and her brother will take us there but I would like to go there to-day.' Brigitte didn't wheedle but it was clear that she wasn't going to take the trip on her own and was asking Aisling for support.

Aisling felt rising resentment. 'Wait up, Brigitte,' she thought, 'you don't catch me out so easily. I'm not your daughter or servant or anybody else whose strings you can pull.' She said nothing for a moment then asked very casually, 'Where and how exactly?' with her head cocked sideways, biding her time.

'Well, I thought I could order a taxi to take us there and he would pick us up again after a short time.'

Aisling noted the 'us' and weighed it up. A quick look at a graveyard wasn't going to take more than ten minutes, so why not? She could hop out of the taxi on the way back at a convenient point and Brigitte would be ready for one of her dozes.

'So let's get cracking,' she said and saw Brigitte's eyebrows lift dramatically opening her face again. Brigitte rang right away and moved as fast as she could but they were barely ready by the time the taxi arrived. Aisling had forgotten just how long it took her to do simple things.

When she heard Brigitte give the name of their destination, Alter St.-Matthäus-Kirchhof, she had a blast of missing Matt. He'd enjoy hearing that the graveyard had his name. Maybe they would get a chance to be together in Berlin sometime. Brigitte prattled on a bit about living in Schöneberg before the war. The taxi-driver clearly knew Brigitte and was happy to humour her especially when she asked him to drive around Schöneberg to where she used to live before going to the cemetery. They stopped in the street where the house was bombed and Brigitte insisted they get out and read a sort of memorial sign which said stuff about Jews living in this street. Brigitte nodded and said, 'The Goldmanns.' Nothing more but with a satisfied tone. A sign still there – a reminder of the horrors hidden by what looked like a normal street.

Finally they were at the entrance to the cemetery. The taxi-driver explained there was a café where he could meet them. Aisling looked pointedly at her watch. This ten minute trip was turning into a marathon. She spotted the café beside a little shop selling flowers. Brigitte promised coffee and cake after they found the grave. Aisling grinned to herself – coffee and cake in a cemetery – another story worth telling back in Dublin. She wished she'd brought a sketch pad or camera.

Brigitte headed straight for a grave where there was another old woman planting flowers. Aisling took the chance to stroll around. She came across the Grimm brothers. Not far away a big gay grave. Matt would have kicked her for thinking, 'how appropriate' so she didn't but mentally winked at him and wondered how he was doing. She was impressed at the blend of old and modern in this corner. There was lots of genuine stuff about people who had died of AIDS. Tasteful.

She rejoined Brigitte who was deep in conversation with the other old woman. Both of them leaning on their sticks – putting the world to rights or talking about the weather. No, not the weather, 'Wurzeln'. Aisling searched her vocabulary – nothing to do with death or the weather. The sight of the plant reminded her – 'roots' – and she realised then why Brigitte looked pleased. She was getting confirmation that tree roots really did cause a problem in some graves. The old woman knew the grave of Monika's family – one of the old graves – one that was properly looked after. She told them some of the old graves, which were no longer in use, had new people buried in them. That explained one of the graves Aisling had found where there was a tribute to someone who was clearly transsexual right in the middle of a grave from yonks ago.

The old woman pointed with her stick to the memorial for the German resistance fighters. That was a trigger for Brigitte to give Aisling the general gist of the story about Germans who had tried to kill Hitler in 1944. The resistance were buried first in the graveyard but the Nazis had them dug up and cremated in the next borough to humiliate them. Another possible sequence to add to Brigitte's story because Von Trott ,who had dined with Delia and Dieter, was part of the resistance. It would be cool to have a cemetery sequence in her graphics. She'd have to come back with a camera.

When they found Monika's family grave, there was a hole dug, ready and waiting. Aisling could imagine Monika kneeling there and felt a pang for her. She looked at Brigitte, surely that would elicit a bit of sympathy. It was time somebody banged their heads together. They were obviously the ones who grieved most for Katharina. You'd think they could share it more.

Next stop the chapel. Brigitte nodded her approval at the neo-Romanic style and the empty platform covered in black – ready for the urn. Aisling was surprised to find the walls and wooden pews breathed resignation and peace. Good choice, Monika. Surely there was nothing Brigitte could take offence over. Brigitte looked at her watch. Time for coffee and cake in the café. The tables outside were full. Stepping inside, they blinked into the shade for a couple of minutes before what looked more like an old-fashioned lacy living room than a cafe took shape before them. A young friendly Christian type was shuttling coffee and cake from the little kitchen and helped Brigitte into a seat.

Not a likely place to find tourists. It was worth an entry in an alternative guide. Brigitte was silent. She ate the coffee and cake as if she was absorbing everything around her. The cake was a sort of lemony cheese cake. It tasted good and was clearly home-made. When they left, the taxi-driver was waiting as promised. Aisling had lost the urge to be dropped off somewhere. She promised herself time out after Abendbrot instead.

## Chapter Twenty-Two

# Funeral and Beer

Sinful sunshine – the words came into Aisling's mind uninvited. Sinful – a word that sounded like it was sent from Gran who had already rung this morning to say that she was having a special Mass said in the local church and would go there with Dad in memory of Katharina. Brigitte sat at one end of the breakfast table without tears and Aisling sat at the other end of the breakfast table watching the sunshine make patterns on the white cloth – strong enough sunshine to mock the transparent shade of the window's voile cloak. It wasn't the sunshine's fault that Katharina was dead so why did it seem disrespectful?

The early lunch was already cleared away. Yola had been and gone. She would come to the funeral but she would travel there herself. Aisling couldn't work out if it suited her or if she was pulling back to allow space for the family.

Brigitte watched the clock, 'Why is she not here yet? It is 1 o' clock already.'

'It's only five past twelve,' Aisling had to point out. She wished again for more of Brigitte's family. The phone calls yesterday evening from her brother Joe and even James from America had helped.

'Uncle Liam didn't ring yesterday, did he?'

'He hates the phone. It makes him stammer. I hope I die before him; I'd hate not to make it to his funeral. If I do die before him, I should make sure they don't tell him until it is too late to come to my funeral. Tell them. Tell who?' she sighed.

'Where is Monika?' she said for the 100th time.

Monika had insisted she would come to pick them up and came bang on 1 o' clock as arranged. At least Monika looked the part – she looked like death warmed up in spite of the 28 degrees. Her brother, in a dark navy BMW, was their chauffeur to-day. Just back from his holiday, his relaxed tan jarred with his black suit and tie. Aisling could see his reflection in the driver's mirror, the crown of beads of perspiration on his forehead. Brigitte had never met the brother either so that helped ease the tension between her and Monika. He was leaning on the car waiting and came forward to shake their hands before ushering them into the back seat. After some words of sympathy, he apologised for his poor English. Yet on the drive there he proceeded to offer more fluent English to the collective conversation than anyone else.

She felt stilted. It wasn't her clothes: the black dress her mother had selected for her was perfect. She worried a bit about her legs. It was too hot to wear tights – funeral or no funeral – but she was sure there were streaks in the self-tanning lotion that she had smeared on last night to try to soften the whiteness of her legs against the black. She'd decided to put the imitation Phillip Treacy headgear in her hair after all. Her auntie Liz had given it to her the day before she left –'I'll never be able to look at it again without crying about Michael.'

'Thanks a bunch,' Aisling had thought, 'So what about me?' Today she felt like she was going to Michael's funeral again so why not wear it? Her mother had insisted she bring it and found a suitable cardboard roll so that it didn't get squashed in her rucksack. 'You don't know what the Germans are like when it comes to funerals – maybe everyone has to wear a hat and this way you don't have to go out looking for one at the last minute.'

Brigitte wasn't the hat wearing type in any situation – a pity really because she looked formidable in the black suit. She looked even more mannish than usual in the black jacket and white shirt underneath, in spite of the skirt in place of her usual trousers. Yola had insisted on taking the aunt to the hairdresser's first thing ignoring Brigitte's insistence that Katharina wasn't there to care and Yola could do it perfectly well at home. Aisling had heard Yola whisper something about her family from Ireland. She knew how to press buttons, Yola did. Brigitte's hair had a bit more body than usual and it lifted her broad face.

There was stand with an urn on it. Of course, the ashes. Aisling followed Brigitte and placed her hand on the urn too. She was glad of Auntie Liz's waterproof mascara when the unexpected tears came. The service was led by a dykey-looking woman in a trouser suit who looked more like a lesbian than Monika, but then so did Brigitte. Aisling felt a smile at the corners of her mouth which helped keep the tears away. She wondered whether the aunt would feel betrayed or not if she caught that Jules thought. What the hell, she'd be gone anyway in a couple of days.

Monika escorted them to the front pew. The chapel looked bigger with all the seats full. The full seats surprised her. She had pictured a service with themselves only – a kind of secret burial on foreign soil. Maybe Monika even had a wake without telling them. No, of course not, there was no place for the neighbours, the casual acquaintances, or friends of the family calling at the wake to pay a few respects. Here if you wanted to mark the death, you went to the funeral. These must be Katharina's friends.

There were readings – a bit from some Pastor Niemoller. With a name like that he must be German but Monika read it first in English and introduced it as one of Katharina's favourite pieces of writing. At first Aisling thought it was a prayer which would be a bit odd given Katharina was clearly an atheist. Then she realised that it was obviously guilty stuff for what Germans did to the Jews but in the circumstances, listening to it from the aunt's position, it came over really differently.

Whatever way you looked at it, it was tough on the aunt. No wonder there was an unusual gulp from the seat beside her. No tears or tissues though. The black guy who read the Nelson Mandela bit was a better choice. The bit about letting your light shine was a bit soppy but it gave room for a broad enough interpretation of God to suit nearly anyone. A couple of others were short poems in German. The organ music played classical pieces in between –long enough and short enough to match the poetry. It seemed a short step from that to the final words of the dykey pastor and following Monika past the unfamiliar faces out into the sunshine and towards the grave. Or rather following Monika and Brigitte as Monika had engineered Brigitte to walk beside her and checked every few seconds to ensure an equal pace. Both of them stood side by side at the grave after the pastor said the final ashes to ashes bit.

Two pillars of pain stood there waiting. The friends stood around them looking uncertain. Monika had explained to Aisling in the car the German ritual was for everyone to go for coffee and cake after the funeral and she had given directions in the chapel at the end of the service. Aisling hadn't grasped where the coffee and cake would be served but she guessed that it was unlikely to be in the little cafe they had visited the day before.

Meanwhile they loitered at the grave. There were a few of Katharina's friends who hugged Brigitte as if they knew her but Brigitte muttered only, 'Thank you for coming' in English whether she knew them or not and whether they spoke to her in German or English. Aisling stood beside her shaking hands with anyone who offered and saying as little as possible. It was the one part of the whole funeral that really reminded her of Michael's. Did they do this usually at German funerals she wondered, or was it Monika's concession to the Irish dimension? At least it didn't take as long as the endless queues at Michael's funeral and there was nothing like the guard of honour from his college to embarrass everyone to death.

Monika was organising lifts for those who had come by public transport to wherever the coffee and cake was offered. She suggested that Brigitte and Aisling use her brother's services as chauffeur again and was clearly shocked when Brigitte announced that they would take a taxi home

'Then we will take you home,' Monika blurted it out. You could see that she wanted to hang onto Brigitte as long as possible as a way of keeping Katharina with her a bit longer. It had clearly never occurred to her that Brigitte would not come. Aisling wanted to give her lessons – insist, don't listen to her, pretend she hasn't said it but that was the Irish way and probably would not work with Brigitte.

'I have arranged a taxi,' Brigitte had the battle-axe expression firmly installed and headed towards the gate where there was indeed a taxi waiting. She must have arranged it yesterday.

'As you say,' Monika's face reddened — as if she had been given a good slap. She looked almost attractive as she stood under the sunshine, which insisted on finding ways through the flickering green of the trees above.

Aisling wanted to say, 'Take Monika home with you, for God's sake and leave me free to go off with the tasty looking brother who looks even better with the loose tie and the jacket over his shoulder. I'd be happy for him to take my mind off things.' But she stayed silent.

In the taxi, she heard the aunt ask in German if he knew Café Buchwald in Moabit. He did.

'I thought we were going home,' she asked puzzled.

'That was only to put Monika off. We're going for Coffee and Cake.'

The streak of nastiness in this gesture made Aisling smile in spite of herself. She was going to miss the old dear when she left Berlin.

'You don't think that maybe you should call a truce with Monika? You might be glad of her some day.'

'Glad of her: after what she's done to Katharina,' Brigitte practically spat it out.

'Well, the cancer's hardly her fault, is it?'

'Maybe not, but something caused it.'

Aisling gave up: it's not my war she thought. Let them be.

Café Buchwald was like taking a trip in a time-machine back a few decades.

Less retro than the cemetery but retro enough in its own way. The tables and tablecloths, the armchairs were similar style to the stuff in the aunt's living room. It didn't take a lot to work out that this was a favourite hangout for the aunt and Katharina. The aunt even met a couple of old ladies that she knew from the old days who engaged in a conversation about the funeral.

While she was talking to them, Aisling studied the cakes. The Germans certainly knew how to do cakes. The display was a dream feast to someone with her sweet tooth. It was too hard to choose from the selection and she felt rushed in spite of the extra time. She went for a strawberry Torte and regretted it almost immediately when she spotted the chocolate cake that they served up to the aunt. Maybe she'd make a trip back here herself even though it was so old-fashioned. The aunt must have seen the green-eye and made her eat half of hers as well as her own. They sat over the remains of the coffee and cake, both uncertain, until there were no crumbs left to make shapes on the plate. Finally Brigitte looked at her watch. So the taxi was ordered again.

Aisling determined to make her escape as soon as they were outside. When they were in reach of the taxi, she suggested it, 'Would you be all right if you went back on your own. It's so hot; I fancy a look around and maybe going somewhere for a beer. I can get home myself later by U-Bahn.'

'I will go with you to take Schnaps. The taxi can take us where you want to go.' So much for making an escape. There was no arguing with that tone. So Aisling was stuck with her for another hour or two.

'Where do you want to go?' Brigitte added to absorb any doubt. 'All those people and the heat have made me thirsty too. I don't know if I'm still fit to take a beer in a pub at my age, I might wet myself but it might test out my nappy which is still dry.'

Aisling looked at her – was this a joke or was it kind of delayed shock?

Brigitte looked at her with eyes and mouth in matching sarcasm, 'No, my dear child, I'm not joking. At my age you never know when your bladder will let you down. I cried so much last night that I'm dried out and there should be room for a bit of beer. I made good use of the bathroom at Café Buchwald and checked out my nappy. Katharina got me a packet of these disposable nappies for old people once when I had a bit of a waterworks problem and was afraid of wetting the bed. I hate them. But to-day I thought why not use one in case my bladder let me down at a crucial moment. It's surprisingly comfortable – as long as it's dry. Apparently they can hold a litre!'

Aisling laughed so much then she wished she were wearing one herself. She stuck her arm in the aunt's like they were friends for the last few steps to the taxi, 'Well, let's test it then. It's a scientific experiment we're carrying out. I really want to go to this place I've read about but I haven't got my guidebook. I didn't really think I'd need it at a funeral. It's near some well-known station.'

'Ostbahnhof, Zoo, Gesundbrunnen?'

Aisling shook her head, 'Something Strasse.'

'Friedrichstrasse?'

'Yeah, that's it, I think. It used to be the place where people had their papers checked when they crossed from West to East Berlin. I read in the guidebook that they set up a kind of concert place and cafe there. It sounds a bit more human than the museums.'

'Could it be the Tränenpalast, the 'Palace of Tears', at the border crossing? A good name for such a place. But a place with a beer garden there. I have never heard of it. I would be surprised if the Tränenpalast is still there. Katharina told me that everything is changed.'

251

'The guide book might be out of date – it was a bit of a bargain but it said that it has been used for concerts and stuff and there's a bit of a beer garden. According to them it's one of the few places left that you can get a real feeling of what it was like passing from west to east before the developers get at it.'

'Let's ask the driver,' Brigitte suggested.

The taxi driver knew immediately where to take them when they mentioned Tränen-Palast. He was able to tell them that nothing much had changed there since the days when he crossed over himself. Everything was very temporary because there's some dispute about what they are going to do with it. It was due for development but, as far as he knew, you could still get a beer there. He dropped them off near a bit of scaffolding which almost concealed the beer garden. The sun was still strong enough for them to be glad of a bit of shade. They both laughed again when Brigitte ordered a Pils. Must look a bit bizarre to the waiter she thought, who squinted a bit facing the sun, but it was hard to phase these Berliners.

That was one of the things Aisling liked about the city. Anything goes. She left the aunt sitting on her nappy to locate the loo. She was side-tracked then to the place where you had to show your pass – just empty like they had just stopped using it that day. It was possible now to imagine a queue of people waiting in a warehouse type place to show their passports. She'd come back and take a photo to show Dad. It was the only the second time she had felt the story of the wall as real – not just something from a newsreel or a history book. The other time was the memorial to the young guy who was shot while in the river. She could imagine that too.

She went back to get Brigitte to show her that the window

where you presented your pass was still there. It was a bit like a really old railway station window – one of those that hadn't changed in a lifetime. She hoped they wouldn't pull it down. She liked the mix of the low-key pub with the big empty warehouse style structure used as a music venue. Far better than a museum as long as they didn't tart it up or make it official. She wished she had her camera now; it could be gone the next time she came.

Brigitte refused her offer of company as far as the loo – waving the stick she had unearthed the night before. 'I've got this.' At least she was able to send her off in the right direction.

'I'm glad you brought me here,' she said when she settled again. 'It hasn't changed much since I was here thirty years ago to watch Katharina and Monika queue there. It is a good place to say goodbye to Katharina one last time. To have someone from Ireland –and from my family – means a lot to me. No-one ever came to visit us here.'

'Not even Gran?'

'Peggy's not a big traveller, is she?'

'Not now, but she did make it to Boston once.'

'Well, that was to James, wasn't it? James with his big house and bathrooms with gold taps. But I can't complain. Peggy has kept in touch more than any of them, even Liam, to give her her due.' The last phrase was such a good imitation of Gran's condescension, it made both of them laugh.

They had one and then another. And then another. The beer, the aunt's deep chuckle and the wicked glow of the sunshine warmed Aisling inside out.

Too good to last, of course. In the taxi home, the sense of holiday persisted but felt a bit false. By the time Aisling came into the living room behind the aunt, now back in her chair, she realised it was over. Maybe the beer had only loosened the tears now tripping off the strong jaw.

'Monika arranged it all. She claimed Katharina for her own. Now Katharina will be there with her forever. I have nowhere and no-one. There will be no Katharina to arrange my funeral.'

Aisling's first instinct was to make a run for it. Out anywhere fast. To leave on the memory of wicked laughter and a nappy that could take a litre of beer. But there was no-one else now. No Yola until to-morrow morning.

'Look, I'm sure Dad would be happy to give you a hand to sort something out. You're not really on your own completely.' Brigitte looked at her with a look that said she knew that was a false promise.

'O.K. O.K. It might depend too much on the football season,' Aisling laughed weakly but her attempt to lighten the atmosphere fell flat. Her next words were out before she knew what she was saying. 'I could do it. It can't be that hard to make arrangements for whenever. This is Germany. You could sort out stuff on the telephone and I could do the running around buying graves or whatever you have to do.'

Brigitte's eyes focussed again – her pupils dark and bright against the watery blue but she said nothing – just looked hard.

'I couldn't stay now but I could come back. I like Berlin'

'You are too young to have to deal with these things,' Brigitte's tone was hopeful but you could hear the doubt behind it too.

'I'm old enough – older than you were when you had Katharina. It would be good practice for my German and I would have no problem asking Monika for help. I want to come back anyway. I found a brochure about a course in Mitte for comic-book design. It is part-time so I could get a job to pay my way. It would suit me perfectly, better than going back to Uni to do a degree in marketing. The first year was bad enough and next year looks like a recipe for total boredom.'

'If it suited you then it would be different. You could stay here as long as you wanted.'

'Just a few weeks until I get my own place. Let's have a wee whiskey to settle it'.

Chapter Twenty-Three

# A Promise

Plans for a complete change. It was beginning to work out. Even if the parents didn't stump up an allowance, she would get waitressing work. Smiling to herself under the sheet, as she closed her eyes for images of Berlin cafes, clubs, and a new set of friends. No shadow of Michael or snub from Maeve to bring her down. How much did she say to the aunt after one beer too many? How much had she guessed? 'You weren't anywhere near him when he died,' Brigitte had said. Guilt buried with Katharina's ashes. After a pause, Brigitte had added, 'You have a strong imagination and a strong will. Don't waste them on feeding the devil in you.' A weird death rattle laugh followed. Aisling laughed with her.

She fell asleep but woke again out of a dream where she was behind Michael in the queue at the station where they had to show their passports. The border guard wouldn't let her through. She tried to shout to Michael to tell him to come back but she couldn't get the sound out. He was waving to her and smiling. She woke up wondering if she had called his name out loud. No sound from the aunt's room. Then she heard her shout, 'Das Badezimmer ist frei.'

All ready now. Aisling dropped her backpack and satchel in the hall and went into the living room to say good-bye. The aunt sat in her usual chair looking stern in her attempt not to cry. I hope she manages to save it until I'm gone, Aisling thought.

'Do you want me to get you anything before I go?' she asked. Brigitte examined the little table beside her; everything was in its place. Aisling could see the packet of paper hankies, the packet of cigarettes, the bar of chocolate, the bulky purse, her glasses case, the remote for the TV that she never watched, the glass of water and of course the fly spray.

'You promise you will come back?'

Aisling didn't know whether to laugh or cry at the thought of making a promise to arrange a funeral. Genuine Goth or what! 'A promise is a promise,' she said aloud.

'My door is always open to you.' The aunt pushed an envelope across the table. 'For you to come back.'

'Oh you don't have to do that. There's no need really,' Aisling dithered – to take it, or not to take it? What if she changed her mind?

'Please take it. If you take it, I know you will come back one day.'

Aisling stuck the envelope in the inside zip pocket of her gilet. She looked at her watch. She knew she had plenty of time but she needed to get out now. She gave the aunt a hug –easier than the pecking experience with Gran. She was surprised when the aunt followed her out to the door of the apartment to see her off: she was using the stick inside now too, Aisling noticed.

She felt her eyes on her from the window as she headed off down the street in the direction of the U-Bahn. Round the corner she had a peek in the envelope – green ones – 100-euro notes – 5 of them. She was better off after this Berlin trip than if she had been working. What with her father's subsidy, the cheap flight, all her food paid for while she was there. She still had the savings from the holiday job. It was a good omen; she would use some of the money to come back to set things up for a year out.

Now she could look forward to a private reckoning session when she got to the airport. For a moment she saw Michael quizzing and teasing her about it when she got home. Let him dare! She hated anybody to know that she cared about money. She made sure that none of her friends knew by making flagrant generous gestures from time to time to counter any danger of being seen as a skinflint. None of them knew the depth of that secret pleasure of treasure mounting in her. Michael was the only one who had guessed her obsession with adding and subtracting her daily expenses. He had a string of nicknames he used to wind her up about it but no-one else ever picked up on it. For the first time the feeling of missing him was stronger than guilt, or anger at him for leaving her an only child, with their mother more and more of a limpet.

Brigitte had sensed more about Michael than anyone even though Aisling hadn't told her much. Aisling could hear the words again now in her head. The short sentences. 'You did what you did. Whatever it was. He's dead and you're alive. Forgive yourself.' The aunt had said some more too pooh-poohing the idea that Aisling had tortured him. 'The pain of living must have been awful if it was easier to face death.' If that was true then Michael's pain must have been worse than hers so far. Aisling had never thought that maybe Micheal's death was a relief for him.

She had something to do with his death but everybody else had something to do with it too – himself most of all. His broken heart over Richard was probably more important than anything. And then whatever happened between him and Richard's dad. Maybe the aunt was right. None of that had anything to do with Aisling. There was nothing she would do differently if he was alive now.

She looked out the window of the train. No goodbye for Berlin – see you soon, she said. She would have liked a closer look at those apartments with the lop-sided windows. She laughed out loud. There was a lot in the way you looked at things but if something is lop-sided, accept it as lop-sided.

Chapter Twenty-Four

# Loyalty

It was so cold that her very bones felt bare to it, in spite of the layers of clothing. She had the church and Alexander TV Tower in the background in her sights before she asked herself, 'Maybe I should have gone straight to the hospital?' Another Berlin. It was hard to remember the heat making her rucksack stick to her back when she looked back as she left in summer. It was better to come here first to orientate herself. Anyway she didn't know where the hospital was, or where to find Yola if she wasn't at the apartment as Monika said she would be. And all she had of Monika was a mobile telephone number.

But Yola answered the entry phone and stood in the hallway of the apartment when Aisling reached it. Standing in front of the first image of Brigitte in August.

'Deine Tante ist krank,' Yola said. Aisling felt anger rise in her, ready to spill aloud,. Why the fuck do they think I travelled through the night to get here? And why do you say aunt? She has a name. She had tried loads of times to tell Yola Brigitte was not her aunt. She had even got Brigitte to explain their relationship in German but still she persisted.

She was even angrier with herself. All those plans to come to Berlin for a year out hadn't materialised. Her parents thought the whole thing was a crazy idea and made her promise to stick Uni one more year. It was still only January. That would teach her to make plans around somebody with one foot in the grave. She was angry at Brigitte too. Why did she have to go and get ill before Aisling had a chance to come and make arrangements as she had promised? She'd fixed a visit for the Easter holidays and her plan was to set things up for the September following.

'She's not my aunt,' Aisling said now in English. Yola looked at her, 'Krankenhaus,' she said hopefully and repeated it again, 'Krankenhaus?' with a question mark this time. Aisling had her sick and hospital vocabulary ready and just nodded to confirm whatever it was Yola wanted to communicate. Brigitte is in the hospital or will we go to the hospital? She dropped her bag in the hall and offered a handshake. Yola seemed really out of her depth. In a way that was reassuring. 'Welches Krankenhaus, Yola?' She needed to know which hospital so no point in wasting energy on being mad at Yola.

Now it was Yola's turn to fumble for words. So Aisling took out her map of Berlin and spread it carefully on the dining table, while congratulating herself on remembering it. Yola just shook her head then and said, 'I too go with you.' So they went together.

Yola led her to the ward where Brigitte was lying asleep but with a drip in her arm and some machine that went beep, beep like a neglected mobile phone. Aisling felt a flicker of hope. It could be all a big fuss about nothing. Brigitte would wake up. Aisling could visit her the odd time until she got better and spend the rest of her time enjoying Berlin with no death, wakes or funerals. It would be the excuse she needed to drop out of the course. She took Brigitte's hand on the arm that was free of attachment to machines.

261

'It's me, Aisling. I'm back again. I've come over to see you as I promised. Gran sends her love. Oh and Mum and Dad too.'

Brigitte took a deeper breath, more like a sigh, but didn't open her eyes.

Her mother had warned her, 'Aisling, Aunt Bridget has had a stroke. You don't have to go there. It might be too much for you. She's unconscious: she might never come round again. People can last ages with a stroke and then die or they can go quickly. Mostly they never get back to themselves again. If Aunt Bridget survives, she will probably have to go to a nursing home. You can't go and stay there in that apartment by yourself. Your father and I will go at the weekend; you don't have to do this. You were good to her when she needed it.'

The more her mother went on, the more Aisling was determined to get on the net, book a flight and go. Now that she was here, the decision felt odd when there was no response from Brigitte.

They sat in silence. After a while, Yola looked at the clock. Aisling sent her home. She had already taken the spare set of keys hanging in the cloakroom in the hallway. They had been her keys for her trips out on her last visit. She would sit here for another while and then decide what to do.

She sat by the bedside. There was a space where another bed should be. Someone who wasn't coming back? When a nurse about her own age came to fiddle with the beeping machine, Aisling introduced herself. The nurse shrugged when Aisling asked what was likely. We must wait and see. So wait and see it was. Another hour later, Aisling went out for air and passed a little Turkish cafe which reminded her of how hungry she was. She came back and there was no change. She decided not to stay much longer.

Home to bed alone in the apartment. She checked all the rooms before going to bed and found a cardboard box with a paper on top and Aisling written on it in Brigitte's room. Inside there was the cracked enamel jug and inside it another envelope with her name on it. She knew the jug all right – it was Anna's enamel can from the Lager. When she touched it, it brought with it those hours of waiting and the stories of Ravensbrück. A visit to Ravensbrück was part of her plan for Easter.

She wished now that she had told Brigitte she had kept the dirty yellow pages. She wished she had told her that she hadn't managed to put them in Katharina's coffin. She still had them in the drawer of her desk at home. There hadn't been a time to get shot of them. It felt weird opening the envelope inside the can, in spite of her name on it. Inside, five 100 euro notes. Nothing else. Was that the money needed to bury her or what? She had no idea what a funeral cost but it was unlikely to be enough. She left the jug on the chest of drawers with the empty envelope. She put the money in her jeans pocket.

Later, she lay in bed wide-awake thinking she would never sleep. Suddenly it was the next morning and she was startled to hear Brigitte's voice, 'Das Badezimmer ist frei.' She shook herself awake and realised she had imagined it. Better not tell Mum that one, she thought. In need of ritual, she went for Brötchen even though Monika had asked to meet her for brunch at the cafe at Hackescher Markt.

She almost didn't recognise Monika when she got there. Monika looked younger and fresher – her cheeks rosy from the cold and wearing a terracotta and burgundy striped scarf with a burgundy beret. Winter suited her or she'd had time to get over Katharina, but after they had ordered food and got over the polite pleasantries, a glimpse of last summer's look came back. So how did it come about that it was Monika who had been the one to call Aisling about Brigitte's being taken to hospital? Aisling had been turning the question over and over. When she'd left, Brigitte had given the impression Monika was the last person she wanted to see.

'I hope you were not too shocked,' Monika said carefully. 'Brigitte asked me often to be sure to let you know when she died. You became her family when Katharina died. You meant a lot to her but I think you know that.'

Aisling shrugged off the emotion in her throat, 'Well we didn't have a lot of contact since.'

'No, she didn't expect it. She was pleased to get your letter telling her your plans to come to Berlin.'

'So when did you see her last?' Aisling asked.

'Last Saturday. I visited her every Saturday as Katharina did.'

Aisling raised her eyebrows and Monika smiled back a crooked smile, her head a little to one side showing off the silver sheen from her hair now in a well-cut bob.

'Yes, I knew she thought she could keep me away and at first she was too angry to talk to me. I would go and bring her some chocolate or some cake and leave again without speaking to her. But I knew she needed someone to talk to about Katharina as I did. I also needed to call to make sure she was O.K. I promised Katharina I would. One day, she asked Yola to offer me coffee and cake as Katharina predicted she would. Then I would always go for coffee and cake on Saturday. Sometimes we sat in silence. Sometimes we talked. Sometimes we would look at photographs together. Often we spoke about you.'

'About me?' Aisling laughed.

'Yes, she said that you helped her put together the times in Ireland, the times in the Lager and the times with Katharina. In the end, all the times became one time.'

Aisling wasn't sure she could believe Monika – the two of them sitting talking cosily together about old times. It seemed a bit unlikely.

'You know that she asked me if she could be buried with Katharina?' Monika added.

'Now that I don't believe,' Aisling thought. 'She asked me if I would make arrangements for her when I came back,' she said aloud.

Monika sighed, 'I know so. She told me and she also said it was unfair to ask you such a thing. And she was also afraid she would die before you came back. I told her I had promised Katharina to make sure she was looked after while she was alive and when she died too. I suggested she be cremated and buried with Katharina. She laughed then, a strange laugh, and nodded. That was some weeks ago.'

'Do you think she will die soon?' Aisling asked.

'I do think so,' Monika said. 'When I saw her on Saturday, she complained about being so tired. She said she was tired of waiting for death. I reminded her about your letter and there was life to wait for too but she said, "Aisling will come in any case." I wasn't so shocked when Yola rang me on Monday morning. She found her half way out of bed and already unconscious. We don't know for how long. Sometimes Yola stayed with her in these last months but on Sunday she had sent her away.'

Aisling wished she knew how Brigitte's change of heart came about. Hopefully she'd come round and tell her all.

Monika offered herself for whatever Aisling would need. She was softer than she seemed under the stiffness.

Aisling was glad of the empty ward when she got back to the hospital. She could sit there and chat quietly to Brigitte. She went over it all. The waiting and waiting. The wake that wasn't a wake. The relatives who didn't come. The Jules turned angel of mercy. The cemetery. Anna and the Lager. Irma and the escape. So much of it coming all together now as Monika said. Happy times surrendering to sad times and sad times to happy times. She would sit quietly then chat a bit. Go off into the grey winter day to find lentil soup and come back again. Sit a while, chat a while. Off again for spaghetti and sauce or Bratwurst swallowed down with a beer. The little Turkish place again for her favourite lamb kebab. Phone calls in the evening to her parents. After two days of it, she felt like she could keep it up forever.

On the third day, she arrived back in shaking off some flakes of snow, feeling fresh. There was a nurse at the bed and she looked at Aisling. 'Es ist nicht viel Zeit'. Not much time for what? And the answer came by itself. Not much time left to live.

Aisling had more she wanted to say but not in front of the nurse. When the nurse left, she sat again holding the hand now free of machines. How long is not much time to die? She watched the breathing change. The nurse came back and took Aisling's both hands. 'Gut gemacht. Sie ist von uns gegangen.'

Aisling looked at her, 'She's gone?'

'Gestorben,' the nurse said. Dead? Aisling thought. It's not possible. Dead already Brigitte looked pale but not a lot different from yesterday evening when she was just sleeping – no blood, no guts, no scary white balloon face, no death. How did the nurse know she was dead?

'Tot?' she asked. No breathing. A woman doctor came, blond and tall and efficient. No heartbeat. She spoke English, 'The nurse said that you did well. Your voice was reassuring and you helped her go. They say that the hearing is the last thing to go. She probably knew your voice. Not everyone can speak as you have done.' Aisling felt a strange warm whiskey feeling in her gut.

She sent her father a brief text and then rang her mother, 'Dad's Aunt Bridget just died... ' It felt weird describing Brigitte like that – it didn't fit her somehow even dead. Aisling heard the panic in her mother's voice and Michael's face bobbed in front of her for a few seconds while she listened to the stream, 'Oh you poor baby. Oh god! Are you OK? You poor baby – in bloody Berlin. We don't even know anybody. You did say that she's gone, didn't you? I told your father he should go and that she wouldn't last long. It's the best thing for her. I told him it wasn't fair on you to be alone there. I'll ring him right away. I just knew this would happen. It's not right.'

'What about Granny – should I ring her?' Aisling cut in.

'Oh no you'd better wait until your father goes over to see her. It might be too much of a shock for her on the phone. He can ring you from there.'

Aisling wished she could ring Gran. She wanted a job. She didn't want to stand by, feeling useless and empty. Monika had turned up from somewhere and was jabbering away to the nurses, arranging god-knows-what. Two orderlies came – asked her to wait outside – of course to clean up the body... No-body said anything about a priest and Aisling didn't either – she didn't even know how to ask that in German and she didn't want to ask it in English or to ask Monika to do it. She'd been sent into a waiting area, so she sat there and said a decade of the rosary. It felt stupid but she didn't know what else to do and didn't want to go back to the apartment. There must be more to do and she wanted to see Brigitte once more.

Her phone rang making her jump. Her mother never did text.

'Your father called and told Gran on his way home. You could ring her if you like, he said. He is going to get us on the first flight to Berlin. He's on the internet now. Diarmuid – what time did you say it leaves at?' Aisling heard her father in the background. 'It gets in at around ten o'clock local time.'

'Hang about, not so fast,' Aisling interrupted. 'You know the funeral is not likely to be for a couple of weeks at least. She's going to be cremated.'

'Oh god! We hadn't thought of that. Diarmuid, Diarmuid, what shall we do? Better to go to the funeral. But we can't leave Aisling there alone.' Aisling heard them muttering together then her mother's voice again, 'Yes, you're right; Aisling can come home now and come back with us.'

'Look, leave it to this evening and we'll sort it out then.' Aisling felt better taking charge. She didn't want her parents coming and taking over everything.

'I'll ring you later. The priest has just turned up and is waiting for me.' She could see Yola standing by the staff desk with Monika and a man in dark clothes – some sort of priest for sure. Time to go and join the hypocrites, she thought. Or maybe Yola is a real Catholic.

'The priest, of course. Oh you poor baby,' her mother's voice was panicky yet.

Aisling cut her mother off and went over to give Monika a stiff hug. 'How did you hear?' Monika pointed at Yola who had the aunt's book of numbers in her hand. Aisling reminded herself to get it back. 'Why and who for?' she didn't know but she'd deal with that later.

Yola had located a Catholic chaplain who knew his prayers in English better than Aisling. She wondered if he spotted how she forgot the words of the Our Father. Monika wasn't much help just standing there silent. Luckily Yola mumbled away anyhow and Aisling recovered some automatic mode from earlier days. The priest asked then about the funeral arrangements. When one looked at the other, he offered his card, 'Let me know if you want anything – it's got my handy on it too.

Monika and Yola stood then looking at her like she was in charge.

'Let's go back to the apartment and have coffee,' Aisling suggested.

The three of them sat around the table, drinking the coffee made by Yola who sat sideways not sure of her place in all this. Suddenly her shoulders started to heave and she came out with a mixture of German, Polish and English. Her grief was real enough and Aisling and Monika both comforted her and sent her home.

When she'd gone, Monika said, 'You should have Brigitte's testament?'

'Come again? Testament? Do you mean her will?' Aisling asked.

'Yes sorry about my bad English,' Monika looked tired now.

'You have Brigitte's will?' That must have been some change of heart, Aisling thought.

'No, but Brigitte asked me to take her to the lawyer and she showed me where you will find her copy.'

It was in the locked bureau and Aisling knew well where

the key was kept hidden. She wondered if they shouldn't wait for the funeral and some solicitor person but thought the better of it. This wasn't a film but real life. If Brigitte wanted her to have it, then she should have it. She read it then to Monika. Nothing complicated. Yola was to have all her clothes or get rid of them and 3 months wages. Aisling was to have what was left after the funeral expenses. Monika explained Katharina had already arranged for her to pay the funeral expenses so whatever was in Brigitte's bank would be Aisling's when the solicitor had sorted it out. Aisling was glad that there was nothing about papers or other belongings. It would be up to her to decide.

'What about the apartment?' Aisling asked blushing – would Monika think she was greedy? Monika was matter-of-fact about it. She and Brigitte had spoken to the landlord. Brigitte and her family had the right to live there. So as long as Aisling wanted to stay in it, it was hers and there would be enough money to pay the rent for a year.

When Monika left, Aisling went through the apartment. Could she live here for a year – or even more maybe? She sat in Brigitte's chair, willing her ghost to come and be with her. She would have enjoyed a Schnapps and a bit of a story from the old bat and a chat about this and that. She had enough Schnaps for both of them and fell asleep then. When she woke the curtain waltzing in the draft gave her a fright. Well she'd asked for a ghost.

She went through the apartment again. This time, in her mind's eye, she imagined how she would have it. She pictured it with most of the furniture gone and it felt better. She resolved to try it.

Monika came back the next day around noon. Arrangements

were made. The same procedure as for Katharina. She made a few more phone calls and they agreed the date for the funeral. Aisling debated whether to stay but decided against it. She would go home and come back again with her parents and then she would stay for the year. No argument.

Back in Dublin, she was glad to meet Matt on his halfway visit, brown and beardy from his six months in Venezuela. He kept looking at her.

'Something has changed. Or somebody has changed you.'

'For better or worse?' she demanded laughing.

'For the better: you're more human. No sign of the spoilt child. Who was it? '

'There's nobody to compete with you. I've lost more friends than I've made in the last year.'

'And what about Berlin?'

'I spent most of the time with Brigitte.'

'"Brigitte" not "the Aunt" or "the awl Biddy?"'

'I'm going to go back over there. Maybe stay in her flat until I find a place of my own.'

'Stay in an old flat like that. Something has changed.'

'I'm giving up the course.'

'No more marketing?'

'Naw. I'm going to do comic-strips and maybe a graphic novel. I've got information about courses in Berlin. I'm hoping I can start in January. I haven't told the parents yet.'

Matt cocked his head sideways, 'So not everything has changed. But I like the sound of you doing something creative. More likely to keep you out of mischief. You've been unbearable since you stopped doing your comic-strips.'

Aisling grimaced at him. 'I'd like to go with you to visit the concentration camp she was in.'

'Tourist trips to concentration camps are not my thing. Making entertainment out of somebody else's suffering.'

'It's not my trip either but she was there and she never went to the memorial even after the wall came down. I want to go to connect to her.'

'For her? Mmhuh, you have changed.

Aisling tried to persuade him to come to the funeral.

'No way, I'm not going to the funeral of somebody I've never met. You're going to stay on after it aren't you? I'll be on your doorstep soon enough. We'll visit her grave.'

'It's worth a visit and there's a great café there.'

Three weeks of tidying up loose ends. Withdrawal from the course. Saying goodbyes. Her parents postponing the big talk. She knew they would do their best to bring her back with them. More denial. Travelling to Berlin with them felt awkward. Prattling about Berlin and missing Christmas markets. Making time for a bit of sight-seeing. They insisted on taking a taxi from the airport even though they had no luggage worth talking about. They had planned to stay in a hotel but changed their minds when Aisling insisted that she was staying in the apartment.

Aisling regretted it when they took over Brigitte's bedroom. Her mother found clean sheets, made the bed and started rooting around in the dressing table, 'Let's have a look at what she's left you.' She rifled the jewellery box in the top drawer. 'Nothing very valuable here and the styles is more your Gran's. I suppose we'd better give her some of it. You know what she's like.'

She looked in the drawers.

'The clothes are for Yola,' Aisling said, impatiently. Her

mother taking charge annoyed her. She'd had a look herself but it felt different. And her mother hadn't even met the woman whose funeral she'd come for. It made Brigitte seem like just so much baggage.

In the living room, Aisling set up the little tray of Schnaps glasses and sat in Brigitte's chair before her mother could. Time to face the reality of her decision to stay after the funeral.

'You're not going to come back and stay in this old woman's apartment all on your own?' Her mother's voice scaled up to panic. 'You can't be serious. It would be bad for you. And this fantasy about developing your drawing. Cartoons and comic books are all very fine and well in their place but you'll never make your living from cartoons.'

'People do,' Aisling muttered.

'Rare, talented people who stick at it. You've hardly opened a sketch book for ages.'

'I did when I was here. I can't do it in Dublin. There are good short courses near here in the Volkshochschule in Mitte.'

'Volkshochschule? What's that?'

'A place for adult education. They run lots of interesting courses which don't cost much.'

'Adult education? That's for the unemployed or housewives or retired people. It's not further education.'

'In Ireland, maybe. It's different here. The course on graphics sounds really upbeat.'

'Is your German up to it?' A more practical question from Dad.

'The tutor speaks English. And I will take a language course as well.'

'And how will you keep yourself?'

'I have this apartment for a year. I can do waitressing or

bar work to feed myself. And I told you, the courses aren't expensive.'

'Come on, Mary, Aisling is talking about taking some time out, learning more German. Even the experience of living in another country for a while would be good for her C.V. She's not happy in the marketing course at university. It's a waste of her time to carry on there. Things are cooling down. It's not like the days when Dublin was hopping with opportunity. I'm not convinced about this comic-strip idea but if she enjoys it, it would give her something for the CV while she makes decisions.'

'What – you mean you would agree to her staying here in this mausoleum with the belongings of a musty old woman, all on her own?' Her mother's disgust was palpable.

'It's not any more of a mausoleum than home and I've already withdrawn from the course,' Aisling muttered. Dad sent her a leave-this-to-me-if-you-want-to-win-this-match look. So she did.

'The apartment is in a good state. It's not such a bad idea: she's got a place to live paid for her for a year. She could rent out a room to bring in a bit of money. We could come over and give her a hand to get it ready.'

Aisling hoped her glance cut into that, Whoah there Dad, there's no way you're gonna do that and you're not palming Mum off on me.

She was relieved when Monika turned up with the ingredients for "Abendbrot". It was a chance to tell Monika her plans to stay on after the funeral. She'd have a few weeks. Monika could help with enrolment on the course on comic-strip design. They speculated whether it would be possible to join in January or whether she had to wait until September.

Monika was encouraging. She offered a lift from her brother in the morning for Aisling and her parents. He would attend the funeral in any case. She smiled and hugged Aisling as she left.

'Brigitte asked me to give you this.' Monika gave her an envelope.

She was barely out the door when Aisling's mother started checking out the rooms and cupboards.

'There's a lot of rubbish to clear out,' she said lifting Anna's enamel can from the shelf in Katharina's room. 'Will Yola or Monika arrange all that too?'

Aisling snatched the can out of her mother's hand, 'That's mine. She said. It's actually a really valuable antique.'

Her mother went quiet: she could see the battle with tears. Aisling let her hug her.

Her father came in and joined the hug. When her mother headed for the bathroom, he took his chance, 'Look I know it's hard on you but this funeral is good for your mother too. You have a life of your own to live and she has to get used to it. I think there was a bit of the old green eye with Aunt Bridget. It's clear to a blind man you did something special for her by coming to Katharina's funeral and she appreciated it. I'm sorry now that I never met her myself. But that's life.'

'That's death, you mean,' Aisling retorted but returned his hug and he laughed. 'You're right, that's death. Do you want me to stay with you while you read the letter?'

'Letter?'

'The one in your hand.'

'Yes, yes, that letter. I mean no, I don't want you to be with me. I'd rather read it alone, if you don't mind.'

'O.K. And Aisling, just by the way, I am proud of you.'

'Dad, I've not done anything. Don't.. .'

'No, I mean it really . You've grown up in these last months. I trust you now to make your own mistakes and learn from them.'

'So you think moving to Berlin is a mistake?'

'No, no, no. Me being clumsy... I think it's a good idea. I trust you to find out what you want.'

'O.K. Dad, thanks and good night.'

Hug a bit cursory in the impatience to open the letter. Not fat enough for money, so what?

"Aisling" on the envelope in Brigitte's shaky handwriting but inside a different handwriting.

Sylvester, 2005
Dear Aisling,

A last letter to you from the hands of Monika and in the handwriting of Monika as mine is no longer legible. I hope it makes you smile to learn we have become friends. You should smile because you helped. When we could not talk about Katharina, we could talk about you, but that was later. We both treasured the life you brought with you into those difficult days.

Monika and I cried and fought together many times before it hit me. I could cry and fight with her and she would come back. She became a friend to me like Mary, like Anna, like Irma and Adelheid. Did I tell you that Irma died too before Christmas? All dead, and now me too. I learnt in these last months how Monika helped Katharina prepare for death. She did not tell me but she showed me because she did it for me too. I could never have helped Katharina to die peacefully. I understood too late how my jealousy and anger made her last days harder. Monika helped me to forgive myself. Forgiving yourself is hardest of all but it helps.

Monika is no saint. We said harsh things to each other on those days she came bearing cake. There were days when I refused to open the door. She told me she carried on with it because she promised Katharina she would. Monika has a strong will and she can help you. The last time we visited Katharina's grave together, we had a meal at a small Italian restaurant called Aroma near the cemetery. I like to think you will one day go there with her and eat the pizza you love so much. Accept her help if you can.

All my best wishes for your future.

Yours,

Signed '*Biddy*' in her own shaky handwriting.

# Acknowledgements

This book would never have emerged without the inspiration of the survivors of Ravensbrück and the many pathways leading to and from that inspiration. Along the way I had sustenance and encouragement from key people. I acknowledge with gratitude the suggestions, tips, corrections and help with research they have given me. The final product has also benefitted from professional expertise in editing and design and finally the publication by Matador. The specific contribution of the following, at crucial points, has fuelled my enthusiasm and overcome my doubts:

Schorse Rennert my life partner for more than words can convey; Heike Thiele, friend, photographer and designer; Pam Wright, friend and website designer; Cressida Downing, editor. I am grateful to my friends Sabine Antony, Iris Lyle, Carmel Roulston and Nora Hughes for their engagement in the process; and appreciate the family support I have experienced throughout.

# Acknowlegement to Memory and Memorials

While all characters and personal details in the novel , Bone and Blood, are fiction, I have been inspired by the following factual accounts which have kept memories alive:

*Ravensbrück: Everyday Life in a Women's Concentration Camp 1939-1945*: Jack G. Morrison pub. Markus Wiener Princeton ISBN 1-55876-218-3

*God Remained Outside*: Geneviève de Gaulle Anthonioz pub. Souvenir Press ISBN 0-285-63530-1

*Journal de Ravensbrück*: Nelly Gorce, pub. Actes Sud ISBN 9-782742704866

*The Past is Myself*: Chrisabel Bielenberg, pub. Corgi ISBN 0-552-99065-5

*Tag der Angst und der Hoffnung*: Delia Müller und Madlen Lepschies pub. Stiftung Brandenburgische Gedenkstätten/ Mahn-und Gedenkstätt Ravensbrück ISBN 3-910159-49-4

*Die Klempnerkolonne in Ravensbrück*: Charlotte Müller pub. Dietz Verlag Berlin ISBN 3-320-00808-0

*A Woman in Berlin*: Anonymous pub. Virago Press ISBN 978-1-84408-112-7

*Through the eyes of Survivors*: *A Guide to Ravensbrück Memorial Museum* pub. Lagergemeinschaft Ravensbrück /Freundeskreis e.V (BRD) ISBN 3-89657-467-1